"Raven? Darling?" a woman's voice called from somewhere outside the dining room.

Darling?

Adrian registered the gleam of smug satisfaction in Thorne's squinty eyes just before the same intriguing female voice spoke again, this time from just inside the dining room.

"There you are." The woman threw open her arms and smiled at him as if they were alone. "Surprise, darling, I'm home."

Adrian gaped at her, frozen in his seat even as the other gentlemen at the table leapt to their feet. It was she. Leah. *His wife.*

Oh sweet Lord.

What was she doing standing in his dining room?

Hell, what was she doing *standing* anywhere?

She was supposed to be . . . well, dead.

He placed his palms flat on the table and pushed himself upright on leaden legs, only distantly aware of the expectant hush all around him.

This woman was most definitely not dead.

She was breathtakingly alive. With hair the color of blazing chestnuts and eyes like fields of clover. My God, his wife was a beauty.

His wife.

Oh sweet Lord, what the bloody hell was he going to do now?

Also by Patricia Coughlin

LORD SAVAGE

PATRICIA COUGHLIN

MERELY MARRIED

BANTAM BOOKS

New York Toronto London Sydney Auckland

MERELY MARRIED

A Bantam Book / October 1998

ISBN 0-553-57521-X

Published simultaneously in the United States and Canada

Bantam Books are published by Bantam Books, a division of Bantam Doubleday Dell Publishing Group, Inc. Its trademark, consisting of the words "Bantam Books" and the portrayal of a rooster, is Registered in U.S. Patent and Trademark Office and in other countries. Marca Registrada. Bantam Books, 1540 Broadway, New York, New York 10036.

PRINTED IN THE UNITED STATES OF AMERICA

OPM 10 9 8 7 6 5 4 3

MERELY MARRIED

1

—❧❧—

Westerham, England 1819

Adrian Devereau, the sixth Duke of Raven, among other things both laudatory and not, staggered to a halt dead center of the rutted country lane and thrust his jaw into the air with the reckless abandon of a man well into his cups.

"Bygod, I've got it," he declared. "I shall enter a monkastery."

"Monkastery?" echoed Sir Colin Thornton, glib barrister by vocation and bon vivant by nature. "D'you mean monastery?"

Adrian shrugged. "Monkastery. Monastery. I'll do it."

There was no need to explain further, even if he'd been able to. Sloshed or not, both Colin and Will Grantley, his closest friends since their first days at Eton, understood what had driven him to this point.

He was one and thirty and blissfully unwed, a decorated war hero, a peer of the realm and rotten with wealth. In other words, a tantalizingly ripe plum dangling before the marriage-minded ladies of the *ton*, most of whom were as eager to pluck him from the thorny branches of bachelorhood as Adrian was determined not to be plucked.

The more he attempted to live up—or rather, down—to his nickname, the Wicked Lord Raven, the more he was pursued. It appeared, much to his utter confusion and disgust, that he had come to be regarded by a number of brainlessly romantic females as a Worthy Project, and they vied for the privilege of undertaking his "salvation."

All evening he had been brooding about the current season and with each tankard of ale at the Black Dwarf Pub, his proposals for dealing with the feminine threat to his freedom had grown more creative. Now this.

"Brilliantidea," Colin mumbled, running his words together with teetering savoir faire.

"Yes, brllnt," agreed Will, dropping his syllables like autumn leaves. "Let's drink to Rave's 'coming a monk." He waved a hand in the air. "To . . . to . . . What the heck to call a duke who 'comes a monk?"

"Brother?" Colin ventured.

Will shook his head. "A bit too familiar. How 'bout BrotherYourGrace?"

"Got it," Colin exclaimed. "Your Celibacy. Get it? Your Celibacy." He and Will surrendered to a fit of laughter, jostling each other in their efforts to remain standing.

"Idiots," muttered Adrian, and continued walking.

"Maybe monking it wasn't such a brillntidea after all." said Will. He and Colin shuffled rapidly to catch up to Adrian. Their mounts forgotten in the stable behind the pub, they were making their way back to the rectory at St. Anne's-on-Clayton. It was one of two comfortable livings Will held, mainly by virtue of being a friend of the Duke's.

" 'Spose not," Adrian conceded gloomily. "I've no gift for celibacy."

" 'Sides which, you don't have a monk's girth. Or the proper hairline." He waved toward Adrian's tall, lean frame and thick, dark brown hair. "They'd have to be always shavin' that little circle at the back to make you fit. Boundtogettedious."

"Would flick off the ladies though," Colin pointed out. "Thazyour problem, Rave. Too damn pretty for your own good . . . and in spite of our trying to fix things by smashing your nose that time in Naples." He slapped Will on the back. " 'Member Naples?"

They shared another loud laugh, then Colin said, "Could always have another go at the old muzzle, Rave, if you like."

"Thanks, but no."

"Wouldn't work anywayz," added Will. "The mamas are more interested in your azzets than your face."

"Did you have to mention the mothers?" grumbled Adrian. "I'd sooner face Lucifer himself than a mother charging across a ballroom with her sweet-young-thing in tow."

"Mothers ought to have the good sense to keep their sweet-young-things away from the likes of you," remarked Colin.

"I've certainly done my part to convince them," stated Adrian. "Then there's the assortment of aunts and other females who aid and abet. Hell, the bloody world is set against the poor sod who wants only to be left alone."

"Well," said Colin with a conspiratorial leer, "not completely alone. Else you really would be monking it."

"No, of course not *completely* alone." Adrian broke into the very grin that never failed to dazzle feminine hearts and get him into trouble. "No fun in that." He sighed. "I prefer to bake my cake and eat it . . . find a cake and need it . . . Ah, hell, you know what I mean."

"I do. The cake, I mean. Having and eating." Will awaited their full attention. "S'called heaven."

Adrian snorted. "Ha. Now there's a subject you would know precious little about, *Rector.*"

Will managed an indignant expression, drawing himself up in a comical attempt at the solemn air he ordinarily reserved for those rare occasions when he was actually called upon to perform some ecclesiastic duty. "Know 'nough to minister to your lost soul, my son."

"Leave my lost soul out of this," Adrian retorted.

Colin moved between them. "Why not do what Plimpton did?"

"Reginald Plimpton?"

"The very one." He paused to belch. "Women chased him same as you till he went and got himself wed."

"Plimpton's not wed."

"Was so," Colin declared. "All happened while you were off in France winning brass buttons and defending . . . whatever it was you were off defending. Old Reggie met some sweet-young-thing from Dorset one week and married her the next. Juzlikethat," he concluded, with several failed attempts to snap his fingers.

"That's success? You want me to avoid the shackles of marriage by getting married? Damn clever, barrister." He made an exaggerated bow. "No bloody wonder you have so much free time for hunting if that's the way you treat your clients."

"Let me finish," protested Colin. "Plimpton got married, then he got widowed. Or is it widowered?" He gave a careless wave. "Whatever you call it when a fellow's wife dies on him."

Adrian frowned. "But how did he manage it? He didn't . . ."

"Kill her?" Colin shook his head. "Course not. Heard Reg was devilish fond of the old girl. Nearly threw himself into the grave after her, they say. That saved him, you see."

"What did?"

"His grief, Rave, his grief. Even the vultures of the Marriage Mart understand grief."

"Of course." Adrian's quiet, almost reverent tone was broken by a sudden hiccup and then a soft whistle between his teeth. "A grieving widower would be out of play for . . . why, no telling how long. Sweet-JesusColin, that is clever."

It was a long walk home from the pub and the cool night air cleared the men's heads slightly. Though not enough to prevent them from joining voices in a spirited rendition of a favorite drinking song as they approached the rectory, a pretty three-story stone dwelling surrounded by beech trees and dogwoods just starting to bloom.

The window above the front door opened and Mrs. O'Hara, the housekeeper, leaned out.

"Shush, shush, the lot of you, coming home at this hour, screaming like boiled cats . . . Why, 'tis enough to wake the poor souls sleeping 'cross the way." She waved toward the adjacent parish cemetery.

"Mrs. O'Hara, 'tis a sight for sore eyes you are," Will called to her in an abysmal attempt at a brogue. "Would you believe I forgot me door? I mean I doored me key. I mean," he said, squaring his shoulders and grinning, "I forgot—"

"You'd forget your head if the good Lord hadn't attached it so well." Mrs. O'Hara shook her own gray head in exasperation. "I'll be down straight away. And mind you, no more singing."

The door opened and the three men crowded into the narrow hallway. She looked from one to the next with disdain. "Now what have you to say for yourselves?"

"I say you are an angel," declared Adrian, reaching for her plump, work-roughened hand and bringing it to his lips as deferentially as if she were a queen. "Truly a rare gem of womanhood and—"

"And you, your reekin' Grace, are a disgrace. Don't you be laughing at me behind your mustache, Sir Colin." She swung her gaze his way. "Fancy barrister like yourself, coming in smelling like a common sod. And you," she went on, focusing on Will next, "a man of God. And needed here so desperately. I vow if you hadn't come soon I was going to send the cook's boy over to the pub to fetch you. How would that have looked, I ask you?"

"Needed for what?" asked Will.

"To do the work God called you to do, that's what. We've a sick woman here." She lowered her voice and waved a hand toward the heavy oak staircase behind her. "A real lady. Leah Stretton, her name is. She was traveling to London when she took sudden ill and her driver brought her here. This was the first place they passed, and a lucky thing it was. At least here she'll have someone to see to her passing from this world to the next."

Will paled. "You don't mean to say she's . . ."

Mrs. O'Hara nodded. "That young fellow who helps out when Dr. Wellstone is away says it's a rupture inside her somewhere and she likely won't last the night. The laudanum he gave her has the poor thing drifting in and out, so she don't even know where she is most of the time. I just thank the good Lord she'll have someone to tend her in her hour of need."

"You don't mean me?" blurted Will.

Mrs. O'Hara glared at him. "Now who else would I be meaning?"

"Brindley. Why didn't you have Brindley handle it?" he asked, referring to Cole Brindley, the curate who oversaw the actual running of the parish while Will was off doing other things.

"Because Mr. Brindley is away visiting home, same as he always does whenever you decide to favor us with a stay."

Will grimaced. "Yes, yes, of course, I forgot."

"That's what a pickled brain will do for you," sniped the housekeeper. "I'll put on a kettle for tea. *Strong tea,*" she added, raking all three of them with her gaze. "Now go along with you," she urged Will. "You'll find her in the room just to the right of the stairs."

"Is she alone?" asked a very nervous Will.

"Yes. Her lady's maid sat with her most of the night, but I finally persuaded the poor thing to get some rest herself. See you don't go tripping over your own feet and waking her."

Will nodded and started up the stairs, with Adrian and Colin trailing. The crisis had left all three men, while not quite sober, at least somber, and slightly ill at ease.

"You *can* do it, can't you, Will?" asked a dubious Colin.

"I'm an ordained minister, aren't I?"

"That's no answer," Colin persisted. "I mean, hell,

Will, have you ever actually done any ministering of this sort before?"

Will's eyes were a little too wide and too bright to inspire confidence. He gulped hard.

"Maybe not *precisely* this sort, but—"

"Of course he can do it," Adrian interjected. "He can do anything any other minister can do. Isn't that right, Will?"

"Of course, I can do it." Will grasped the newel post at the top of the stairs for balance before pacing along the hallway. "All I need is a Book of Prayers. Now where . . . ? "I know. Cole's room. He's sure to have an extra lying around."

After appropriating a prayer book from the curate's room, Will started back down the hall, riffling the pages, mumbling to himself.

"Let's see. Blessings, Baptism, exorcism, where the . . . Ah, here it is. Final Rites." Will faced the closed bedroom door and took a deep breath.

"Hold on," Adrian said impulsively. "By any chance, does that prayer book also contain the marriage ceremony?"

"Probably, but why would I need . . ." Will blinked rapidly, then stared at his best friend. "What are you thinking, Rave? Not what I think you're thinking. Please not that."

"I'm thinking of the Plimpton Solution."

"Oh no. Oh no."

"Stop groaning," Adrian whispered. "You don't want to wake her maid, do you?"

"I'd rather wake the maid than hear this," Will hissed. "It's madness is what it is. Just the sort of lunacy you're forever thinking up at night and regretting in the morning. Believe me, you'll thank me tomorrow for saving you."

"I won't thank you, and I don't want to be saved. I want to be married."

"To a woman you've never so much as set eyes on?"

Adrian reached past him to open the door a crack. He glanced inside.

"There," he said, closing it. "I've set eyes on her. Now will you perform the ceremony?"

"No. And don't try telling me it's a case of love at first sight either."

"I wouldn't dream of it. You know I don't believe in love at first or any other sight." His eyes gleamed with reckless determination. "What this is, is an omen . . . and please don't start that infernal groaning again. Her being here tonight is an omen, I'm sure of it, and it is your solemn ecclesiastical duty to act on it if I so request. Which I do."

"Oh, no." Will shook his head forcefully. "Don't go pulling rank on me, Rave. That wouldn't be right, would it, Colin?"

Adrian frowned with indignation. "I never pull rank. Do I, Colin?" He nudged the man propped against the wall beside him, eyes at half-mast.

"Never," he blurted, then blinked. "What was that again?"

Adrian looked back at Will. "I'm simply asking you, no, *imploring* you, as a friend."

"And as a friend I'm telling you that I am honor bound to do the right thing for this poor woman."

"Did you even bother to consider that this might be the right thing for her?" Adrian was just sober enough to know he was being absurd, but since the question gave Will pause, he instinctively jumped in with both feet. "Think of it, Will, a woman traveling to London, alone, unchaperoned but for her maid, forced to seek refuge with strangers. She may well be a lady, as Mrs. O'Hara claims, but I cannot help but think her situation is not the rosiest."

Will's forehead puckered, a sure sign of confusion.

"I could change all that," Adrian continued, calling on a natural gift for persuasion. "As the lady's husband I would handle all of her . . . final arrangements, as well as settle any debts. Wouldn't that be a blessing for the poor family she leaves behind?"

"B-but you've no license," Will sputtered.

Adrian swept that objection aside. "We'll worry about that later. This is an emergency. In the meantime, Colin can draw up some sort of legal papers. Isn't that so, Colin?"

"Right away," said Colin, obviously struggling to keep up. "You ought to sign a letter stating your intentions toward her, and relinquishing a husband's claim to whatever she might possess, so it doesn't appear—"

"Yes, yes," Adrian broke in, waving him to silence. "I'll relinquish whatever you like. So, Will, it would appear that the future of this unfortunate woman rests in your hands."

Will pondered that.

"There's a bumble in your logic somewhere, Rave," he said finally." I know there is, but cursed if I can pick it out with my head pounding this way."

"So you'll do it?"

"I'll do it . . . but not here." His expression turned mulish. "You said *lawfully* married and that means the vows have to be spoken inside the church."

"The church it is then," Adrian agreed. "Colin, see to the necessary papers. Will, fetch the parish register for the signatures, and I'll bring the bride."

I'll bring the bride.

Easier said than done, he discovered, as he stood over the bed and stared at the woman lying there. She looked pale and fragile and a less impulsive, more sober man would no doubt have had second thoughts. The burnished mahogany of her long hair against the pillow was the only color visible. Then she opened her eyes and he was assailed by a gaze the green of a summer hillside.

"Hello," he said, feeling suddenly like an absolute idiot. "You don't know me, madam, but—"

"Christiana," she said, growing agitated. A small V formed between her dark brows, marring an otherwise flawless complexion. Adrian felt a quite improper urge to smooth it away with his thumb.

"Christiana," she said again, tossing her head. "You must finish dressing. The dresses must be right . . . your hair . . . the ribbons . . . everything . . . just so . . . perfect . . ."

Mrs. O'Hara was right. The woman had no clear idea of where she was or with whom.

"Shhh," he said. He bent and slid his arms under her, gathering the heavy layers of bedclothes and lifting her against his chest. "You have no need to worry."

She twisted anxiously. "But Christiana—"

"Christiana will be fine," he assured her, wishing he knew who the hell Christiana was. "Everything will be fine. I promise you."

He hurried downstairs to find his friends waiting by the front door.

"That's her then?" queried Colin, peering at the woman cradled in Adrian's arms, her head resting with a disconcertingly trustful air against his chest.

"It would appear so," Adrian whispered. He would prefer not to let the righteous Mrs. O'Hara in on what was happening. "Would you mind getting the door?"

"You're sure about this, Adrian?" asked Will. "Really sure? Because it's not too late to—"

"I'm sure."

But then, he had also been sure the last time he set out for a church to be married. And look how that had turned out.

The ceremony was mercifully brief, the longest interval being when Will dropped the prayer book and lost his place. Not that it mattered all that much since most of it was improvised, to allow for the bride's state of semiconsciousness.

After reading the opening prayer, Will turned to Adrian.

"Wilt thou, Adrian Devereau, Duke of Raven, Marquis of Haverill, Earl of—"

"Skip the titles," Adrian ordered, when his bride moved restlessly in his arms.

"I can't skip—"

"We'll be here all bloody night if you don't."

"Besides," added Colin, "we all know who he is."

"Very well," Will snapped. "Wilt thou take this lady, Leah Stretton, as thy wife, to live together after God's ordinance, in the holy estate of marriage?"

"I—"

"Not yet. Wilt thou love her, honor her, comfort and keep her in sickness . . ." He paused to give Adrian a pointed look. "And in health, and forsaking all others keep thee only to her as long as ye both shall live?"

Adrian nodded. "I will. Go on."

"Do you, Leah, take this man, Adrian Devereau, Duke of Raven et cetera, et cetera, to be your husband—"

"She does. Go on."

"But she didn't say anything."

"She did," insisted Adrian. "I heard her."

"*I* have to hear her," maintained Will.

"But . . ." Adrian noted the stubborn set of his friend's chin and gave up. "All right, drat you. Listen." He bent his head and spoke gently. "Leah, do you hear me? You must say yes if you do. Say yes, Leah."

"Christiana? The dresses . . . the carriage . . ."

"Yes, that's right, Christiana and the dresses. You do want the dress to be right, don't you?"

"Christiana . . . yes—"

"There," Adrian exclaimed triumphantly. "You heard her that time, I wager."

"I heard," muttered Will. Squaring his shoulders, he continued, blessing Adrian's signet ring and instructing him to slip it on his bride's finger. It was so big on her, Adrian had to hold it in place and he felt a funny rustling in the pit of his stomach when her slender fingers curled around his in turn.

At last Will said the words Adrian had thought never to hear, at least not with anything resembling joy.

"By the power invested in me et cetera, et cetera, I now pronounce ye man and wife."

"That's it?" Adrian asked. "We're married?"

"Reasonably so," Will replied.

"Thank God. Let's go. I want to get her back and tucked into bed before she freezes to—" He caught himself and the three men exchanged uneasy glances. "Before she gets any colder."

Once *his wife* was safely back in bed and all the legalities attended to, there was naught holding Adrian there. Certainly there was no reason for him to spend what was left of the night sitting by Leah Stretton's bedside, sponging her forehead with a cool cloth, soothing her when she became restless and holding her hand until she drifted into sleep once more. And growing utterly, irrevocably sober.

Near dawn, he paced the small room, trying to outmaneuver the second thoughts that lay in ambush at the edges of his mind. He wasn't one for regrets, mostly because he never worried about consequences. He'd forfeited his heart years ago and said good riddance to it, and he'd given death more than one go at him on the battlefield. What was there left to fear? Certainly not his conscience. He didn't have one.

The lady's belongings had been neatly arranged atop the bureau and on the dressing stand beside it. Adrian absently trailed his fingers along the silver handle of her hairbrush and examined the dove-gray dress she must have been wearing when she took ill. Fashioned in what he knew to be the latest style, the narrow waist and full bodice suggested it had been fitted for a woman who was slender, but shapely. But then, he mused, recalling the feel of her in his arms, he already knew that.

The dress held the same warm, beguiling scent that engulfed him when he leaned over Leah Stretton to sponge her face or stroke her temples. He couldn't put a name to the fragrance. Nor did he care to, he told himself, abruptly dropping the dress back onto the stand.

As he turned away, his gaze fell on the crimson and gray tapestry bag at his feet. He shouldn't look, he thought, even as he realized he was going to do exactly that. He couldn't help himself; he needed to know about the woman who was his wife in name only. It wasn't merely morbid curiosity. He wanted more to take away with him than a memory of a few barely coherent syllables and an unconscious woman. He owed her that much.

Curious, he drew it out and glanced at the handwritten pages inside. His inquisitiveness changed to bewilderment, then amusement as he read.

The walls of Castle Faraway were tall and strong . . .

Several times his lips twitched and when he reached the final page he chuckled softly.

A fat lot of good the King's walls did him, however, for as surely as Princess Olivia grew more beautiful, she grew more restless. She was not the sort of princess to sit in her tower and wait for some prince to scale the walls.

In fact, Olivia wasn't entirely certain she wanted a prince in the first place. The few who had made it past the drawbridge all had long, thin noses and fussy velvet tunics and were forever adjusting their crowns. All in all, she found the frogs in the palace pond to be a more interesting lot, but since she had no desire to wed a frog, she decided to steal away from the castle and go in search of the most handsome, courageous, honest and true prince in all the world.

"You're making a big mistake," warned the teakettle as Olivia tiptoed through the palace kitchen early one summer morning, for in Faraway even teakettles have an opinion.

"You'll be sorry," added the feather duster from its hook near the door.

"Humph," said Olivia, without breaking stride. "Perhaps. But I'd rather be sorry than bored."

Adrian grinned and gazed at the woman in the bed with new interest. How much was the audacious Princess Olivia modeled on her creator? He would never know, he reminded himself, feeling an odd twinge as he returned the manuscript to the valise. Though he'd be drawn and quartered before he admitted it, he was beginning to wish he'd listened to Will last night.

At first light Mrs. O'Hara entered the room and

found him there. With a mixture of surprise and suspicion she hustled him out. Adrian refused her offer of breakfast, wanting to be gone by the time she discovered what he had done. Besides, he had a distinct lack of appetite that morning.

Colin was to ride with him back to town as planned, while Will would remain behind as long as necessary to *handle matters.* Adrian was grateful for that. For all that they teased Will about being ill-suited for his calling, he was a kind and gentle man, the sort Adrian wished to have by his side in his own final moments.

Adrian handed Will a full purse as he waited for his horse to be brought around. "This should take care of everything, including persuading her maid and driver not to say a word to anyone about all this."

"I'll take care of it." Will's furrowed brow suggested that Adrian was not the only one feeling serious morning-after pangs.

"If she needs anything," Adrian said. "Anything at all . . ."

"I know, Rave. I'll be in touch as soon as . . ." He swallowed hard. "I'll be in touch."

The very last thing Adrian did before leaving was find a pretense to bound back upstairs for a final glimpse of *his wife.*

She was alone. He approached the bed and took her hand in both of his, amazed to find that already the texture of her skin and the fineness of her bones were familiar to him.

He was vividly aware of the pulse beating rapidly at her wrist. How was it possible? he thought. She felt so warm, so *alive.* Slowly he lifted her hand to his lips, kissed her palm, and watched, transfixed, as her fingers curled over the spot his mouth had touched.

He had to get out of there.

With morning had come the inevitable clearing of his head—and the sharp, unshakable suspicion that this time even he may have gone too far.

"God be with you, Leah." He trembled slightly as he added, "And with me.

2

“More sherry, Lady Meredith?”

Meredith Gidding, wife of Sir Arthur Gidding and a prig beyond redemption, smiled warmly at Adrian, something she had not done for years prior to that evening. “No, thank you, Your Grace. I am quite content at the moment.”

He doubted that, though he understood that it was not sherry she thirsted for, but information. She and the other wives present at the small gathering in his Grosvenor Square home had come in hopes of learning more about the woman who had at long last snared the *ton*’s most elusive bachelor. And so they would.

All evening he had been dribbling fictional details of his whirlwind courtship and sudden marriage. That, after all, was his reason for inviting these three particular couples to dinner. Confiding in Lady Meredith and her bosom friends, Lady Hockliffe and Lady Torrington, was tantamount to placing a notice in the *Times*, announcing that he had wed and that his bride, who was to have joined him in town as soon as he had prepared his bachelor abode to receive her, had fallen ill and was convalescing with her sister in the country.

It was more or less the truth. As soon as he heard from Will, he could safely and sorrowfully reveal the final chapter in the story of his ill-fated "marriage" and then settle into the gloriously unfettered existence of a grieving widower.

The thought of it should have filled him with anticipation. Instead it caused an increasingly familiar tightness in his chest. He resisted the urge to tug at his collar. It had been over a fortnight since he'd returned and still no word from his friend. Surely it couldn't be much longer.

Or was she suffering still? he wondered, seriously troubled by the possibility, and by his own prickly misgivings over the whole thing. What was done could not be undone, but he'd be relieved when it was all behind him. Damn Will for not keeping him informed. He would have sent for news by now if not for his fear of putting the gossipmongers onto the scent. Not to mention an irrational, but still unsettling dread of somehow *rushing* matters.

"Enough of your war stories, Torrington," admonished Lady Hockliffe, giving the earl's arm a firm pat. "We simply must hear more from Raven about his oh-so-mysterious bride."

Adrian gave a small, suitably pensive smile. "There is no mystery, Lady Hockliffe, simply another case of Cupid finding his mark. I only wish Leah could be here tonight, for no mere words from me can ever capture her beauty and her spirit."

Lady Meredith gazed at him with amazement and approval. "Gracious, Raven, I had no idea there was such a romantic hiding beneath that notoriously sinful persona of yours."

The Marquis of Hockliffe, who knew him a great deal better, eyed him with suspicion.

Adrian graced them both with a self-effacing smile. "Nor did I, madam, nor did I."

"Tell us, Raven, is she as great a beauty as everyone is speculating?" inquired Lady Hockliffe.

He nodded. "Truly a vision. Almost, one might say, otherworldly."

"I must have details. What color is her hair?"

He closed his eyes briefly, allowing the corners of his mouth to turn up just a fraction. "The color of blazing chestnuts."

"And her eyes?"

"Like summer meadows, the clear, rich green that soothes and warms at once. Her complexion is as flawless as fresh cream, her lips as soft and alluring as the petals of a rose." Good God, he was nauseating even himself.

But not Lady Hockliffe, apparently.

"How poetic," she gushed. "So it was her beauty that finally captured you and brought you to your knees?"

"Only at first." He remembered to lift his hands with a sort of bewildered earnestness. "The instant she spoke I was ensnared by the velvet chains of her gentleness, her generosity of spirit, her goodness . . . But please, I beg you, no more of this. It only makes it harder to be without her."

"I'm surprised you can bear it at all," said Lady Meredith. "Why do you remain in town instead of joining your new bride?"

"Only at her impassioned request, I assure you, madam. Her sister writes that Leah is adamant that I not see her looking so pale and wan, and though I am equally fervent in replying that she could never appear less than perfect in my eyes, I am too besotted to deny the woman anything. Even my reluctant absence."

He allowed the chorus of feminine sighs to abate before continuing. "So I can only wait, and dream of the day when my beloved will join me here and I will hear her angelic voice fill these empty halls."

"She sings?"

"Like a nightingale," he replied.

"And does she play as well?"

"Masterfully. She was taught in Rome."

"So she attended school abroad?"

"Yes. A convent school actually."

Lady Torrington laughed outright, while the others limited themselves to surprised chuckles. "Good God, Raven, this is too rich. You, of all people, brought to heel by a convent girl."

"Yes. Lucky me." He hoped he wasn't straining credibility with the convent bit. "But now I really must insist that you cease this torment. I invited you here tonight in hopes of distracting myself from my loneliness, not wallowing in it."

"I must confess your invitation did come as a bit of a shock," said Lady Torrington. "You've never been much for formal entertaining."

"But I daresay he's done more than his share of *informal* entertaining here, and not in the dining room either," remarked Lord Torrington, the victim of one too many glasses of wine.

"Arthur," scolded his wife. "Please remember yourself."

"Of course, of course." The Marquis ducked his head like a child who'd had his knuckles rapped.

Of course, thought Adrian disdainfully. Thou shalt never speak the truth . . . unless it's behind someone's back. That was the *ton*'s first commandment. How tacky of Torrington to have broken it.

The Marquis cleared his throat and looked sternly at Adrian from beneath lowered brows. "What I meant to say was that it's time you put all those shenanigans behind you, past time really. A man in your position can't be too discreet. Isn't that right, Hockliffe?"

"Just so. A gentleman always puts marriage ahead of pleasure." He glanced quickly at his wife. "Sorry, my dear, that didn't come out quite right. But, well, you know what I mean, Raven."

Adrian nodded. He knew exactly what both men meant. Their hidden message was that it was perfectly all right for him to go on with his amorous liaisons, but he must now do so in secret while presenting to the world the facade of a faithful husband. Exactly as the men sitting at his table that evening did. As most of the married men of the *ton*—and more than a few of the married women—did as well. As his father had done and had expected him to do. With disastrous results.

Their remarks touched a raw nerve deep inside him. They also stirred his loathing for the hypocrisy that seemed to be the glue holding society together. He enjoyed chipping away at that hypocrisy. In fact, if his rather useless life had a mission, he supposed that was it.

Adrian thought about his latest pet project, still in its infancy. A jest of the first order, a scheme so scandalous, so abominable, it would forever cast him outside the ranks of the socially acceptable. A worthy goal, in his estimation. Now his guests' admonishments convinced him there was no time like the present to put things in motion.

"You've read my mind, sir," he said to Torrington,

shaking his head in feigned wonder at the other man's insight. "In fact, I intend to go beyond discreet. It is my goal to become a model of decorum and propriety . . . No, no, don't look at me that way," he said to the circle of raised eyebrows. "I mean every word I say."

"And just how do you propose to go about this?" inquired Lady Meredith with a muffled hint of laughter.

"By putting my, shall we say, frivolous pursuits behind me and applying my energies to more worthy undertakings."

"My my, this *is* a remarkable transformation," observed Lady Torrington. "Have you ever witnessed such a metamorphosis, my dear?"

"Hell's whiskers, no," muttered her husband, fishing out his quizzing glass to peer at Adrian.

"I have changed, Lady Torrington," said Adrian, "and you and these other good ladies must take some of the credit for it."

"We must?" she countered, startled. "What on earth can you mean?"

"By encouraging your husbands to refuse my participation in the fledgling Society for the Protection of Animals, you managed to shock me to my senses."

"Oh. That." She squirmed, clearly surprised that he knew who had spearheaded the movement to blackball him. The slight had occurred several months earlier, and in truth, he could not have cared less about it.

"Yes. That." Adrian expelled a self-recriminating sigh. "You forced me to ask myself what kind of man I was that decent ladies considered me unfit even to serve as a benefactor for the most miserable of four-legged beasts."

Lady Torrington exchanged a look with her friends. "Perhaps we were a bit hasty in our—"

"No, no, not at all," he interrupted. "I cannot deny that in my wasted past I have made a practice of over-indulging in liquor, cards and—if I may be frank—women of dubious nature. I insist you not make light of my shortcomings, but rather allow me to prove to you how determined I am to overcome them."

He glanced around the table, savoring his visitors' awkward and astonished expressions. "I have decided to follow your philanthropic example, gentlemen, and establish the London House of Birds."

"Did he say birds?" inquired Hockliffe, twisting in his seat so that his good ear faced the head of the table.

"Yes," replied Adrian. "Birds. Rare species from all over the world. Exotic birds with the most colorful plumage imaginable, brought together in one place for study, exhibition and—most important—the wholesome enjoyment of the masses."

"An aviary," exclaimed Lady Meredith, clapping her hands together.

"I suppose one might call it that," agreed Adrian with a straight face.

"What an absolutely marvelous idea."

"Yes, indeed," concurred Lady Hockliffe. "Why, it's the most exciting proposal I've heard in ages. I insist on being part of it, Raven. You must allow Harvey to contribute. Isn't that right, dear?"

"Yes, yes, of course," said her not nearly as enthusiastic husband.

"I was hoping you would pledge your assistance," said Adrian.

"Tell us how we can help," urged Sir Arthur.

He smiled. "In the simplest way possible, by becoming benefactors and lending your good names to the project. Your involvement will doubtless attract other notables to our cause. As for the more practical arrangements, I insist on proving my resolve by personally overseeing the organizational work and the acquisition process."

"You've already proven yourself to me," Lady Torrington assured him.

"Thank you, madam, and you have my word that you will be left speechless by the final result of my efforts. I predict that the grand opening of the London House of Birds will be the talk of the town for years to come."

All three women beamed at him as if he had suddenly sprouted angel wings. Adrian beamed back. If all went well, he would succeed in killing two birds at once . . . so to speak.

First, he would teach a well-deserved lesson to London's most narrow-minded hypocrites. At the same time he would also be enhancing his own scandalous reputation. After all, he had to think ahead to that day when his widower's immunity would expire. The House of Birds was guaranteed to convince even the most optimistic ladies of the *ton* that, beneath his title and his wealth, he was wretched husband material. And damn proud of it.

The simple truth was that, unlike most noblemen who looked to marriage to broaden their connections and fill their nurseries with heirs to be shaped and molded in their own image, he had neither use nor desire for a wife. And he fully intended to live, and die, without one.

"Would you be wanting some advice, ma'am?"

Leah glanced across the carriage at Bridget Granahan, the middle-aged maid who had been looking after her since the first day she arrived in Baumborough.

"Not really," she replied.

"A pity, since I'll be giving it to you just the same."

"Somehow I knew that you would."

"If you ask me, which you haven't, I'd tell you I think you're making a big mistake. You should not be going into the house of that madman."

The carriage was stopped outside Raven House, the London home of the Duke of Raven. The large brick dwelling was located in the most fashionable part of the city, but the house itself did not strike Leah as fasionable, or even particularly well kept. If she hadn't sent her driver, Rowland, to ferret out the information that the duke was in residence, and was in fact hosting a dinner party that very moment, she might have concluded the place was deserted. It had that air about it.

"Bridget, need I remind you that that madman, as you persist in referring to him, is my husband."

"Husband?" echoed her maid. "Pooh. A blinkin' stranger is what he is . . . and a daft one at that. Just ask yourself what manner of man would think to wed a lady who—"

"That's enough, Bridget. We've been over this time and again. What's more, I know that Mr. Grantley rewarded you and Rowland handsomely for your promise to remain silent about the circumstances surrounding my . . . marriage."

"As if I needed rewarding." Bridget's expression was indignant and wounded at the same time. "Or Rowland either. We'd both of us do anything for you and Lady Christiana, you know that, and no extra coin is ever needed."

"I do know that." Leah reached across the carriage to squeeze her maid's hand. "But I want you to have the reward just the same. After all, the coins came from the duke's purse and that's the least he owes us under the circumstances."

"He owes you, is more like it. An apology, for starters."

"Don't worry, Bridget, I shall collect from *His Grace* in my own manner."

"You're sure about going in there then?" asked the maid.

"Very sure," Leah lied.

Truthfully, she wasn't sure of anything except that she was not about to let anyone, not even the infamous Duke of Raven, destroy her sister Christiana's chance for happiness.

When Mr. Grantley first revealed to her what had transpired during her illness, her disbelief had given way to indignation, and then anger. For days, her feelings had been a raging inferno, inflaming old wounds, laying bare other heartaches and resentments she thought she had left behind. Gradually reason returned. She was accustomed to dealing with injustice, she told herself, and she would deal with this.

But how? What could be done about a husband one had never seen and didn't want? If the blackguard even was her husband, after such a sham of a service. On the other hand, if he wasn't legally her husband, and had indeed spent the night by her bedside, she was ruined. And Christiana along with her.

As she lay in bed convalescing, she'd vacillated between a desire to see Raven suffer for his sins—something suitably creative and horrid, such as being staked out atop a hill of ants—and a cowardly but equally tempting desire to return to the uncomplicated safety of home and pretend the whole thing had never happened.

When she could no longer avoid making a decision,

she'd done the only thing that made sense at the time; she'd resorted to asking herself what Princess Olivia would do in her place. The answer had come to her instantly. Olivia would take action. Somehow she would turn the whims of fate to her advantage, Leah realized, resolving then and there to do the same.

What in God's name could she have been thinking? That she, who was far better at writing about romance and adventure than living it, could turn the tables on one of the most ruthless and debauched men in all of England?

She stared at the imposing wrought-iron gates of Raven House, embellished with fierce bird of prey finials that, in her opinion, would look equally at home on the gates of hell. Olivia could keep her adventures, she thought. At that instant, given a choice, Leah would prefer to be bored than sorry.

Unfortunately, thanks to the duke's arrogance, she had not been given a choice. She was determined to secure Christiana's future, and if that meant venturing deeper into the lion's den than she had originally planned, so be it.

Marshalling her courage, she turned to Bridget. "However, my being sure of bearding the lion in his den is not enough," she said. "I also need to be sure of you. If I can't count on you to back me up, how will I ever manage to keep the truth from Christiana?"

"Wouldn't it be simpler to just come out and tell her what's happened?"

"No." Leah shook her head. "That's out of the question. You know how impulsive she can be. She would be so indignant on my behalf that there's no telling what she might say or do. I fear that within hours of her knowing, the whole humiliating story would be all over London, sordidly embellished along the way, you can be sure, and all my planning and scrimping and saving to give her a glorious, unblemished season will have been for naught. Perhaps someday I will be able to confide the truth, but not now."

"If you say so."

"I do."

"In that case, my lips are sealed." Bridget pressed her fingertips to her lips to illustrate.

"Well, please unseal them long enough to wish me luck."

Bridget's eyes widened. "You're going in now?"

Leah nodded.

Bridget flinched. "Perhaps it would be better to wait till morn . . ."

"No. I prefer for our little *reunion* to take place in front of witnesses."

She summoned the driver to assist her, arranging the cloak around her shoulders, breathing deeply to steady her nerves and hoping desperately that if she managed to *appear* confident, sooner or later she would begin to *feel* confident.

Her last sight as she left the carriage was of Bridget making the sign of the cross.

Adrian was still savoring the praise being heaped on him by his guests when the crusty manservant who managed his household appeared by his side.

"What is it, Thorne?" he asked.

Thorne bent to whisper close to his ear. "A problem, sir. You ought—"

"You handle it," ordered Adrian, reluctant to have his amusement interrupted.

"Yes, sir. But you really ought to—"

"Not now, Thorne."

The servant set his jaw and glared at Adrian.

Adrian glared back. He understood that formal entertaining was a rarity in Raven House and a bloody strain on everyone, but Snake, the former infantry-man who passed for a cook, had turned out an edible meal and a pair of feckless footmen had managed to relay it to the table with a minimum of mishaps. The least the old crank could do was *pretend* to be proper and heedful.

Instead he continued to glare. "What I am trying to say to you, Y'Grace, is—"

"Raven? Darling?" a woman's voice called from somewhere outside the dining room.

Darling?

Adrian registered the gleam of smug satisfaction in Thorne's squinty eyes just before the same intriguing female voice spoke again, this time from just inside the dining room.

"There you are." The woman threw open her arms and smiled at him as if they were alone. "Surprise, darling, I'm home."

Adrian gaped at her, frozen in his seat even as the other gentlemen at the table leapt to their feet. It was she. Leah. *His wife.*

Oh sweet Lord.

What was she doing standing in his dining room?

Hell, what was she doing *standing* anywhere?

She was supposed to be . . . well, dead.

He placed his palms flat on the table and pushed himself upright on leaden legs, only distantly aware of the expectant hush all around him.

This woman was most definitely not dead.

She was breathtakingly alive. With hair the color of blazing chestnuts and eyes like fields of clover. My God, his wife was a beauty.

His wife.

Oh sweet Lord, what the bloody hell was he going to do now?

He squared his shoulders, his usually quick wits slowed by shock. Instinct made him certain of only two things. First, if Leah Stretton was standing there calling him "darling" and apparently presenting herself as his wife, he'd damn well better start acting like a husband in a hurry. And second, when he got his hands on Will Grantley, England was going to be minus one inept, disloyal botchbag of a rector.

"Leah. My sweet," he said, forcing his facial muscles to form a smile. "You have taken me totally by surprise."

"Good." She captured his gaze and held it. "That was my intent."

The look she gave him left no doubt that she had meant to ambush him with her sudden appearance and was enjoying his discomfiture to the hilt.

But why?

Why indeed, he thought, recovering his senses. He should probably count himself lucky she'd come alone—and unarmed. Belatedly it occurred to him to wonder if the woman had brothers. Large brothers. Belatedly it occurred to him to wonder any number of things he should have considered a fortnight ago.

At the moment however, his first order of business was to wipe the increasingly speculative looks from the faces of their audience.

Striding across the room, he grasped Leah by her shoulders. "God, how I've missed you. When you first walked in I thought I must be seeing things . . . that loneliness had driven me mad and you were but an apparition. But now . . ." He ran his hands down her arms, then up, finally sliding them around to her back to draw her closer and press her stiff body tightly to his. She blinked rapidly, signaling a crack in her composure.

Good, thought Adrian. Spring herself on him, would she?

"Now that I am convinced you are real, my own flesh-and-blood Leah," he went on, "I must do what I have been dreaming of doing since I left you in Devon what seems like years ago."

Their gazes remained locked as he lowered his head. He saw resistance flash in her eyes and felt it in her tensed muscles, but she didn't flinch or try to pull away. Had she, his urge to conquer might have been satisfied and he might have gone easy on her. As it was, he tightened his grip and opened his mouth, using his tongue to claim her the way any randy bridegroom would want to, but would doubtless restrain himself from doing before onlookers.

Adrian seldom restrained himself, and he certainly wasn't about to start now and give this presumptuous chit the notion that she had the upper hand. He kissed her hard and long, nearly forgetting that they were not alone and that it was merely a performance. His blood heated rapidly and one of his hands moved to rest on the pleasing curve of her hip, as naturally as if he had every right in the world to put it there.

When he finally remembered himself, he lifted his head slowly, watching her long, dark lashes flutter and open.

"Westerham," she said, her tone steady and audible enough for everyone in the room to hear.

Adrian frowned. "What did you say?"

"I said you left me in Westerham, not Devon. Have you forgotten already?"

Westerham. Saint Anne's. The rectory. Of course. Devon was where her *fictional* sister lived. But she had no way of knowing that, or the countless other details about her life that he had fabricated that evening. That could be a problem.

Could be a problem? He nearly laughed out loud at his own absurdity. This entire affair was turning into a debacle right before his eyes.

"No, no, of course I haven't forgotten," he assured her gently. "Though when you are close to me, it is a wonder I can even remember to breathe."

"Don't worry, darling. If necessary, I'll prompt you. I happen to be a most accomplished breather."

"Yes, I can see that," he murmured, aware of the impudent glint in her eyes as she gazed up at him with seeming adoration. He released her and turned to his guests. "Please forgive my lapse in manners. I totally forgot myself for a moment."

Sir Arthur raised his hand. "Perfectly understandable under the circumstances, Raven. Think nothing of it."

"Yes, allowances must be made for newlyweds," his wife chimed in, her eyes as bright as those of a hound circling a meaty bone. "Especially when they have been separated for so long. But now, Raven, I insist you make us acquainted with this surprise addition to our party."

"Of course." He handled the introductions as succinctly as possible. Try as his overtaxed brain did, it could not come up with any way to avoid using the words *my wife* in presenting her. Though the phrases *long-lost sister* and *recently acquired ward* did flit through his mind.

The damage was done now. The best he could hope for was to limit the repercussions as much as possible. To that end he proceeded to push the chairs nearest him back to the table before any of his guests could resettle themselves.

"I know you'll understand if I beg to end the evening prematurely," he said when they persisted in lingering, inquiring about Leah's health and her journey to town, precisely the things he intended to inquire about the instant he had her alone. "I fear if sh . . . Le . . . *my wife* overtaxes herself she will suffer a relapse."

His wife slipped her arm through his. "Your concern is touching, darling, but altogether unnecessary. The doctor assures me that kidney stones rarely afflict women my age and a recurrence is unlikely."

Stones? thought Adrian.

"Stones?" exclaimed Lady Hockliffe. "Is that what ailed you? Why you poor dear, that is a horror." She swiped at Raven with her closed fan. "You beastly man. If I were your bride I should never forgive you for abandoning me in my hour of need."

"I shall spend the rest of my life making amends," vowed Adrian, kissing the back of Leah's hand before tucking it inside his arm once more. Gently. There would be time later to squeeze the truth out of her.

3

The Duke of Raven dispatched his guests with a lack of delicacy that Leah found appalling, though not surprising. She had spent hours questioning the remorseful Mr. Grantley and learned, to her chagrin, that she was wed to one of the most arrogant, self-indulgent rakes in the land.

Threatened with swooning—a bluff, since she was not an accomplished swooner, or even a passable one—Mr. Grantley had reluctantly revealed that her *husband* had a dreadful reputation and was notorious for living down to each deplorable nuance. He was generally thought to be heartless and wicked, though Grantley loyally maintained that the duke had a caring, generous side that he kept hidden.

Well hidden.

He was, in short, the very last man Leah would have chosen to wed, had there been any choosing involved.

All of that was beside the point now, she told herself, as she watched his guests depart. Her one advantage lay in the fact that even a man of Raven's ilk would not want to be publicly associated with the gruesome deed of which he was guilty.

"Come with me," he ordered the instant they were alone.

Having recovered from the aftershocks of being manhandled and kissed so audaciously, Leah planted her feet on the floor and watched the duke's rapidly disappearing back.

He reappeared and stood glaring at her from the far end of the hallway. "Are you deaf as well as ill-mannered?" he demanded loudly.

Heart pounding, Leah contrived to glance unhurriedly to her left, then her right. "Are you by chance addressing me? I was certain from your tone that you must be speaking to your dog."

"No," he replied, his smile quick and nasty. "I was able to teach my dogs to respond to a whistle."

"How exceedingly clever of you. What other tricks can you do?"

His brows shot up. In his eyes she saw annoyance edging toward anger, but still she stood her ground.

For the longest moment of her life, he stared at her. Then, executing an exaggerated bow, he swept his arm in a wide arc. "Madam, will you please do me the honor of accompanying me to the library so we may discuss privately a certain matter of importance to us both?"

She smiled, thrilled by this first, small victory. "I'd be delighted."

This time he allowed her to precede him upstairs into the library, situated at the back of the spacious, if somewhat gloomy, townhouse. Raven House. Humph. Raven's lair was more like it. She made a quick inspection as she passed and, as always lately, found herself calculating how it fit into her plan. The place was in sore need of a thorough remodeling, but there was no time. Thanks to her illness, she was already weeks behind schedule. A top-to-bottom cleaning, some flowers and perhaps a fresh coat of milk paint here and there would have to suffice.

If all went well that evening, she would send for Christiana to join her as planned. The difference was that instead of launching her into society from a modest house in Knightsbridge, which was all their budget had allowed, she would be firing her off in style, from one of the most prestigious addresses in all of London. Not to mention having the considerable resources and influence of the Duke of Raven behind her. If her *husband* thought he could buy her off with a few gold coins, he was due a lesson in paying the piper.

"Please be seated." He indicated a leather wing chair as he shoved aside newspapers and betting slips to make room for himself on one corner of the desk. She took off her cloak and sat.

Silence.

Leah folded her hands in her lap and gazed around as she waited for him to speak. Two walls of the room were lined with leather-bound books, which her fingers itched to explore. A massive fireplace was centered on one of the remaining walls and a bank of tall windows on the other, overlooking, she surmised, a sizable garden, no doubt as poorly tended as the rest of the house. That would have to be remedied as well, she noted, imagining a colorful oasis of flowers and greenery where Christiana could entertain suitors on warm afternoons. Oh yes, this was going to work out splendidly.

The continued silence afforded her ample time to

note in detail the framed maps, the subtly patterned Persian rug and the . . . nudes. A pair of them, one hung on either side of the door. She could hardly miss them. They were an explosion of crimson in the otherwise somber room, featuring the most voluptuous and hungry-looking women she had ever seen.

Leah managed to regard them as placidly as she did everything else around her, according them no more—or less—attention than the crystal decanters or wooden globe, as if erotic paintings were something she encountered with tedious regularity. When in fact, she would love nothing more than to get up and take a closer look.

She also managed to slant several quick glances at the man staring at her. He was quite tall and flawlessly proportioned. His dress was what she had once read described as the fastidious and simply elegant style of Brummell. At the time, the words had conjured in her mind a dashing and darkly romantic image and Raven did not disappoint. Black boots, snug black trousers, black waistcoat and jacket, finished off with a snowy shirt and cravat that set off to great advantage his bronze skin and the bluest eyes she had ever seen.

He looked like what he was, a man who bred scandal and broke hearts with callous disregard for anyone but himself. Any sane woman would have picked up her skirts and fled the instant he tried to kiss her. Unfortunately for Leah, fleeing was not an option.

"Well," he prompted, breaking the silence abruptly. "I am waiting."

"For . . ." she prompted in turn.

His gaze went from aloof inquiry to sharp and penetrating. "For an explanation of why you saw fit to barge in here without notice or invitation."

"I see. Actually I had rather expected to be on

the receiving end of any explanations that were proffered."

"Me? Explain?" He folded his arms with a short, incredulous laugh. "Do you have any idea who I am, madam?"

"I know exactly who you are. I regret to say you are my husband."

"I am a duke," he corrected impatiently.

"Which clearly makes me a duchess," she responded quietly, but with equal vehemence. "*Your* duchess, to be precise, Your Grace. I have your signed letter of intent and this ring to prove it."

She held out her left hand, willing it not to tremble. The heavy gold signet ring, according to Mr. Grantley, had been placed on her finger as she lay semiconscious in Raven's arms.

"That proves nothing. It doesn't even fit properly."

"It does now." She turned her hand palm up to illustrate. "Mr. Grantley was kind enough to arrange for a goldsmith to fit it."

"Did he now? Well, Mr. Grantley is a—"

"A decent man," she interjected. "He deeply regrets the role he played in this matter and has assured me that he will do whatever I desire to make it right. I bear him no ill will. We all make mistakes."

"Do we ever." He got to his feet and began to pace.

"I think you are a bad influence on him."

"Is that so?" He turned and cornered her with his wolfish stare. Leah braced herself, expecting him to bare his teeth at any second. "Tell me, *Duchess,* do you have any other insights into my character you'd like to share?"

"Yes, but they can wait."

He laughed harshly and ran his hands through his dark, wavy hair, dragging it back so that the chiseled planes and angles of his face were bathed in golden candlelight.

He was too handsome, she decided. Distractingly so, the way a fine painting was distracting, compelling one to look again and again. Leah could not, however, imagine a mere painting causing her heart to hammer the way it was hammering now.

"This is insane," he said at last, dropping his hands to his sides.

"My sentiments exactly."

"You'll never get away with it."

She raised her eyebrows. "With what?"

He made an impatient gesture. This . . . whatever brings you here, that's what."

"Only two short weeks ago I would have agreed with you. But then, I also would have believed it impossible for a woman to fall ill and wake up several days later to discover that she is wed to a man she has never met. A man, I might add, of questionable character."

His mouth curled into a mocking smile. "I thought that could wait?"

Leah conceded the point with a nod.

"All right." He grabbed a straight-back chair, spun it around and straddled it, facing her. "I made a mistake and I regret it. What's it going to cost me?"

"Cost you?"

"Yes, yes, get on with it. Name your price."

"Oh, I see." She studied his countenance. "Tell me, sir, do you regret your action because it was a sneaky, despicable thing to do or because you ended up with a wife instead of a corpse?"

He had the decency to look uneasy. "See here, Lady . . . Stretton . . . Raven . . ." He growled with frustration. "I don't even know what the devil to call you."

"I see no harm in your calling me Leah." She paused. "We are married, after all."

His perfect mouth curved in a rueful smile and something warm and unfamiliar unfurled in the pit of Leah's stomach. Nerves, she told herself.

"All right, *Leah.*" He tugged at his cravat. "What I started to say was that I do regret, very much actually, what occurred. I never intended you any harm. On the contrary, I arranged to handle all your needs and expenses. Did the kind and decent Mr. Grantley bother to tell you that?"

"He told me everything."

"Traitor," he muttered.

"Because he serves a higher master?"

"Will? Ha! He serves himself more often than not."

"Mr. Grantley is an ordained minister."

"And just who do you think ordained him . . . or at least made it possible?"

"He explained to me that you are his benefactor."

The duke nodded with satisfaction.

"That only makes it more reprehensible for you to have coerced him into aiding and abetting you in such a fashion."

"Coerced?" he retorted. "I was half-foxed at the time. So was the rector. Did he confess that? We all were. Colin had just finished going on about how Reggie Plimpton had been widowed almost as soon as he was wed. And I thought—"

"You thought *how convenient,*" she broke in sharply, provoked by his attempt to rationalize his actions. "Oh yes, I know all about your little plan. You thought you'd found a way to use marriage as a shield against unwelcome female attentions without suffering the actual bother of a wife."

He shrugged. "Something like that."

"And there I was, *conveniently* unconscious, so you

didn't have to contend with petty details, such as my consent or my feelings about the whole thing. Oh no, what I thought or wanted or felt didn't matter a twit to you. Why should it? After all, you are a man, a *nobleman* at that, a high and mighty peer of the realm. And I am only a woman, whose life—and death apparently—are subject to your whims. Your drunken whims, I might add."

She was trembling, Leah realized with annoyance. She was not given to temperamental outbursts. In fact, she deplored all extremes of emotion. She had purposely delayed this meeting until she had brought her initial turmoil under tight control once more, anger replaced with common sense, and bitterness with careful planning. Or so she'd thought. Now, when she most needed to think coolly and appear confident, her emotions threatened to overwhelm her.

She would not permit that to happen. She was no longer fourteen years old and this man was not her father. She was not going to cry or beg him to let her stay. She was going to compose herself and get on with the business that brought her there.

A few deep breaths helped to revive her determination.

Looking up, she found Raven watching her with cynical amusement. That helped even more.

"Finished?" he asked.

"Quite."

"Feel better?"

"No. I will not feel better until we have settled this unfortunate dilemma which you have thrust upon me."

"So now it's an unfortunate dilemma. Just a moment ago you seemed to think it something far more meaningful, *Duchess,* as you so passionately brandished your ring to illustrate."

"*Your* ring," Leah corrected. "But passionate? Meaningful? At the risk of disappointing Your Grace, may I point out that we are merely married, not lovers."

"Perish the thought."

"I have."

"I never entertained it in the first place." His mouth hardened. "Enough sparring. Let's get on with it, shall we? What is it you want from me, *Duchess*? Money? Jewels? A cozy little setup of your own here in town?"

"None of those things," she replied, steeling herself for what lay ahead. "I want only what you promised me before man and God."

He frowned in confusion.

"A husband," she said.

He shot to his feet, flinging the chair aside. "You cannot be suggesting we continue this farce?"

"I'm not *suggesting* anything. I'm demanding you honor your pledge."

"That's absurd. We don't even know each other."

Leah also stood. If he wanted to glare at her he would have to do it eye to eye. "The fact that we are strangers is something you ought to have considered before we spoke our vows."

"*We* didn't speak any vows," he argued. "You were barely conscious, for pity's sake."

"Says who?"

"Says me," he roared. "Says anyone who was there."

"Not I," she countered. "Nor Mr. Grantley. He claims that had he not heard me affirm the vows, he could not have legally proceeded with the service."

"What he heard was . . ." He stopped and shook his head with exasperation. "It's not worth discussing. The entire marriage is a sham and any claim you make to the contrary will never stand the scrutiny of the court."

"Precisely."

Her placid agreement obviously took him by surprise. In fact, for a moment it appeared he had forgotten which side he was on and who had started this in the first place.

He shot her a probing look. "What, exactly, are you after, madam?"

"Exactly what I said a moment ago. I want you to honor your pledge to me . . . at least for the time being."

"And if I refuse?" he demanded, his arms crossed and his jaw thrust out.

She understood then, if she hadn't before, that showing any hint of weakness or vulnerability would be her undoing. She squared her shoulders. "Then I shall be forced to ruin your reputation as deliberately as you have ruined mine."

He laughed. Loudly.

"It's hardly a laughing matter," she admonished, her temper rising.

"I beg to differ," he said, laughing again. "If your goal is to ruin my reputation, madam, all I can say is good luck. I've taken a stab or two at it myself through the years and I fear my good name is as besmirched as it's likely to get."

"I'm well aware that you have the reputation of being something of a—"

"Miscreant? Degenerate? Satan's spawn?"

"Rogue. But surely, wedding a dying woman, without her consent, will not be tolerated even from a titled nobleman."

His mouth twisted. "You would be amazed at what is tolerated if the price is right."

Leah gaped at him, alarmed that this was not going

at all the way she had planned. "But people will talk. They always do."

He shrugged. "Let them."

"Do you mean to say you don't care at all what people say about you?"

"Not a whit."

He meant it, Leah was certain. As certain as she suddenly was that Mr. Grantley's depiction of his friend, as appalling as it had been, did not come close to being the whole truth. The man was a knave, through and through. Still, she told herself, struggling to regroup, even knaves have weak spots.

"What of your friends?" she demanded. "Mr. Grantley could find himself in serious straits. What is the penalty for officiating at an unlawful marriage? Fourteen years transportation, I believe."

His smile was mocking. "Nice try, wrong target. You see, at the moment, I would be most willing to row the rector's sorry hide all the way to Australia myself."

"I hope you feel as antagonistically toward your other friend, the barrister. I daresay he will also have some explaining to do . . . not the least of which is how your own signature came to be on a back-dated license."

"Old Colin is like a cat," he told her, his deepening smile eroding her confidence even further. "Nine lives. Colin will land on his feet. As for the license . . ." He shrugged. "That shouldn't be too expensive to resolve."

"A pity you can't buy off all of London," she snapped.

"Who says I can't?"

There was a stretch of stunned silence as she let that sink in and hit bottom.

"Well," she said finally, "you're in luck then. Because that's what you'll have to do once word of your macabre stunt gets around. That is, if your friends don't take offense at being lied to in the first place." There was just the slight tensing of his jaw, and she hoped that meant she had hit her mark. Concealing her trembling hands behind her back, she peered at him with great interest. "I'm curious, what *did* you tell them about me? They all seemed so pleased to make my acquaintance this evening."

"Chalk it up to curiosity," he managed to reply offhandedly. "I told them you were a runaway nun."

She inhaled sharply. "You're joking, of course?"

He gave his head a careless shake. "For all I know, it's true. You definitely kiss like a nun."

"I most certainly do not," retorted Leah. "Though one must wonder how you could possibly have knowledge of—"

"You don't want to know," he interjected.

"You're right. I don't. I do, however, want an answer to my question. Do you or do you not intend to honor your vows?"

"You mean, do I or do I not intend to go on paying, for the rest of what would no doubt be a miserable life, for one drunken mistake?"

"I have no interest whatsoever in the rest of your miserable life," she told him. "Only in the duration of the current season."

His eyes gleamed with new interest. "Why?"

"Because it suits my purposes. Surely self-interest is a motive you can understand."

"To what purposes do you refer?" he asked, ignoring her barb.

"I have only one purpose for this trip, and a quite simple one at that. I'm here to provide my younger sister with a season in town."

"Christiana," he said quietly.

"Yes." She regarded him with suspicion. "How did you know her name?"

"You mentioned it that night. In your sleep."

Leah quickly lowered her gaze, her cheeks warming. "Mr. Grantley said you spent the night by my side."

"Yes, I did. You were very feverish. You seemed to sleep easier if I sponged your forehead with a cool cloth."

The picture painted by his words fixed itself in her mind, joining the fragmented memories that had been teasing her ever since she regained consciousness, quick, unsettling flashes of a deep, soothing voice and a strong, tender touch. She *must* have been feverish, she thought tartly. Soothing and tender are not the words she would choose to describe the man standing before her.

"I suppose you are waiting for me to express my gratitude," she said, as the silence lengthened. "So I shall. Thank you for ruining my life."

Amusement tugged at the corners of his mouth as he gave a small bow. "All in a day's work, madam. Now, tell me why your sister isn't here with you."

Leah hesitated, reluctant to reveal more than she absolutely had to. "The plan was for me to get settled in town and send to Baumborough for her to join me."

"Baumborough?"

"Yes, our home is there. I'm not surprised you haven't heard of it. It's a small village on the western border. Very small," she added, "and very near the border. In fact, if you miss our turn, you're in Scotland."

"That is a long journey for a woman alone. You wouldn't have preferred to travel together?"

"That would be my preference, yes, but Christiana

is barely eighteen and has no patience for the mundane details of setting up a household. I decided that by coming ahead, I could handle all that and be ready to devote myself to Chrissie when she arrived. Since both our parents are deceased, I feel even more responsible for her than an older sister ordinarily would." That concluded her preplanned explanation.

"I see." Raven's expression had grown thoughtful and skeptical. "Tell me, madam, is your sister's interest in London of an artistic nature? Touring the great museums and galleries?"

"I'm sure we shall visit a gallery or two," said Leah, thinking that a tour of the shops on Bond Street was more Chrissie's style.

"Or perhaps her pursuits are in a more quiet, intellectual vein."

Quiet? Intellectual? Chrissie? Leah had to bite the inside of her cheek to keep from chuckling as he continued.

"In which case, she may choose to confine herself to the reading rooms or one of the societies dedicated to a particular discipline. Astronomy or botany, perhaps?"

"Actually," she said, "Chrissie is a very lively, outgoing girl. When she was younger she found ways to keep herself happy and entertained at home, but now she needs to be around people more."

He feigned surprise. "Are there no people in Baumborough?"

"Of course there are, but in London she will be able to go to balls and parties and meet gentlemen her own age." When he continued to stare at her blankly, she heaved a sigh and added, "*Eligible* gentlemen."

"Ah, we come at last to the truth. You're here to trap a husband for your sister."

Leah bristled. "Trap a husband? I think not. Help her to be trapped? Now that is more like it, given the inequities of the marriage contract. But if marriage and a family of her own are what Chrissie wants, then that is what I want for her. And I shall do whatever necessary to make my sister happy."

"Even if it means being my wife?"

"Even so."

"How revoltingly devoted of you." He reached for a bottle of brandy and held it aloft with a questioning look.

Leah shook her head.

He poured himself a generous portion and downed it. "Not that I have much firsthand knowledge of familial devotion. My own experience runs more to a father who proved he would go to any lengths to *stop* me from having what I wanted most in life. And a mother who devoted herself to looking the other way. Always."

"I'm so sorry," she said quietly.

Adrian turned away abruptly. He had no idea what had prompted him to make such a revealing remark, much less what he expected her response to be, but the straightforward compassion in her tone was very unsettling.

"Don't be," he advised, keeping his back to her. "It all turned out for the best. And what about your happiness, dear wife?" he inquired over his shoulder. "Did you perhaps set out from Baumborough hoping for a double wedding?"

She laughed, a little self-consciously it seemed to him, and he found himself turning to see her expression. "Not quite. I'm a bit past the age for a season. Besides, I have all I want waiting for me at home, thank you very much."

"Such as?" He was conscious of an undercurrent in her tone. Wistfulness? Or relief? He couldn't be sure.

"I do some writing, and gardening, and of course there's the running of the household."

"How romantic," he observed dryly.

"I'm afraid I'm not a very romantic person."

"Really?" He surveyed her closely, recalling the pages he'd found tucked in the bottom of her valise. "What about us?"

"Us?"

"You know, till death us do part and all that rubbish?"

She rolled her eyes. "Please. No, I have something eminently more reasonable and of shorter duration in mind for us."

"Tell me."

"You agree to allow our *marriage* to stand until I see Christiana wed. For the benefit of the rest of the world, we must appear to be the perfect couple, attentive, devoted, and *faithful.* Please, don't scowl. Our sudden marriage is bound to cause speculation as is. I know your reputation for womanizing and I refuse to have you fanning the flames by catting around behind my back."

"What if your sister doesn't land a husband?"

"She will. Christiana is beautiful and an accomplished flirt and not overly interested in anything of an intellectual nature, which should make her pleasing beyond all reason to the young men of the *ton.*"

"Only a fool would argue with that," he said, his tone sardonic. "And if I agree to this charade?"

"Then I shall agree to an annulment immediately following Christiana's wedding, and shall return home never to darken your door again."

He crossed the room and dropped into his chair

behind the desk. Leaning back, he propped one booted foot on the desk as he studied her. Everything in his experience warned him not to believe a word she said, that women were master manipulators and invariably had a hidden agenda. If his new bride was willing to admit that she was seeking a husband for her sister, it was a safe bet that wasn't all she was after.

She was good, he'd hand her that, from the very convincing mix of determination and nervousness in her manner to the way she had responded and yet hadn't to his welcoming kiss. She may well be from the back of nowhere, as she claimed, but there was more to her than that. She didn't look or speak like a country miss and no innocent, inexperienced maiden could have devised such a solution to her problem, or sauntered in to deliver it so smoothly.

He didn't trust her. He hadn't trusted any woman in years, ten years to be exact. Even if he were foolish enough to change now, he would never choose this woman, who so obviously harbored ulterior motives.

Still, her proposal was tempting. In more ways than one. Leah Stretton was beautiful, and she intrigued him, and the thought of having her right under his roof, at his disposal, was not at all unpleasant. Especially knowing it was strictly temporary. It was almost too good to be true, and certainly more than he deserved after the stunt he'd pulled.

Then too, there was his reputation to consider. Though he'd refused to concede the point to her, there was a crucial distinction between being thought a scoundrel and being branded a liar. He *had* spoken openly about his marriage. Hell, he'd bragged about it. More damning yet, he had welcomed her that evening as if she were his bride and introduced her as such to six of the most influential gossips in all London. It would be awkward to explain her away now.

Lastly, there was his plan for the London House of Birds. Masquerading as a devoted husband would not only allow him to go forward with his plan, it would also lend credence to his claim to have abandoned his wicked ways.

Adrian was well aware that he was trying to talk himself into accepting her terms. But the reason, to his surprise, had less to do with her desirability or his latest scheme than with the small, worried V that had formed between her brows. She sat, pitched forward, hands clenched on the arms of her chair, waiting for his decision.

Not that he would have wasted time considering her proposal unless it served his own purposes as well, he assured himself. What she suggested was straightforward enough, and relatively painless. Foolproof even, since he would see the sister wed by season's end even if he had to buy her a bloody groom. A few short months of captivity and both their problems would be solved. And he would never have to think about Leah Stretton or that misbegotten night again.

"You said we must appear the perfect couple when the rest of the world is watching," he began, reaching for a cigar from the humidor. He held it up. "Do you mind?"

"Not at all." She smiled. "A man's home is his castle after all."

That was an encouraging attitude, he thought as he lit his cigar. "What about when the world is not watching?"

If she understood the implication of his question and was flustered by it, it didn't show. "When no one else is present, we may have as little to do with each other as we please. However, I must insist that no one, not even your friends Mr. Grantley and Mr. Thornton, know the truth about our arrangement."

"Isn't it a bit late for that?"

"Not if we employ a bit of ingenuity. We shall tell them simply that we have decided to make the best of a bad situation, which is close to the truth, and request that they keep the circumstances of our wedding to themselves. Christiana will have to be handled more delicately, however. She and I are extremely close and she will be quick to suspect if anything is amiss."

"In that case, why not simply tell her the truth?"

"Because she would be outraged on my behalf. She would fret and feel guilty that I was undertaking such a charade for her sake and that would ruin everything. This is her one chance for the kind of life she longs for and for the happiness she deserves, and I will not have it spoilt for her in any way. Nor will I permit the loose tongue of a friend or servant to ignite gossip. The illusion must be complete."

"Of course," he murmured, running his gaze over her slowly as he savored the prospect of playing the role of her husband, in every way.

"Does that mean you'll do it?"

"Ordinarily, if confronted with such a blatant attempt at blackmail, I'd tell you to go hang. I happen to enjoy being the object of a good, steamy scandal. It enlivens the season and serves to keep the most faint-hearted of the husband-hunters at bay. However, at present I am about to launch a . . . business venture of a delicate nature, one that will not be well served by gossip. So, yes," he concluded, offering her his hand, "it appears we do have a deal."

"Excellent." She took his hand and shook it, not a second longer than what politeness dictated.

That was still sufficient time for Adrian to register

the soft, familiar contours of her palm and the way it fit comfortably against his own.

"I'll write Christiana at once with the good news of our marriage and to tell her how eager you are to have her join us here at Raven House," she said.

"Here?" He was on his feet, tossing the cigar into the marble tray on his desk. "Do you mean you intend for your sister to stay here?"

She shook her head as if he were a not-too-bright child. "Of course. Where else would she stay?"

Adrian shrugged. How the hell should he know? He was ignorant about sisters or the launching of them into society, and would prefer to keep it that way.

"Where had you planned for her to stay?" he inquired.

"I took a small house in Knightsbridge for the season, but there is no question of Chrissie staying there unchaperoned. Besides, even if that were an option, that house does not compare with this one as a place to receive suitors and host soirees."

"Suitors? Soirees?" Adrian felt queasy.

"Of course. I daresay that is the silver lining to this nightmare," she declared, looking very pleased with herself. "Being under your protection should advance Christiana's cause considerably."

Under his protection. Now there was a picture. He was saddled not only with a wife, but with a sweet young virgin to protect. Him. It was as if some cosmic jester had picked up the world and turned it upside down.

"She may stay here," he said, "but let me make one thing abundantly clear. I will not take an active part in any husband hunting."

"Very well." She reached for her cloak and tossed it over her arm.

She stood with her back to him as she arranged the folds of her cloak, and a tendril of hair came loose, a dark, gleaming ribbon that fell softly across fine shoulders that were generously revealed above the neckline of her pale green dress. Adrian had a sudden image of himself sprawled in a chair, watching as she stood before the mirror in the chamber adjoining his, unpinning the rest of her hair and letting it cascade down her slender back. It was not an unpleasant prospect. Not at all.

His mind peeled away the sash of her dress and unlaced the frilly chemise he imagined beneath, letting both float slowly over her rounded hips and bottom and long bare legs until they settled in a frothy pool at her feet. He was rising from his imaginary chair, his hands reaching to turn her around to face him, when she actually did turn.

"As it appears our discussion is finished," she said, "perhaps you would be so kind as to have someone show me to my chamber."

"Your chamber. Of course. I'll have Thorne see to it right away."

"Thank you."

"Leah," he said as she turned away.

She glanced over her shoulder at him. "Yes?"

"Your plan sounds reasonable, but what if you fall in love with me before it's over?"

"That won't happen."

"How can you be so sure? Most women seem to find me irresistible."

"And for all the wrong reasons," she countered drily. "Which no doubt accounts for the swollen condition of your head . . . and the very level state of my own. Forewarned is forearmed and all that."

He laughed softly. "Arm yourself, by all means. Six

years under Wellington and I never did develop a taste for an easy victory."

"That's just as well, because you won't be claiming victory this time, easy or otherwise. Trust me, Raven, there is more chance of *you* falling in love with *me.*"

His smile left him. "I don't believe in love."

"Then neither of us has any cause for concern."

"Apparently not. Still, I feel compelled to warn you . . ."

She eyed him warily as he let his voice trail off. "Warn me of what?"

"You asked earlier if I knew any other tricks. I'm certain that if I put my mind to it, I could teach *you* to come when I whistle."

Her eyes widened, then narrowed, and for several seconds she stood with her teeth biting her bottom lip, looking for all the world like a schoolgirl who'd forgotten her lesson. Then her chin came up, and that clear, placid gaze swept from the top of his head to the toes of his boots and back, taking in all six feet, two inches of him.

"You could try," was all she said.

Adrian grinned as she turned and walked out.

You could try.

Was that a challenge? Or an invitation? He would soon find out, he thought, anticipation mingling with a general feeling of contentment. True, he'd suffered an uneasy moment or two at her hands this evening, but he had everything back under control now.

What idiot couldn't play the perfect husband for a few months? While he was at it, perhaps he would even show his poor married brethren how a wife ought to be handled. He was definitely looking forward to *handling* his wife, in every sense of the word. Now that she was awake and recovered, the woman was a great deal more alluring than he had realized when he made her his bride. And with plenty of spirit. He'd meant what he said about easy conquests.

Instinct, he thought with satisfaction, leaning back and reaching for his cigar. When it came to women, a man either had it or he didn't. And he had it.

4

Leah was shown to her chamber by Raven's very aptly named manservant, Thorne, who had a slight stoop and gray-whiskered chin. He did not appear pleased by the news that she was staying and Leah wasn't sure if he objected to women in general, her in particular, or was just of prickly disposition.

The bedchamber was spacious, but cluttered, with too many pieces of dark, heavy furniture. There were too many of *everything,* in fact. An extra washstand, several mirrors and even a quick count turned up no fewer than eight lamps. The chamber appeared to be a resting place for castoffs, as if the very last thing anyone expected was for someone to turn up and claim the room.

Surprise.

"Tell me, Thorne," she said as she ran a fingertip over a particularly horrendous porcelain owl, leaving a streak in the dust, "what exactly are your duties here?"

"Little of this, little of that."

"I see." From what she had seen thus far, she decided *little* was the operative word.

"If you're needing anything, ring the bell." His shaggy gray head bowed in the general direction of the brocade bellpull by the black walnut, canopied bed.

"Thank you. My maid will see to whatever else I might need tonight."

He muttered something, his own gracious form of agreement, she supposed.

"I do have a question, however. Where is the duke's chamber located?"

"Right through there." He indicated the connecting door between her chamber and the adjoining one.

"I see." Her troubled gaze focused on the lock. "And the key would be . . . ?"

"Gone," he said. "Lost years ago. Not that it matters none. I once seen His Grace kick in a brick wall 'cause he was in a mood for what lay on the other side."

"What a charming anecdote," she remarked drily. "And thank you for the warning. I shall take care not to sleep too close to the wall."

His eyes didn't exactly widen in surprise, but they did gleam a bit. There was no question he was taking her measure anew.

"You do that, Y'Grace. Ain't too much in this world worth getting clunked in the head with a brick for."

Your grace? Leah's first instinct was to glance around to see if the duke had crept up behind her; then she remembered who she was, the Duchess of Raven, and as such the new mistress of Raven House.

"Thank you, Thorne. That will be all." She dismissed him with a nod worthy of a duchess, even a temporary one.

"*Your grace,*" she whispered as soon as she was alone. "Well, la de da."

Catching sight of the full-length looking glass in the corner, she curtsied to her reflection, then shook her head with a self-conscious laugh.

"Best not get too accustomed to all this *Your Grace* nonsense," she muttered to herself. "It will be ended as quickly as it began."

Bridget arrived, followed by a small regiment of footmen with Leah's bags and trunk, and immediately began unpacking. She grumbled the whole while about how the place reminded her of a cave and how Thorne had asked her where she left her broom when she'd done no more than inform him of precisely when and how her mistress's breakfast was to be served.

"If that little weasel wants to see a witch, I'll—"

"That won't be necessary, Bridget. I can handle Thorne," she promised, hoping she was right. True, she was accustomed to running a household, but at home the servants were devoted and cooperative, almost family.

Almost.

Regardless of their affection and concern, they could never truly satisfy her yearning for a real family, or for the sense of closeness and security that had been stripped away from her so suddenly. It was a yearning she had learned to live with, but she was not nearly so acquiescent when it came to Christiana's fate. Chrissie deserved to have a loving husband and children. That was why the season in town was so important.

"That's it," announced Bridget as she hung up the final garment. "And a good thing too, since there's not room enough for an onionskin left in either the wardrobe or dresser."

"Let's hope Christiana's chamber has a larger closet," said Leah. "She has twice as many of everything I have."

There was little of fashion in Baumborough, so months earlier, she had retained a fashionable modiste from Bath to create a new wardrobe for Christiana, and for herself as well. She'd been resigned to the role of spinster elder sister, but she refused to indulge those who would love nothing more than to titter and chortle over what a dowdy item the glamorous Dava's elder daughter had turned out to be. Now she was doubly glad she had made the investment. If she was going to play the role of a duchess, she had to look the part.

"I'll undress and do my own hair tonight, Bridget," she said as the maid lifted her silver-handled hairbrush from the dressing table. "I want to write to Christiana before it gets any later. You must be as tired as I am, so run along to bed."

Bridget nodded and withdrew.

Alone, Leah crossed to the window and pulled back the heavy burgundy drape, wrinkling her nose at the small cloud of dust that arose. She gazed out over the city, and her breath caught in her throat. Back home at this hour, everyone would be long tucked in their beds, but here fine carriages still clattered along the streets and there was even an occasional gentleman stroller. Thoughts of the balls and concerts and theatrical performances where they might have spent the evening filled her head.

She had undertaken this venture solely on Chrissie's behalf, but now that she was actually in London, she was eager to see and experience for herself everything it had to offer.

It was an effort of will to tear herself from the window and seat herself at the writing desk tucked in one corner to do what had to be done.

Dear Chrissie, she wrote.

You'll never guess . . .

Happy news!

Are you sitting down?

Ten minutes later, the floor around her was littered with crumpled sheets of parchment and she had nibbled the left corner of her lower lip raw.

It was not easy to lie to the person closest to you in the whole world. A person who knew her well enough to detect when something was amiss from forty paces—or, in this case, half a country away. Not that she wasn't determined to lie. She was. She had no choice.

Dear Chrissie, she wrote, *I am married.*

There. That was true.

If that news has not landed you squarely on your posterior, I implore you to hurry and sit down before you read any further. I am married to—take a deep breath—none other than the Duke of Raven.

Leah read what she had written, imagining Chrissie's response.

I can see your eyes going wide and hear you shrieking. My sister and a duke? How on earth did this come about? That, dear sister, is a very good question.

Leah wished she had a very good answer, one that she could safely reveal. She dipped the pen and thought and dipped the pen again.

There I was . . .

It was the oddest thing . . .

You'll never guess . . .

Gad, this was even more difficult than she'd feared. Especially since at that moment she wanted nothing more than to spill everything to Chrissie and hear what she had to say about Raven's despicable stunt.

Chrissie would say that Raven was a selfish, unprincipled cur, which he clearly was, and that he had abused Leah beyond all respectability and endurance, which he had, and that she must publicly denounce him as the scoundrel he was . . . which she could not do.

A fresh scandal would only stir up the past and put an end to Chrissie's hopes of making a suitable match. What's more, she thought irritably, she wouldn't even have the satisfaction of seeing Raven humiliated, since he was obviously without any shred of concern for the opinion of others. No, she must grit her teeth and make the best of things, even if it meant stretching the truth a bit for her sister's sake.

She ran her fingertip over the feather quill, her expression brightening. Stretching the truth . . . Why hadn't she thought of that earlier? It had a much more pleasant sound than *lying.* Besides, it was what she did best. She wrote fairy tales, for heaven's sake. Her own bizarre version of them, to be sure, but fairy tales nonetheless. She'd written often enough of princesses who found love in unexpected places, surely she could make up a story about herself and Raven. She resumed writing, quickly telling of her sudden, brief illness and how she happened to take refuge at the rectory at Saint Anne's-on-Clayton, where Raven was also staying.

Oh, happy coincidence!, she wrote with a lip curled. She then conveniently skipped ahead to their first meeting—first conscious meeting, that is—and twisted the facts where necessary.

Fully recovered at last, I entered the dining room and locked gazes with the most handsome man ever created, the Duke of Raven, my own dear Adrian.

Sparks flashed, the air hummed and my stomach was tied in such knots I feared they would never come undone.

All true, Leah assured herself, recalling how nervous she had been a few hours earlier.

We took one look at each other and . . .

And? And?

And knew we were destined to be together.

At least for the time being.

We stood as if alone in the world, timelessly and in silence and we knew.

Leah smiled and closed her eyes. How easily the lies came after all, she thought, when you had been secretly rehearsing them in your heart for years.

Then he kissed me and . . .

At least she would not have to invent this, she thought. As she relived the moment when Raven had pulled her into his arms and kissed her, her heart pounded, her stomach clenched and she forgot all about the letter. Again she heard the hot rush of Raven's breath close to her ear, felt his hand sweep down her back and come to rest on her hip, tasted the cognac sweetness of his warm breath.

She used to imagine what it would be like to be kissed by a man. A real kiss, not the cold, tight-lipped peck on the lips a flabby, jowled widower from a neighboring estate had once subjected her to when she failed to turn her head away quickly enough. Raven's kiss had been a real kiss, and it had driven home to her just how paltry the powers of her imagination were.

She shook her head, wincing as she recalled long-ago nights when she had lain in her bed, pretended her pillow was a suitor and *practiced* her technique on it. How young she had been. And how naive. In those days she'd still believed that knights in shining armor existed outside of storybooks, and that at any moment one would come riding up to save her from the harsh fate she had been dealt.

Impulsively, she stood and reached for one of the plump pillows piled on the bed. She no longer believed that anything was possible, but with the vast experience of one incredible kiss behind her, she could at least give her imagination another go at it.

Wrapping her arms around the pillow, she pressed it to her face. The linen casing smelled faintly musty, as if her imaginary suitor spent too much time in a damp attic. Worse, he felt lumpy, as though he had a mouthful of porridge. She felt silly suddenly. This was a schoolgirl's trick, not something a woman her age should be indulging in . . . and a married woman at that.

"What in blazes are you doing?"

Leah jumped and turned.

And froze.

Raven was standing in the doorway between his chamber and hers, staring at her in bewilderment.

She groaned inwardly as she slowly lowered the pillow.

"What did you say?" she asked, stalling.

"I asked what you were doing with that pillow pressed to your face."

"This pillow?" she echoed, holding it aloft.

He eyed her mockingly. "Yes. That pillow. That is the one you had your face buried in, isn't it?"

"Yes. It is."

"Well?"

"Well?"

"What were you trying to accomplish?"

"I was . . . hiccuping," she blurted. "I had the hiccups and I was trying to stop them."

"By smothering yourself?" He arched one dark brow. "Isn't that a bit drastic?"

"Very funny. I was trying to hold my breath. That's an old country remedy and as you can see, it worked. Now may I inquire what *you* are doing in *my* chamber?"

"I saw the light and thought you might have fallen asleep with the candle burning."

Leah gestured toward the desk. "I was writing a letter to my sister."

"Until you were stricken with a sudden attack of hiccups."

"Exactly."

Silence. Leah clutched the pillow and tried not to fidget under his steady, challenging gaze. "It so happens, however, that I am glad you're here."

His mouth curved into a knowing smile. "Somehow I thought you might be," he drawled, moving toward her with a slow, purposeful stride.

He stopped mere inches away.

Leah's pulse skittered and her spine tingled, her body sensing the precise nature of a danger her mind was slower to perceive. Her anxious gaze followed the movement of his hands as they lifted to the pillow.

"What are you doing?" she asked, because her foolish brain needed to hear what her body and her heart and her soul already knew.

"A sack of feathers is a poor stand-in for a flesh and blood lover, Leah." He tugged the pillow free and tossed it aside. "Perhaps in Baumborough you had need of a substitute, but that's no longer true."

A wave of heat that was part embarrassment and part excitement swept over her.

"You can't be suggesting that I was . . . that is, I never . . . surely . . ."

"That's it," he said, his voice a soft whisper, his

gaze focused on her lips as his hands cupped her face and tipped it up to him. "Hold your mouth open for me. Just . . . like . . . that."

As he spoke, his head bent and his mouth came closer and she knew that what she both dreaded and craved was about to happen. His mouth brushed hers, bathing her lips with the faint scent of smoke and brandy, with sensations she could never have possibly imagined.

The pressure of his thumbs kept her mouth open, but she would have cooperated anyway. Some unfamiliar reckless streak inside *wanted* him to kiss her, *wanted* the rough and tender thrusts of his tongue, *wanted* to feel once again that strange and wonderful explosion of pleasure that left her dizzy and breathless.

An experiment, she told herself, to see if her response the first time had been an anomaly, attributable to nerves. She would permit him to kiss her this one time and one time only.

And then . . .

And then . . .

His tongue filled her mouth and the reality of it overwhelmed her senses. Her thoughts drifted away. He licked her lips and traced the straight line of her teeth. He teased her, played with her, running his hands over her shoulders and down her back, drawing her to a place without restraint or regret, a world of pure feeling unlike any she had ever known.

When he stopped kissing her, she was bereft. It took several seconds for her to remember that this had been only an experiment.

"Just what do you think you're doing?" she demanded as soon as she felt steady enough.

"A regrettable job, if my efforts are so totally unrecognizable. But if you must ask, I'll answer. I'm kissing you."

He bent his head to continue, but this time Leah stopped him by bracing her hands against his chest.

"Why?"

"Why?" He sounded incredulous, and a bit annoyed. "I suppose because it seemed more polite than walking in, throwing you on your back and tossing your skirts over your head. But then, you did say you're not a romantic. If you prefer that approach—"

"I don't," she broke in. "I prefer no approach from you at all. Have you already forgotten our agreement?"

"No, but it seems you have. I understood I was to play the part of your husband. Unless marriage customs are very different where you come from—"

Again she interrupted. "In public. Our bargain calls for you to play the role of my husband in public."

"What the hell does that mean?"

"I believe I made my terms very clear."

He released her. "Not clear enough, apparently."

"Very well, *Your Grace,* it means I will not be giving any private performances, tonight or any other night."

"You can't be serious? You actually expect us to live here together, as husband and wife, sleeping in adjoining rooms every blessed night, and never touch each other? That's . . . unnatural."

"Oh, you may touch me." His grunt of relief gave way to a look of even greater disbelief as she continued. "In fact, I think it would strain credibility if you did not do so occasionally. An affectionate pat on the shoulder or a gentle hand at the small of my back will go a long way toward convincing others that we are the most deliriously happy wedded couple in all of Christendom."

"Let me see if I have this straight. I am not to bed another, because that might give rise to gossip?"

"That's correct."

"And I am not allowed to bed you, because . . . because . . ."

When he trailed off, looking baffled, she shook her head.

"Because," she reminded him, "we shall be seeking an annulment when this is over."

He chuckled. "The annulment? Is that all that's holding you back?"

"All? Have you, by chance, thought of some other solution to our problem?"

"I haven't thought about it at all. I'll worry about that when the time comes."

"Oh really?" Her expression dripped disapproval. "That seems to be a habit of yours, acting on impulse and worrying about the consequences later. But not this time, Raven. We shall proceed according to our agreement. As soon as Christiana is safely wed, we shall apply to have this so-called marriage dissolved on grounds that it was never consummated."

His gaze narrowed, impaling her. "Have you lost your bloody mind?"

"Not at all." She tried not to let her voice quiver the way her knees were. "That seems the most obvious approach to take."

"The most obvious approach to making me a complete laughingstock, you mean. Me? Incapable of bedding my own wife?" His loud laugh held no trace of amusement. "Can you imagine the field day the gossipmongers will have with that?"

She could. All too well, in fact, but at the moment she had her own problems with the gossipmongers to worry about.

"I thought you were not concerned with the opinion of others," she said.

"I'm not," he retorted hotly. But . . ."

She subjected him to a small, sympathetic smile he was sure to resent. "I see. You really are afraid of their ill opinion."

She watched the word *afraid* work its magic.

"Like hell," he growled. He eyed her smugly. "There may be another problem, however. The powers that be shall want proof that the deed was never done. Have you considered that?"

"They shall have their proof," she replied tersely.

"I see."

"I'm pleased you do. Then it's settled. That is, unless you are so devoid of self-control that you cannot see our bargain through for even a single night without reneging."

"Self-control?" he echoed, his tone coldly indignant. "If you think this is a question of *self-control,* madam, then you sorely overestimate either your charms or my susceptibility to them."

He gave a stiff nod and turned to go, leaving her feeling stung by his parting shot. Which was ridiculous since his retreat clearly signaled that she had won this round. She had wanted him to leave her. Hadn't she?

When he was almost to the door, he turned abruptly. "Why the hell did you say you were glad I'd come to your chamber, if you were not?"

"Oh, that." She hesitated, the rigidity of his stance suggesting that perhaps she ought to bide her time before pushing him any further. A fig on that. She hadn't time to waste coddling his moods. "I find it necessary to ask a favor of you."

"Ask."

"Would it be possible for you to send a carriage to

collect my sister? My intention was to send my own carriage back for her, but Rowland tells me there is a problem with one of the axles. I'm sure he can repair it as he's often done so in the past, but . . ."

He held up his hand to stop her. "Say no more. I'll send a carriage for her."

"It will need to be a rather large carriage," she advised.

He arched one dark brow. "Why? Is your sister a rather large woman?"

"Not at all," she said, smiling. "Quite slender, in fact. But there are her bags to consider. Quite a number of them, I'm afraid."

His eyes gleamed with smug understanding. "Of course, her armor and weaponry. We couldn't send her out to compete without them. I shall make sure to send my largest carriage to fetch her, and will toss in a couple of brawny footmen while I'm at it. Will that suit?"

"Very well, thank you. I'll inform Christiana of the change in plans in my letter." She waved her hand toward the desk. "If I post it first thing, it should arrive before your carriage."

The candlelight played across his dark hair as he gave a curt nod. "Was that all?"

"Well, as long as you've asked," she said, throwing caution to the wind, "I wonder if you would object to me freshening the house up a bit before Christiana arrives? I thought perhaps some new—"

"Spare me the details," he snapped. "I don't care what you do to the place as long as it does not interfere with me." He glanced over his shoulder at her. "And now if there is nothing further?"

She shook her head.

"Nothing you need?" His mouth curved, taunting her. "A larger pillow perhaps?"

"No," she said tightly. "Nothing."

"Then I bid you good night."

The door clicked shut. Leah sagged with relief.

So much for her experiment. Instead of spending the past weeks trying to anticipate her husband's reaction to her, she should have better prepared herself for *her* response to *him.*

Exactly what had her response been? Indifference? Ha. Curiosity? No. It was something deeper and far more portentous. As much as she hated to admit it, and as personally inexperienced as she was in this domain, her woman's intuition told her that what she felt in his arms was passion. And that was the very last thing she trusted herself to feel with a man, any man, but especially a man as unprincipled as Raven.

Not that she was opposed to passion, in theory and in small, manageable doses. But she was very much opposed to letting passion, or any other emotion, rule her life. If she had learned anything from her mother's tragic fate, it was that passion could easily lead to loss of control. For her mother that had ultimately led to the loss of everything, even her life.

Leah had made up her mind years ago that she would never risk sharing that fate. She steadfastly avoided feeling any emotion she could not govern, including passion. That was not all that difficult to do in Baumborough. Her private yearnings and desires were exactly that, private. That Raven should be the one to threaten to unleash what she kept so carefully bottled up was worse than unfortunate. It was revolting. And dangerous. She could not conceive of a man to whom she'd be more loath to surrender control than the one whose hands had just made themselves at home all over her body.

She pressed her palms to her cheeks and felt the

heat there. Heat that was part embarrassment and part . . . something else.

Her cheeks flamed anew.

Stop fretting, she ordered herself. Nothing had happened, after all. And nothing would. Raven may be clever and smooth, and experienced, devious and totally without scruples. But she was . . . well, she was wiser than she was a half hour ago. And she was determined.

There would be no further experiments.

She finished her letter in a rush, describing Raven House and the little she had seen of London thus far, and ended by urging Christiana to join her immediately. The sooner she had Christiana's life settled, the sooner she could return to the peace and safety of home.

After signing and sealing the letter, she turned her attention to her manuscript. She quickly became so embroiled in Princess Olivia's troubles, she forgot her own.

If Olivia were a more practical princess, she would have run away by carriage. Instead she trudged for miles along the narrow road that curled in such a way, she felt as if she were going in circles. She was tired and hungry and missing one red kid slipper when, at the sound of thundering hooves behind her, turned to see . . .

What?

Closing her eyes, she pictured the scene that an artist would later render for the book's fanciful illustrations.

Olivia turned to see . . . She turned to see . . .

A knight seated astride a tiger. A knight dressed all in silver, but for the black leather mask covering his face. His name was Nevar, and he was the prince of Here-and-Now.

After swinging from his tiger, Zanzibar, he offered Olivia the missing red slipper, with a great flourish of the sort for which princes are known. But the shoe would not go on.

"I fear your foot is swollen from walking," said the prince. "You must allow me to take you back to my castle to rest."

"I haven't time to rest," she told him. "I am Princess Olivia of Faraway, and I am on a quest."

Olivia told him all about the Old Hag and the curse.

"I see," he said when she was through. "What if you found a man who had only three of the four qualities you seek? Would you be willing to compromise?"

Olivia shook her head. "I never compromise. Now I have a question for you. Why do you wear that mask?"

"Because I am cursed as well. I must wear the mask if I am to have any hope of finding a bride."

Olivia felt so sorry for him that when he asked to take her to his castle, she accepted.

They rode with Olivia seated in front of Nevar on the tiger's back. She tried not to think about the face hidden beneath his mask. She liked Prince Nevar and was sorry that he obviously lacked the very first quality on her list.

Ah, but, Princess, the road to Castle Here-And-Now is long and winding, whispered Leah as she stretched mightily, finished for the night. She would see to it that Prince Nevar had ample opportunity to teach the stubborn Olivia the art of compromise, and prove to her that he was courageous, honest and true.

All the things that Adrian, Duke of Raven, Prince of Scoundrels, bane of her existence, was not.

That same night Adrian found Will at Boodle's, a club they rarely frequented. Will was seated at an out-of-the-way table, with his back to the door, in a transparent attempt to go unnoticed. In the mood he was in, Adrian would have hunted him down in whatever hole he sought to hide.

He paused just inside the shadowy room. He was torn. The urge to walk over and knock Will off his seat without warning was a near second to the desire to see him dangling from a noose. Had Will warned him of Leah's recovery in time, he could have . . . He would have . . . Dammit, he would have done *something* to avert disaster. Now it appeared he had a wife who was that most irksome of all creatures, a virgin. One who did not want to be tumbled, but was curious and couldn't hide the fact.

Striding across the room, he did an intentional double take as he passed Will's table.

"Will," he exclaimed, "what are you doing here?"

The color drained from Will's round face. "Where . . . what . . ." His gaze careened around the room.

Adrian let his jaw drop. "My God, man, what am I thinking? Your presence in town can mean only one thing." He collapsed heavily into the seat beside Will and bowing his head, made a hasty sign of the cross. "Just tell me this, my friend, did she go peacefully?"

"What in blazes are you t-talking about?" Will demanded, stuttering as he always did when backed into a corner. "She didn't *go* at all."

Adrian looked confused. "You mean she lingers still?"

"I mean she's here," Will hissed, dropping his voice.

"In Boodle's?"

"In London."

"Of course," Adrian said, nodding with approval. "I

had assumed the burial would be in Westerham, but I see your reasoning. It's natural I would want to be present and what's more, this way there will be a grave nearby where I can deposit flowers and appear properly grief-stricken at regular intervals." He clapped Will on the back. "I can always trust you to look out for my best interests."

"Good God, Rave, she's not here to be b-buried. She's here t-to . . . God, I need a d-drink."

Adrian signaled the waiter to bring a bottle of brandy and poured them both a drink. Will gulped his.

"That's right, steady your nerves," urged Adrian. "I can see this tragedy has taken a toll on you and I shan't forget your loyalty, old man."

Will poured himself another brandy.

Adrian waited until he lifted the glass to his lips. "So where is she?"

Will coughed and sputtered and wiped brandy from his chin with the back of his hand. "Where?"

"Yes, where?" said Adrian, letting a hint of impatience creep into his tone. "The body, I mean."

His friend went from white to gray.

"You must agree that a memorial service of some sort is in order," he went on. "Have you located her nearest relation?"

Will nodded. "Yes, it's you."

"Yes, yes, the devoted and grieving husband and all that. But who is her closest relation *really*?"

Will reached out and grasped the lapels of his coat. "You, it's you, you great menacing dolt." Sandy hair curled damply around his ears and the back of his neck as he began sweating in earnest. "Listen to me, Raven, she's not dead. She's *alive.* And she's here, in town, at your house this very moment. At least, that's where she should be."

At that instant Colin emerged from the card room, sporting a self-satisfied grin, and joined them.

"Congratulate me," he ordered. "I've just relieved that obnoxious young sot Wickerson of half his yearly sum, as well as . . ." He squinted at the signed note in his hand. "As well as a gallery in Soho. What the blazes am I to do with a gallery in Soho?"

He shrugged, folded the note, and slipped it in his waistcoat pocket. The silence got his attention at last. He looked at Adrian, still smoothing his lapels where Will had clutched them, then at Will, then back at Adrian and whistled softly. "Looks like the cat's out of the bag." He leaned closer to Will. "How's he taking it?"

"He's not taking it," Will snapped. "He's no idea she's alive. Which means she never made it to Raven House. Which means she's lost . . . or worse, and it's all my fault."

Adrian listened contentedly as Will rattled on, steadily progressing from alarmed to frantic. Perhaps by the time he approached apoplectic, Adrian would have had his fill of retribution. Perhaps.

"I knew I should have seen her to Raven House myself," Will lamented. "But she was set on handling the meeting with Raven her way, and when the Duchess makes up her mind about something—"

"The duchess?" Adrian interjected.

"Well, I didn't know what else to call her," Will muttered. "Besides, that's what she is."

"Well, now that you've divined *what* she is," retorted Adrian, "allow me to enlighten you as to *where* she is. At this very moment, *the duchess*," he said, every muscle in his body tensing at the words, "is safely asleep in the bedchamber adjoining my own."

Will and Colin stared at him blankly. Colin caught

on first and resumed grinning. "Good one, Rave. You even had me going."

Will wet his lips. "Do you mean to say . . . you knew? All along? You bastard," he snarled. "It's not enough you dragged me into your fiendish little scheme and then left me caretaking an angry woman, now you sink to making sport of me."

"You deserve it," Adrian retorted. "And worse. Why the bloody hell didn't you warn me she was alive before she walked into my dining room and staked her claim in front of no less an assemblage of back-stabbers than Hockliffe, Torrington, and Gidding . . . and their wives."

Colin's mouth twisted as if he'd bitten into a rotten apple. "You had that tedious lot in your dining room?"

"What did you do when she walked in?" Will asked cautiously.

"What could I do? I welcomed her with open arms, and now I'm stuck with her."

"You can't mean you intend to let the marriage stand?" demanded Colin.

"What other choice does he have?" Will challenged.

"The lady has threatened to expose the entire truth about that night," Adrian explained.

"Let her expose whatever she pleases," declared Colin. "We've survived worse."

Adrian regarded him sardonically. "Worse than threats of deportation for the rector, legal charges against you, and my being publicly branded a liar? I think not. Even I have my standards."

Colin exhaled in disgust. "Hell, Rave, she does have you by the jollies."

"So it would seem. The lady and I have resolved to make the best of this unfortunate situation."

Colin shook his head, his expression forlorn, his

tone dejected. "I never thought it would end this way for you, of all people. Married." He washed down that grim thought with what remained in Will's glass and then refilled it. "If you can be run to ground, no man anywhere is safe."

Run to ground? That chafed. Adrian let their pity ooze for another moment or so, then couldn't stand it any longer.

"Of course, there is a bright side to all this," he said.

"There is?" asked Colin, barely lifting his head.

"It occurred to me that I may have embraced the Plimpton Solution a bit prematurely."

"I tried to tell you," Will broke in. "I said you'd regret it, but would you listen?"

Colin shoved the brandy glass at him. "Here, drown your sorrows, or yourself. I don't care which as long as you shut up." He nodded for Adrian to continue.

"Plimpton's approach was right in theory, but it needed a bit of fine-tuning. Which I am pleased to say I have now accomplished. I shall embrace my husbandly status and exploit its benefits until I've enjoyed all the marital bliss I can stomach. *Then,* and only then, shall I send *the duchess* packing, back home to the quiet, solitary life she professes to love, leaving me free to resume my own pursuits here."

"But your vows," protested Will.

"The vows will remain intact, rendering me legally and permanently off-limits. But there will be no annulment. Ever. Not on any grounds."

Colin's forehead puckered as the pieces settled in his mind. "Married and yet, to all intent and purposes, without a wife."

"I like to think of it as the Plimpton Solution with a twist."

"Damn, Rave, that is brilliant. No, it's beyond brilliant. It's . . ."

"Perfect," Adrian pronounced when Colin faltered, and as suddenly as that he realized it *was* perfect. His remarks had been an off-the-cuff effort to make himself appear less pathetic in the eyes of his friends, but as the plan unfolded in his head, he was won over. Everyone would win. Leah would get what she claimed to want, a husband for her sister and the freedom to return home. He would get the immunity of marriage without the complications.

Of course, there was the little matter of her damn annulment, but he knew of one surefire way to eliminate that stumbling block.

He reached for Will's glass and tossed back the contents, savoring the sweet fire at the back of his throat just as he savored the heady prospect and unparalleled challenge of seducing his own wife.

5

Adrian woke mid-afternoon as he always did, groggy from another late night, as always, and wandered downstairs barefoot and in his dressing gown, as was his habit. He picked up the newspaper from its customary spot on the table by the foot of the stairs and read the headlines as he walked to the dining room for his usual two cups of bitter chocolate and six slices of buttered toast liberally sprinkled with cinnamon sugar.

The only difference today was that he stopped abruptly in the door of the dining room, wincing and shielding his eyes with one hand.

"What the devil is going on here?" he demanded. "Someone put out that blasted light."

Thorne stood in his usual position beside the head of the table, a wooden pick clamped between his teeth, waiting to snap his employer's napkin into his lap and pour his chocolate. "Easier said than done, Y'Grace."

"Don't grumble, Thorne, just do it." He glanced around, still squinting. "Where in blazes is it coming from anyway?"

"The sun, Y'Grace."

"The sun?" Adrian glanced at the windows and for the first time noticed they were bare of the voluminous dark blue draperies that had hung over them for as long as he could remember. "Where are the draperies?"

"The Duchess, she ordered them taken down."

"Why?"

"She said they blocked the sun."

"Isn't that the point? Where is that wom . . . my wi . . . the Duchess?"

"Shopping."

"Did she say when she would return?"

"She said she would be away most of the afternoon. I told her that since you always slept most of the—"

"All right, all right," Adrian interrupted. "The woman is obviously insane. How am I expected to have my breakfast here?" He glowered at the windows. "Is it always so bright at this hour?"

"Yes, Y'Grace. Unless it's raining."

"Then let's pray for rain, shall we? In the meantime I'll take breakfast in the library."

There were more surprises awaiting him en route. In the upstairs hallway, he encountered a man using a metal crowbar on the wainscotting. The wrenching sound made him wince.

"What the hell is he doing?" he asked Thorne, who trailed behind him with a tray.

"Prying it loose," replied the servant.

"I can see that, devil take you. *Why* is he prying it loose?"

"The Duchess, she ordered the wainscotting removed to expose the plaster panels underneath. Says they have buttercups on them."

"Buttercups?"

"Yes, Y'Grace, buttercups. Says they'll cheer the place up," he added. "Says the wainscotting was too dark."

"I happen to like dark wainscotting," he declared, though truthfully he'd never noticed the wainscotting was there, much less the color of it. "And I detest buttercups. You may tell her so."

"Yes, Y'Grace."

"Then tell that man to put it back the way it was. Every dark, cheerless inch of it."

Thorne turned to the workman. "You heard the duke. Put it back the way it was . . . and don't be sneaking off for a pint till you do."

"Buttercups," muttered Adrian under his breath as he strode away. "Buttercups. Sunshine. Of all the hideous, revolting . . ."

He settled himself behind the desk while Thorne made a place for the tray amidst the paper and clutter.

"If you'll pardon me for saying so," the servant said as he arranged the plate and cup, "the lady made it plain as a pimple on an arse that you had approved certain changes in the house."

"I never approved *buttercups.* Or blinding lights . . . or that infernal pounding," he added, grimacing. "What the hell is that?"

"That would be the workmen securing the trellis, Y'Grace."

"We don't have a trellis."

"We do now," Thorne informed him. "The duchess desires ivy."

"I'll give her . . ." Adrian threw down his napkin and stomped to the window to see two burly men on ladders mounting a wooden trellis to the brick wall at the back of the house. His gaze traveled over the garden and narrowed. "What are those?"

"In the barrels or the crates?" inquired Thorne without bothering to glance out the window.

"Either," he snapped.

"Rose bushes in the barrels. Lilacs in the crates. The fountain with the bare-arse Cupid is still on the wagon out front. The duchess—"

"Has gone too damn far," declared Adrian. "Not even here a day and already she's costing me a fortune."

"Actually, sir, the fellow from the greenhouse said everything was paid for in advance by the duchess herself."

Adrian felt as if someone had strung a wire along his nerves and drawn it taut. "Oh, did he now? Does the blasted woman think I cannot afford to adorn my own home? I can see her now, raising eyebrows all over town by paying for her own purchases. By God, I won't have it. Did she happen to say where—"

"Bond Street."

"Have my horse—"

"It's waiting out front."

He found her at Thatcher and Swan, who still referred to themselves as *silk mercers*, though their wares had expanded to include fabrics and household goods of all kinds. Leah was at the back of the shop, seated on a high stool, tapestries and fabric samples strewn across the long table in front of her. As eager as he was to set her straight, he slowed his steps as he drew near, appreciating the straight line of her back, almost as much as he appreciated the curvaceous lines of her hips and bottom. Her head was slightly bent and she had removed one glove to feel the fabrics.

He didn't speak and his footsteps on the carpeted floor were silent, yet she lifted her head as he approached, as if his presence alone held the power to command her attention. And she smiled.

Adrian's breath caught. It was like walking into the dining room all over again, except that the smile she turned on him was brighter and warmer than a thousand suns. Immediately he wondered about her motives.

"Raven, what a wonderful surprise," she said.

Adrian was struck anew by the sound of her voice, its smooth texture and husky undertone, and its unhurried cadence, as if exchanging pleasantries with him was the only thing she had to do, not orchestrating the cursed campaign to marry off her sister in grand style . . . and upending his entire life in the process. It was not to be tolerated.

"I never expected to see you here," she added.

"I assure you, madam," he replied with a loathing glance around, "that I never expected to be seen here."

As impossible as it seemed, her expression did not dim. "Well, I'm very glad you're here just the same."

"I hope that remains unchanged after you hear what I've come to say."

"Oh dear." Her smile disappeared, and Adrian remembered one long-ago winter day, when he'd scraped together enough newly fallen snow to make a small snowman. The snow had turned to rain and his creation dissolved right before his eyes. Then, as now, he had the wild urge to do *something* to put everything back the way it was.

His anger abated somewhat, though not, he assured himself, his desire to bring his errant wife into line.

"It's about the house," he said at last. "That is, it's about the changes in the house—the wainscotting, the trellis, the missing drapes."

"You're displeased?"

Displeased? he thought, watching that familiar look of dismay mar her smooth forehead. Of course, he was displeased. The woman was turning his home into some ludicrous showpiece. But, he reminded himself, he must tell her so in a way that would not impede his ultimate goal—seduction. "I wouldn't say displeased exactly. I'm . . . concerned."

That was it. He was concerned. None of this mattered enough to merit a stronger response. It was all simply the means to an end. *She* was only a means to an end, he reassured himself.

"I see." She pressed her lips together. "I was afraid I might be overstepping my bounds by ordering the wainscotting removed."

"Not at all," he was stunned to hear himself say. "Actually I've been intending to have it removed for some time. You've simply saved me the bother."

The impulsive, bald-faced lie earned him another smile. Really, what difference did a few bushes and a fountain make, especially if such concessions paved the way to her bed?

She eyed him uncertainly. "I was afraid you might find the panels underneath too drastic a change."

"No. Buttercups are precisely what I had in mind."

"I'm so glad," she exclaimed, beaming. "In that case I will definitely have them re-created for the ceiling in the drawing room."

God help him.

"The architect Robert Adam considers the ceiling

to be one of the most important features in the design of the room," she went on, "and I think I agree."

"Who would not?" he murmured absently as he watched her mouth.

"He recommends pastel colors on both ceilings and walls, set off with white decorations and judicious gilding. What do you think?"

"It sounds perfect," he replied, having no idea what he was approving.

"So, if not the wainscotting, what exactly is your concern?"

"My concern?" His mind scrambled. "The expenses. I must insist that all future accounts be sent to me for settlement."

"That's really not necessary. I shall be saving a substantial amount by giving up the house in Knightsbridge and it doesn't seem quite fair to ask you to pay for what I requested."

"It is eminently fair," he corrected. "It is my home, you are my wife, the bills will be sent to me. What will people say if my wife goes around paying for the refurbishment of my ancestral home?"

"Do you care?" she asked with a sly look.

It was a good question, and one he felt no more comfortable answering today than he had last evening. Was it possible that he *did* care what people said about him? Or, more disturbing still, about her? The fact that he couldn't answer was one more sign of how very wrong things had gone in a single day.

"Just have the bills sent to me," he ordered gruffly.

She nodded. "Very well. Now, would you like to see what I have planned for the dining room?"

He shrugged. "Why not?"

He listened and watched, lulled by the music in her tone, fascinated by the expressiveness of her eyes, the way they sparkled and crinkled, now intent, now hiding behind a sweep of what were surely the longest lashes in existence. Her references to walls hung with apricot Spitalfields silk, gilded ceiling medallions, and brocade drapes with braided fringe drifted in one ear and out the other.

"So, can you recall the exact color?"

The question came at him without warning, and she turned the full force of her gaze on him, innately sultry with absolutely no effort on her part, and so very, very . . .

"Green," he replied.

She frowned.

Damn, he thought.

"Green? Really? The dining room rug?" She looked perplexed.

Adrian hesitated. Feint or parry? What the hell.

"Not the rug," he said softly, leaning just the slightest bit closer, so that his chest grazed the back of her shoulder and her scent filled his head. It was a subtle smell, elusively floral, all woman. He drank it in, feeling like a starving man given a bowl of porridge, feeling like a complete idiot, telling himself it was all part of the game, that he was in control. "I was talking about your eyes."

"Oh." Her lashes fluttered down. "Oh."

He caught her chin and turned her face toward him. "The softest, deepest, most dangerous green known to man."

"Dangerous?" Her voice was low, her small laugh slightly breathless and unsteady. "How is it possible for one's eye color to be dangerous?"

"Because of the way it draws a man in, and pulls him under, and makes him long to drown there."

"Oh dear." Lashes down, up, and quickly down again.

Adrian felt her chin tremble. Ah, yes. This was very

familiar terrain. Standing behind her, he slid his palm along her forearm to her ungloved hand and laced his fingers with hers. He could feel the pulse in her thumb beating wildly. Almost as wildly as the pounding yearning inside him.

She tilted her head closer to him and whispered something.

Adrian bent to hear. "Pardon?"

"I said squeeze my hand," she whispered again. "It will add a touch of warmth."

A touch of warmth. Was she mad? The length of him pressed against her back was already far too warm for a public place. Nonetheless, he squeezed her hand.

She slanted him a small, private smile. "Perfect. You're frightfully good at this," she murmured for his ears only.

It was then that he happened to glance across the table and for the first time noticed the women, some alone, some in pairs, all pretending to examine fabric and doodads while their gazes were fastened with avid curiosity on the scene being played out at the sample table by the Duke of Raven and his bride.

So, they had an audience, and Leah assumed he was performing for them. What's more, the chit was coaching him . . . using him. No wonder she was so acquiescent all of a sudden. She was playing along for her own purposes. And doing a bang-up job of it, he thought, recalling her slight trembling and lowered gaze. He had been completely convinced, allowing himself to become enthralled, cooing and fawning over her like some callow, lovesick youth.

He had a good mind to give his scheming bride—and the nosy gawkers—a true demonstration of husbandly ardor. And he would, on the spot, he assured himself, if not for the wretched fact that he'd given his word to avoid scandal, not create it. The lesson would have to wait for a more private moment.

He lifted her hand to his mouth and planted a quick kiss on the back of it, drawing at least one audible sigh from across the table.

"Order the materials," he advised, releasing her with a show of reluctance, "or I fear Raven House, like its master, shall never be worthy of you."

"You were wonderful," she told him as they paused outside the shop. "Thank you."

"Simply living up to my side of our bargain."

Leah marveled at his aloofness. On top of everything else, the man was a consummate actor, cool and completely unaffected by their little display of affection, while she was still vibrating like a harp string from his touch. But then, he'd had much more experience.

Thank heavens she'd become aware that they were being watched and had resurrected some backbone in time, before she melted into a puddle at the man's feet. Clearly her resistance technique needed some work.

"There you are." A woman came barreling toward them, wearing a lemon-colored bonnet and a short, black velvet cloak trimmed with fur. Leah recognized her as one of last evening's dinner guests, but didn't remember the name.

"Good day, Lady Torrington," he said, and Leah followed suit.

"Your Grace," the other woman responded. As she made a small curtsy, she took in every detail of Leah's lilac walking dress, topped with a pelisse of deep violet cashmere. "I heard a fascinating rumor that you two lovebirds were shopping together and I've been searching from one end of Bond Street to the other to see for myself. Dear lady, I hope you appreciate what an amazing effect you have had on your husband's, shall we say, habits?"

"I believe I do," replied Leah, exchanging a subtly ironic look with that husband. "But ours is a mutual venture, I assure you."

"Well then, I hope you will mutually agree to attend my ball this evening. You ignored my invitation—again," she said, wagging a finger at Raven. "But you are always most welcome, and I would be honored to be the first hostess in London to entertain the new Duchess of Raven."

They replied in unison.

"We'd love to attend," said Leah.

"We're committed elsewhere," said her husband.

In the awkward silence that followed, she very subtly connected her elbow with his rib cage and explained, "We *did* have another commitment, but our companions were forced to cancel." With a steely sweet smile at Raven, she added, "I must have forgotten to tell you, darling. I hope you're not upset with me."

"Not at all . . . sweetheart." He gave her elbow a slightly painful squeeze. "But since I know how you had your heart set on this evening, I insist we forge on without our *companions*."

"Actually," she said, wrenching her elbow from his grip, "I would much prefer to attend Lady Torrington's ball. Please, say we may go."

Leah noted the irritation in his narrowed gaze and the tic in his right cheek and realized with every fiber of her being that every fiber of his was gearing up to refuse.

"Yes," he said, stunning her by the reply. "Of course we may attend the ball, if that's *really* what you want."

She ignored the warning lurking behind his words. "Yes, it is what I want. Very much, in fact."

"Then it's settled," declared Lady Torrington. "I shall see you both tonight."

As soon as they were alone, Raven turned to her, visibly annoyed. "Now see what you've done?"

"Yes. I saved you from missing out on one of the most important social events of the season."

"A ball?" he said derisively.

She nodded eagerly. "I read of the plans for the Torrington ball in the society pages—"

"Of which paper? The *Baumborough Gazette*?"

"Of the *London Times,*" she shot back. "I've been having it sent to me in preparation for our visit, so that I can—"

"Plot strategy? Set your traps?"

"Something like that." She refused to let his cynicism intrude on her excitement. "I cannot believe I am actually going to be there."

"Nor can I," he said in a grim tone. "I'll have you know, madam, that I detest balls, nearly as much as I detest squabbling with my wife in public."

"Humph."

"What did you say?"

"I said *humph.*"

"That's what I thought you said. What does it mean?"

"It means," she said, opening her orchid ruffled parasol so forcefully he had to duck, "that you talk a good game about not caring a whit what people say or think about you, when in fact, in the short time we've known each other I have already discovered at least three things about which you are extraordinarily sensitive."

"You said all that in a single humph?"

"You will find that I am a woman of few words."

"Not so I've noticed thus far, madam, but then hope does spring eternal."

Silence.

"So," he said as they turned in the direction of her carriage, "what are these three things about which I am supposed to be so sensitive?"

"You wish me to speak?" she countered with mock deference. "I understood that you preferred my silence."

"I shall let you know when I prefer silence. For now, I desire nothing more than the sound of your dulcet tones answering my damn question."

A sideways glance confirmed that his expression matched his tone in exasperation. Satisfied that she had made her point, Leah deigned to reply.

"It is patently obvious that you are loath to have people think that you squabble in public, fail to pay your own bills, and do not sleep with your wife. There, that's three."

He glanced around anxiously. "Sweet Jesus, will you lower your voice?"

"See?"

"All I see is you extrapolating wildly from my simple statement that I detest balls. Which I do. And I especially detest this one, knowing as I do that your primary motive for attending has nothing to do with it being one of *the* events of the season and everything to do with lining up likely prospects for the hunt."

"I beg your pardon?" she said, feigning bewilderment.

"I'm referring to marriage prospects, likely candidates, sheep ready for slaughter."

"How crass."

"My sentiments exactly. That is why I refuse to be a party to your little game."

"Courtship is not a game, it is an art," she informed

him patiently, as if speaking to someone who didn't know the language. "A time-honored art, at that, and one in which you are so obviously lacking that I cannot imagine your participation being of the slightest advant—"

She broke off with a small gasp as he grabbed her and jerked her against him. Leah had been so absorbed in her lecture that she hadn't noticed the older, well-dressed gentleman striding toward them with his head down. Raven's efforts to move her out of his path were too late, however, and the man's shoulder collided with hers.

"I beg your pardon," the man exclaimed. "That will teach me to watch where I'm going. Are you all right, madam?"

"I'm fine," Leah assured him, rotating her shoulders to demonstrate. "I've been known to walk into walls myself from time to time."

"Ah, a kindred spirit. I often—" He halted abruptly, his lined face becoming a mask of horror. "Dava? My God, is that you?"

Leah quickly turned away, feeling as if someone had run an icicle along her spine.

"I'm sorry, I have no idea what you're talking about." She looked at Raven. "Can we please go now?"

"Of course," he replied, taking her arm.

"But . . . but . . ." the other man sputtered.

Ignoring him, Raven quickly led her toward her carriage a short distance away and helped her in.

"Are you certain you're all right?" he asked when she was settled, his anxious gaze scouring her face.

"I'm fine."

"You don't look fine," he argued. "You look as if you've seen a ghost."

"Don't be silly. I'm simply tired and want to go home. Now."

He nodded and stepped back to close the carriage door. "Straight home," he called to the driver without taking his eyes off her. "I'll be right behind you."

Alone inside the carriage, Leah rested her head against the back of the leather seat, closed her eyes and gave way to the panic she hadn't dared reveal in front of Raven. She'd spoken the truth when she told him she hadn't seen a ghost. But she had no doubt the gentleman who'd bumped into her was convinced he'd seen one.

6

She hurried into the house before Raven dismounted, intent on reaching her chamber and pleading a headache in order to have some time alone to gather her thoughts. As she passed the gilt-framed mirror in the entrance hall, she carefully averted her gaze, afraid of whose reflection she might see.

The years had blurred her image of her mother, until she sometimes wondered if she could possibly favor her as much as she'd been told. There was no denying she had the same green eyes, thick chestnut hair, and fine bone structure, but you could fill a cathedral with women who had green eyes, brown hair, and high cheekbones.

Obviously, the gentleman on Bond Street had been struck by more. Was it something in her expression that made him think she was her mother? The way she held herself? Or perhaps a certain light in her eyes as she'd walked beside Raven, a man she had foolishly allowed liberties she now winced to recall.

She folded her arms tightly, aghast at the possibility that in spite of all her resolve, she and her mother shared more than a physical likeness . . . and that it showed.

She paced her room anxiously. This never would have happened back in Baumborough, she told herself. But things were so different here. *She* was different here. Raven made her feel different, more reckless and more vulnerable and more needy . . . and all at the same time.

That had to stop. In the meantime, she must deal with the matter at hand. Clearly, her resemblance to her mother was strong enough to be noticed. Which meant she had two choices: She could tell Raven everything and hope he was willing to continue their charade in spite of it, or risk letting him hear a much more colorful and damning version of the family scandal from someone at tonight's ball.

She would tell him herself, she decided. A public scene would be far more damaging to her cause than anything he might dish out in private. That resolved, she settled herself on the bed to plan *how* to tell him and was soon asleep. When she woke, it was dark outside and she fumbled for the lamp by the bed. Still groggy, she rang for Bridget and began searching her wardrobe for something to wear to the ball.

Sackcloth and ashes, she thought sardonically. That's what she ought to wear. The more ghastly she looked, the less she would remind people of Dava. And the less Raven would look at her with *that look,* all smug and hungry, like a tomcat eyeing a bowl of cream and knowing there's no need to pounce, that he can have his fill anytime he pleased and was rather enjoying the anticipation.

The trouble was, she didn't want to look ghastly. She wanted to look beautiful. That, too, was a new and unsettling feeling. She'd never thought herself the primping and preening type, but it was as if she were a prism and facets that had been hidden in darkness for years were suddenly being revealed. Even more alarming than her wish to be beautiful was her yearning to see the acknowledgment of that beauty gleaming in Raven's eyes. God only knew why. It was frightening and confusing and the absolute antithesis of the woman she thought herself to be, but part of her *wanted* to play the cream to his tomcat.

Play. Period. It would go no further, she assured herself. This was a marriage in name only and it must stay that way. Any notions Raven might be entertaining to the contrary were doomed.

With Bridget's help, she donned an off-the-shoulder gown of vivid blue silk, with a matching lace overlay, its deep hem embellished with pearls and ivory satin rosettes. The same trim adorned her slippers, fan and reticule. The outfit was the *pièce de résistance* of her new wardrobe and she had intended to save it for a very special occasion, perhaps even Chrissie's wedding day. After Bridget tended to a lock of hair that had slipped free of the upswept cluster of curls at the back of her head, Leah strolled downstairs—and made her grand entrance into a silent, empty drawing room.

She found Thorne in the kitchen.

"Thorne, where is the Duke?" she asked.

"Gone." He glanced up at her as he bent over the open oven door, clearly unimpressed by her matching pearls and rosettes.

"Gone?"

He nodded.

"Gone where?" she asked.

"Out."

Leah clenched her fists. "Thorne, do you, or do you not, know the whereabouts of the Duke?"

"Not," he replied, removing a pie from the oven. Fragrant steam wafted as he carried it past Leah to the long pine table at the center of the room.

"What is that?" she inquired.

He pulled a knife from the wood block by the stove. "Meat pie."

Having partaken of Snake's culinary offerings, Leah regarded the pie with less enthusiasm. "Did Snake make meat pie for dinner this evening?"

"No. Chicken Fricassee. Same as every third night."

"What do you mean, every third night?"

"First night is roast mutton, second night is stewed beef, third is the fricassee. Then he starts again."

"He serves the same three dishes, in the same order, week in and week out? You can't be serious."

"The devil you know," he muttered and cut into the pie, releasing more of the heavenly aroma.

"Has he never even attempted a new recipe?"

"Used to. No more. Those three dishes are safe. It would take a braver man than me to down something Snake whipped up on his own."

"I understand," she said, her small smile rueful. "And thus far I've sampled only his eggs."

"That's more than enough," he retorted, and dipped his head.

He was hiding a smile, Leah realized. He was no doubt galled to think that he could share a laugh with the woman who'd invaded this bastion of male chaos.

"Then where did this pie come from?" she ventured to ask.

"I made it."

The reply surprised her. "You cook?"

"Some."

With an exasperated sigh, she moved so they faced each other, the table between them. "Thorne, do you suppose it might be possible for us to have a conversation? A real conversation, with whole sentences passing between us? Instead of me having to pull words from you like ticks off a hound?"

He eyed her suspiciously. "What would a lady know about ticks on a hound?"

"Enough. I haven't always lived in London, you know."

"And why would a lady be wanting conversation with a servant . . . Y'Grace?"

"I know nothing of the wants or habits of other ladies. I would like to establish some sort of communication with you because I'm interested in what you have to say. And because we're living under the same roof, for pity's sake." She tossed her reticule on the table. "And because I'm all dressed up for a ball, with no idea where my husband is and I haven't eaten since breakfast and that pie smells delicious."

"You want a piece?" he asked, his expression and gruff tone incredulous.

"May I?"

He shrugged. "It's your house."

"It's your pie."

For half a minute, he stared at her, as if searching for some hidden motive. Finally he said, "There's plenty. Shall I serve yours in the dining room . . . Y'Grace?"

"Of course not. And you can stop looking at me that way. This is hardly the first time I've taken a meal in the kitchen. Where I come from, things are less formal. To tell you the truth, I prefer a bowl of soup with the clatter of pots and pans around me to sitting for a full-course meal in a big dining room, with only my sister and our governess for company."

"Sit," Thorne ordered, then added, "Y'Grace."

He fetched knives and forks and rummaged in a drawer for a rough linen napkin, then served them each a generous slice of the meat pie. It tasted even better than it smelled. Leah told him so, then waited until they'd both slaked their appetite a little before speaking.

"Will you tell me how you learned to cook?"

Silence. When he finally did speak it was with a decided lack of zeal. "From my mother."

When Leah continued to gaze at him with an expectant look, he added, "She was laid sick for more than a year when I was just thirteen. We brought her bed into the kitchen, where it was warm. She'd lay there and tell me what to do and I learned."

"And very well indeed, if this is any indication of your talents. What happened when your mother recovered? Did she take over as cook or by that time did the pupil outshine the teacher?"

"She didn't recover." He swallowed hard, his flinty gaze fixed on his plate.

"I'm sorry." Without thinking she reached over and briefly touched the back of his hand. He didn't pull away. "My own mother died when I was around that same age."

"Sorry," he responded brusquely, then shoveled a huge bite of pie into his mouth, signaling he'd rather eat than talk.

Leah followed suit until she put down her fork, full on only half the serving he'd given her.

"Tell me, Thorne," she said, shifting to a less emotionally charged subject, "does Snake mind you invading his domain?"

He snorted. "Not hardly. He'd rather be out there talking to the posies."

"Posies?"

"Posies, roses, whatever they are. Snake says when it comes to gardening, Mannington doesn't know his ars—" He broke off, flushing.

Leah nodded. "I understand. Is Snake right?"

"Who knows?" He looked surprised, but flattered to be asked his opinion. "Till you showed up, there was never much gardening to be done, so old Mannington took to spending his time with the horses. Likes horses better than people, that one."

"I see."

Leah thought that somewhere in this jumble of a butler who'd rather cook, a cook who'd rather garden and a gardener who loved horses, there might be the solution to a problem that had been nagging at her. She could tidy and rearrange Raven House all she liked, but unless something was done about the inefficiency with which it was run, it would be in the same sorry state in no time.

"Tell me, Thorne, if you like to cook, how did you end up in your current position instead, while Snake was hired to cook?"

"We drew lots."

"I beg your pardon?"

"Lots. It's when—"

"I understand the concept. What I don't understand is why servants would be employed in such a fashion."

"It was the Duke's doing."

"Oh." That explained nothing, and everything.

To her surprise, Thorne elaborated without prodding.

"We served under His Grace, you see, from the Battle of Salamanca on, and a better or braver commanding officer there never was. Once we were all back home, we needed work and His Grace gave it to us. We weren't about to quibble over our duties."

"But what did he do with the existing staff?"

"Weren't none left. The old duke had been dead and gone for years, with this place standing empty. Truth be told, I think His Grace would as soon have left it that way until it rotted and crumbled, and set himself up somewhere with no ghosts. He's only here to give the rest of us a spot to hang our hats."

"I see." She had attributed his neglect as further evidence of his self-indulgence, assuming he was too busy with the pursuit of selfish, dissolute pleasures to give a thought to the water stains on the ceilings or the inefficiency of the staff. Thorne's remarks made her suspect that the state of the house had more to do with contempt.

But why? she wondered. What would cause Raven to feel such disdain for his own heritage? And whose ghost haunted Raven House?

Cyril Gates's Glasshouse Street office was empty except for Adrian and Cyril Gates himself. He was a modestly successful solicitor whom Adrian called on to handle matters of an unusual or sensitive nature. The man was preeminently qualified for such assignments because he had few scruples and knew how to keep his mouth shut. And he had something lacking in the solicitors who handled Adrian's routine business affairs—connections in all the wrong places.

"You received my instructions?" Adrian inquired as soon as he was seated in a small private office. It smelled of old leather and old tobacco, and was lit by a single lamp.

"I received your note," Gates replied, straightening his wire-rimmed glasses. The lenses were perfect circles and had the effect of making his brown eyes appear the same shape. That and the feathery fringe of dark hair ringing his bald head always gave Adrian the impression that he was conducting business with an owl.

"Your instructions," continued the solicitor, "were a bit vague."

"Intentionally so. There are some details a gentleman hesitates to commit to writing."

"Of course. Then I am correct in assuming that this House of Birds you intend to establish is a very, ah, delicate venture?"

"Precisely."

"I understand. Then I would say our first task is to determine the proper location."

"Actually, I may have already done that. I know of a gallery in Soho that I may be able to acquire in a discreet fashion."

"Very well. That brings us to the matter of the, ah, birds themselves, Your Grace."

Adrian nodded with a small smile. "Yes, and that is the most delicate and critical part of the entire endeavor."

"I take it we are not talking about the sort of ordinary bird that any man with a few quid in his pocket might lay his hand on at any street corner?"

"No, we most definitely are not. I am looking to acquire the most spectacular specimens available. I desire creatures both beautiful and spirited, and of course, no two are to be alike."

"Of course," Gates agreed, scoffing at the very notion. "Your, ah, patrons, would soon be bored if the bird in one cage was just like the next."

Adrian's mouth curved. "Cages. That's bloody brilliant, Gates. I hadn't considered cages."

"It was just a figure of speech."

"No, no, you're onto something. I think cages will provide exactly the sort of ambience necessary to set this establishment apart from every other birdhouse in London. I can see it already, room-size cages, each one designed to highlight a particular specimen. For instance, in the canary cage, everything will be yellow, floor to ceiling. In the cardinal's cage—"

"Red," interjected Gates. "Yes, yes. I see where you're going with this. And I like it. I like it very much."

And so would every other red-blooded man in town, Adrian realized with satisfaction.

"Of course," he said to Gates, "this makes it even more imperative that you do not bring me any two birds alike. You may even need to import specimens from abroad. Are you up to the task?"

"Oh, I can lay my hands on the right birds, all right. But as I said, these aren't pigeons we're talking about, and they won't come cheap."

Adrian flashed a smug smile. "Did I neglect to mention that I have gathered a most generous group of benefactors to fund the entire project? Set your traps, Gates. Cost is no object."

Outside Gates's office, Adrian defiantly turned his horse not toward home, but in the direction of his club. He'd spent the afternoon pacing and waiting, while *the duchess* remained locked in her room with a convenient headache. Now it was her turn to wait.

Colin and Will were already at the club, engaged in a game of cards. Both men were at least one drink ahead of him. Once Adrian had caught up, Colin suggested a visit to Madame Loiselle, whose nearby establishment featured some of the most exquisite prostitutes in London.

"Enjoy yourselves, gentlemen," Adrian responded.

"I have another commitment." He explained about the Torrington ball.

Both his friends stared at him.

"A ball?" inquired Colin, his expression progressing from startled to amused. "*You're* going to a ball? Of your own free will?"

"Of course, of my own free will," snapped Adrian.

"Are you feeling all right?"

"I feel fine. The duchess desires a proper introduction into society and I decided it was the least I could do under the circumstances."

"That's decent of you, Rave," declared Will, nodding encouragingly.

Colin reached for his glass and emptied it. "And so it begins. First you allow yourself to be dragged to a ball, then a recital by somebody's tooth-faced niece. The next thing you know you're traipsing down Bond Street after her, cooing over the latest silks and lugging packages like a pack mule."

Adrian eyed him suspiciously. Had Colin seen him on Bond Street earlier? No. He would have crowed about it straightaway if he had. Besides, he had not been lugging any packages. Thank God.

"My thanks for the warning," he retorted. "And now, if you gentlemen will excuse me . . ."

"Not on your life," Colin said, rising along with Adrian. "I hadn't thought to attend the Torringtons' ball, but damned if I'm not suddenly feeling a yen for pickled quail eggs and a waltz. How about you, Will?"

Will clambered to his feet. He rarely initiated a jest, but he also seldom sat out one of Colin's. "I think I could force myself to partake of a quail egg or two."

Colin grinned. "It will also give me a chance to get a look at your bride with her eyes open."

"Don't you two think you're a bit old for this sort of

nonsense?" Adrian inquired with his most patronizing air.

"No," they replied in unison.

"So then," said Colin, "shall we go collect the duchess?"

Privately, Adrian hoped that "collecting the duchess" was not going to present a problem. Leah was unpredictable, and she possessed a disconcerting tendency not to respond to anything the way a woman ought to.

In retrospect, he realized he'd left her hanging for quite a while this evening. She might well have taken it in her head to go to the ball without him. On the other hand, she might have given up and gone to bed. Or she might be waiting by the door to tell him exactly what she thought of him. Any one of the three could prove awkward in front of his all too easily amused companions.

How many times had he himself snickered at a husband in just such a humiliating predicament?

Too many to count, a fact that Colin and Will would not fail to toss in his face.

No matter how uncomfortable things became however, he would not react in any way that might jeopardize his campaign. He must remember at all times that his ultimate goal was the duchess herself, in his bed, warm, willing and consummated like no woman had ever been consummated before.

He entered the house braced for anything. Anything, that is, except for the sight of his wife seated in the kitchen, laughing and sipping tea with one of the most cantankerous men ever dropped on earth. He ought to know. He'd saved Thorne from a military tribunal once, a knife in the back at least twice, and from his own orneriness countless times, and it had taken all of that to win the man's unswerving loyalty.

Leah rose gracefully at the sight of him and he was swept by desire as swift and hot as it was untimely. Her hair was pinned up, revealing a slender throat, gorgeous shoulders and an absolutely perfect bosom. She was a confection wrapped in deep blue silk, a very special present he couldn't wait to open.

She smiled, apparently pleased to see him in spite of his unexplained absence.

Where was the woman's resentment at being kept waiting? Her indignation? Her God-given wifely wrath, for pity's sake?

Not that he wanted her to be angry with him. He simply didn't like surprises. Or trust them. And Leah was proving to be one damn surprise after another.

7

"Duchess, may I present Sir Colin Thornton?"

The tall, lean man by Raven's side stepped forward and bowed. He had eyes that sparkled like amber glass and a masterpiece of a grin.

A rascal, Leah decided as he pressed his lips to the back of her hand, and yet could not help liking him immediately.

In a dry tone, Raven added, "I believe you and Mr. Grantley are already well acquainted."

Leah smiled warmly and returned Will Grantley's stammered greeting.

"Your Grace, this is truly a pleasure," said Colin. "May I be permitted to say that you are the most exquisite creature I have ever encountered? Certainly much more than this lucky devil deserves." He tipped his head toward Raven.

"You may say it," Leah replied, "but I don't know if I shall believe you, Sir Colin. Your ease around a compliment suggests you encounter *most exquisite creatures* on a regular basis."

He chuckled good-naturedly. "Ah, beauty *and* intelligence, a rare and intoxicating combination."

"If you're through flirting with my wife," said Raven, "perhaps we can be on our way."

"Raven loves balls," Colin confided in a tone she didn't trust. "You must have him tell you about the time he single-handedly brought the dancing to a complete halt at the Earl of Penwick's birthday ball."

Leah turned her curious gaze on Raven.

"Some other time," he growled, taking Leah's arm. "Make haste, gentlemen, if you're still bent on coming with us."

"Wouldn't miss it for the world," drawled Colin, as Leah hid her dismay over the fact that Raven's friends would be accompanying them. She'd counted on having time alone with Raven before they arrived at the ball. More than ever she regretted not telling him everything at the start.

"I will leave as soon as the Duchess promises me her first dance of the evening," declared Colin.

"Out of the question," retorted Raven. "It is already promised to me."

His friend made a scoffing sound. "You hate to dance."

"Not anymore."

"Is that true, Duchess?" Colin demanded. "Are you going to commit the ultimate social sin of dancing with your own husband?"

She glanced at Raven, his head tilted slightly back, his expression magnificently arrogant, and a shiver of pure, sensual awareness ran through her. At that instant, it was as if no bargains existed between them, and no compromises. *You are mine,* his dark gaze seemed to say, *and I will dance with you when and where I please.*

"I'm afraid I am," she told Colin.

"In that case," he countered easily, "I claim the second dance."

"And I the third," added Will.

Leah grinned, flattered and quite amazed by the novelty of being the center of so much male attention.

"Provided there are three dances remaining by the time we finally arrive," grumbled Raven, as if he were not the one responsible for their being late in the first place.

He really was an impossible man, Leah mused as he helped her with her black velvet wrap and then shepherded them all out the door. His hand rested possessively on the small of her back, its heat and weight causing a pleasant whirling in her stomach. The sensation was not unlike what she'd felt a few moments earlier, when he walked in and gave her a look that was more hungry lion than lazy tomcat . . . and everything she'd secretly hoped for when she'd chosen to wear this dress.

He kept his hand on her as they entered the carriage, shamelessly maneuvering to claim the seat beside her. He sat so close, his hard thigh pressed against hers through the layers of silk and lace, and sent a steady stream of warm tingles coursing through her. It was all she could do to keep up her part of the conversation. No matter how hard she tried to focus, her thoughts were drawn to the man beside her, to the scent and heat and overwhelmingly masculine allure of him.

Leah shivered. It was a dangerous game she was playing. Instinct warned that Raven was not like any other man alive, and that to become involved with him would mean, sooner or later, surrendering everything.

The Torrington home was grand even by London standards. Set well back from the street, a large courtyard provided a buffer from the noise of Picadilly, except when the great iron gates were thrown open, as they were tonight, to receive guests arriving in their carriages.

They were not the only late arrivals. Seeing the stream of finely attired gentlemen and ladies reminded Leah of the balls her parents had hosted when they all still lived together in a big house near Hyde Park. She would slip from her bed and peer through the banister at the deliciously grown-up scene below. Then, as now, the air around her was filled with laughter and excitement. The difference was that back then, she had only longed to be part of it, and now at last she was.

Why, if not for the proverbial ax hovering above her outstretched neck, she would be thoroughly enjoying herself.

"So," said Raven as he led her across the crowded dance floor in a ballroom with a magnificent high gilt ceiling and burgundy silk-sheathed walls, "how does it feel to be steeped in social sin?"

Leah stumbled, thrown off balance by her own guilty conscience. "I beg your pardon?"

"Social sin. Isn't that how Colin described the act of dancing with your own husband?"

"Oh, that." Her laughter was tinged with relief. "I suppose we are being dreadfully boring."

"Not judging by the amount of attention we are attracting."

"Really?" she said, hoping he couldn't feel the

nervous tremor that raced through her. "I hadn't noticed."

At least she had *tried* not to notice. It only added to her anxiety to meet all those curious gazes and wonder what nasty thoughts and questions lurked behind them.

"You didn't notice that every head turned as we walked past? Or that, even now, at least half the people on this dance floor are stumbling over their own feet trying to get a closer look at you?"

He did not sound at all pleased that his new bride was the object of such intense scrutiny. Leah didn't even want to think about what his reaction would be when he learned the real reason for it, and that she had hidden it from him when they struck their bargain.

"I imagine I was too busy being dazzled by my first London ball to notice. And frankly, I wish you hadn't told me. I'm sure they're all staring and thinking what an absolute country bumpkin I am, gaping all around and dancing with my husband."

He shot her a sardonic smile. "I assure you, madame, that the half of the dance floor I was referring to—the male half—are not looking at you in that dress and thinking anything nearly that innocent."

She gazed up at him with astonishment. "Why, Raven, you sound jealous."

"Don't be absurd," was all he said.

The irritation in his gruff voice was unmistakable, and Leah tucked away the possibility of what it might mean, intending to examine it at some future time.

When the music stopped, he surprised her a second time by taking her hand and preventing her from leaving the dance floor.

"What do you want?" she asked, excruciatingly aware of the speculative glances they were drawing and the hushed voices that seemed to ripple around them like a whirlpool.

"You," he said, making her breath catch. His gaze locked with hers as the orchestra began another waltz. "Right here, where you belong."

She glanced around uncertainly. "But Sir Colin . . ."

"Hang Colin. You're mine." Leah's pulse raced as he pulled her even closer than before, closer than was proper, certainly far closer than a woman intent on avoiding scandal should allow. But Leah found herself not able, not *wanting*, to pull away. "Bore me some more."

His husky whisper was just loud enough to be heard by those standing near, with just enough of a suggestive edge to merit repeating to every person in the room. Soon everyone would be saying what a devoted bridegroom the Duke of Raven was. Was that his intent? Was he simply playing the role she had demanded of him? Or was it something more? Was it possible that he felt what she felt when they touched? And that he was merely pretending to be pretending, the same way she was?

No. It was not possible. A man of Raven's habits and experience did not go all tingly inside at the touch of a country spinster with more imagination than sense. It was she who was confusing fantasy with reality. And who could blame her? It was difficult enough to think clearly when her head was swirling from his heat. The growing gaggle of lies and pretenses she had to keep track of made it nearly impossible.

"Well?" he said eventually, regarding her with mock reproach. "Have you exhausted yourself flirting with those worthless friends of mine and now have nothing left to say?"

Nothing to say? She had plenty to say to him, but a

crowded dance floor was hardly the place for confessions and explanations. "Not at all. I was simply following your instructions, as I imagine a good wife ought to."

"And those instructions would be . . ."

"Why, to bore you, of course. Am I succeeding?"

"Frankly, no," he told her with a rueful laugh. "I have a hunch that *boring* will never be one of the words I'll choose to describe our time together."

"What words will you choose?" she asked impulsively.

He shrugged. "Challenging. Infuriating. Surprising. And memorable."

"Memorable," she echoed, turning the word over in her mind and smiling. "I'll settle for that."

"How will you describe it?"

The question directed her thoughts to the future, when she would be safely home in Baumborough, looking back on her ordeal. The prospect should have filled her with anticipation, Leah thought, instead of this curious, unnamed longing.

"Challenging," she said finally. "Infuriating. Surprising. And dangerous."

"Dangerous? In what way?"

In every way, she thought, in ways she hadn't dreamed existed before he charged into her life and taught her that she didn't know herself nearly as well as she thought.

"You have to admit our situation does involve a certain amount of risk," she replied.

"You mean because it is all a charade?"

"Shh." She glanced around. "Don't even say that word in public."

"Why? It's been a while since I made an appearance at one of these things, I admit, but last I knew the *ton* didn't infiltrate the crowd with lip-readers."

"You never know." Leah gazed around with barely concealed suspicion. "I wouldn't put anything past some of these people."

"Any particular reason?"

She quickly brought her anxious gaze back to meet his. "Why do you ask?"

He spun her around with effortless grace. "I suppose because you suddenly went so stiff I felt as if I were dancing with the corpse you once accused me of wishing you to be."

"Very funny. And I am not stiff," she argued, trying to relax her shoulders. "Merely cautious. As you should be."

"Why?" He moved his hand on her back. So much for trying to relax. "Think about it, Leah, would it really be so bad if we said the hell with it and abandoned the charade?"

"Bad?" Leah was appalled, fearing he meant to renege on their deal. "It would be worse than bad. It would be a nightmare. It would ruin everything."

Suddenly she felt as if she were the one dancing with a corpse.

"By *everything*," he said in a voice as rigid as his arms, "I assume you're thinking of your purpose in coming to London."

"Of course. What else would I be thinking of?"

"What indeed?" he muttered. "You can relax. Far be it from me to ruin your sister's prospects of landing herself a plump pigeon."

"I prefer to think of it as ensuring my sister's ability to meet a decent, honorable man and to be wed in a church with flowers and music and a proper ceremony."

"The way you would have wished to be wed, is that it?"

"Yes." She caught herself. "I mean no. Oh, you

make everything so difficult, I don't know what I mean."

"Perhaps I can help. It's clear that in spite of your claim not to be a romantic, you are as susceptible to legalized sentimentality and empty promises as every other member of your sex."

"And it is equally clear that you are as given to cynicism and self-serving prevarication as every member of yours."

"Smile when you say that," he advised. "Our audience may not read lips, but they'll certainly recognize a lovers' spat when they witness one."

He waited until she managed to shape her lips into a tight smile before bending his head to nuzzle her. The small, negligent gesture incited in her a rush of warmth that quickly exploded into something more perilous when he pressed closer and swirled his tongue in her ear. The touch was hot and wet and so audacious that if not for the way her knees were buckling, Leah would not have believed he had done it.

"What do you think you're doing?" she demanded.

"Convincing our audience that I'm mad about you. That was our agreement, was it not?"

"No. Our agreement called for *tasteful* displays of affection."

"*Tasting* you is exactly what I was doing."

"You're impossible," she snapped.

"And you're delicious. And just for the record," he added, his smile filled with lazy satisfaction, "*that* is how I brought the dancing to a halt at old Penwick's birthday ball. Of course, the trick is that it was Penwick's wife I was tonguing at the time and not my own. Now where were we before I gave in to temptation?"

It galled Leah that he could be so nonchalant while she was still light-headed.

"Of course," he continued. "Now I remember. We were discussing your secret longing for a church wedding with all the trimmings. Tell me, Duchess, did you have a groom picked out along with the flowers? Is there perhaps a gentleman farmer eagerly awaiting your return?"

"If there were, *Your Grace,* you can be assured he would not have to render me unconscious to get me to the altar."

"Ah, ah," he chided. "Smile. Much better. Has it occurred to you that perhaps I prefer you unconscious?"

"Less of a challenge?"

"Less of a shrew."

"Lord, you two are sickening."

They both turned to see Colin Thornton beside them.

"I swear, you haven't taken your eyes off each other since the music started." Grinning at Raven, he added, "But if you thought that would discourage me from cutting in, you're mistaken. She may be your wife, but she's promised to me for this dance." He held out his hand. "May I?"

"She's all yours," Raven replied, releasing her.

Too abruptly, Leah thought peevishly, and after taking such pains to warn her to smile and keep up appearances.

"That was easier than I expected," remarked Colin. His arm circled her loosely, with far more deference than Raven's and, she noted with irritation, with none of the same impact. Though to be truthful, she wasn't sure which fate would be worse—responding indiscriminately to any man's touch or coming alive only to Raven's. "Though I must say he didn't look too happy to share you," Colin pointed out.

"On the contrary," she assured him, "I believe he

was very happy to be rid of me. It's me he is not pleased with."

"What? A lovers' quarrel already?"

"Certainly not," she replied indignantly, then realized she probably ought not appear offended by the suggestion that she and Raven were lovers. "It was simply a slight difference of opinion."

"Well, fear not, Duchess, you shall find me a most agreeable partner. In fact, I hereby make it my life's purpose—well, at least for this evening—to agree with your every utterance." Leah was amused in spite of herself. Noting her smile, he furrowed his brow. "You're giggling. You don't trust me?"

"Should I?"

"Probably not. No, make that definitely not. A woman should always require a man to earn her trust. So go ahead."

"I beg your pardon?"

"Go ahead. Put me to the test. Say something, anything and I shall concur, no matter how ridiculous. In fact," he said, flashing an infectious smile as he whirled her enthusiastically, "the more ridiculous it is, the more sickeningly agreeable I shall be."

Leah shook her head, hardly in the mood for games. Then she caught sight of Raven among the onlookers at the edge of the dance floor. He was watching, glowering really, so fiercely she wondered if it was the power of his gaze that had drawn her attention to him in the first place.

With a defiant toss of her head, she directed her most dazzling smile at her partner. "Let me see. I have it . . . the moon is made of green cheese."

He nodded. "And always has been. Would Your Grace care to step into the garden with me and confirm that fact?"

"You're incorrigible," Leah said, laughing with genuine enjoyment.

"Not totally," he protested. "For example, a totally incorrigible man would fail to seize this opportunity to apologize for his role in your recent marriage . . . whereas I do, and most sincerely. Can you ever forgive me, Duchess?"

"Of course, I forgive you."

He immediately stepped on her toe and uttered a quick apology. "You forgive me? Just like that?" His expression was such a mixture of hope and disbelief that Leah had to laugh again.

"Yes, just like that. What did you expect?"

"Torture, a couple of spins on the rack perhaps, tar and feathers at the very least. Seriously, most women of my acquaintance would let me dangle at the end of my apology until they'd extracted their pound of flesh."

"Then the women of your acquaintance are far more talented than I, for I would have no idea how to make you dangle, nor what to do with you once I had you there."

He drew back slightly and studied her as if not quite knowing what to make of her remark. Probably because it was so blatantly inane, she thought. She hardly needed to underscore her lack of sophistication in such matters.

She added, "However, perhaps gentleman-dangling is a skill I will acquire now that I am in town."

"I hope not, Duchess," replied Colin, his smile rueful. "I sincerely hope not."

By the time the dance ended, she had agreed to call him by his given name and had impulsively extended him the same privilege. And she had decided that her first instinct was right; Colin Thornton was a thoroughly likable man. And loyal to a fault. Contrive though she did, he refused to reveal any further details about Raven's dance floor spectacle with Lady Penwick. He insisted it was because he liked his own tongue exactly where it was, thank you very much, but Leah was convinced his silence had less to do with fear of her husband than with friendship.

Will Grantley appeared to claim her as soon as the music ended. The next dance was a cotillion, which limited conversation. He still managed to make it clear he was concerned for her and that she should feel free to call on him if she ever needed him for anything.

"Not that Rave's a bad sort, not at all," he assured her at one point, when the intricate steps of the dance brought them side by side. "Just difficult. Sometimes, when things don't go precisely as he thinks they ought to—"

"Meaning his way," she interjected drily.

"Meaning his way," Will concurred ruefully. "Then he can be like a great lumbering bear with his hand caught in a beehive, and do a lot of damage without meaning to."

"You don't have to convince me that the man is given to acting on impulse. Or that impulsiveness never leads to anything but regrets."

Her mother's fate had taught her all she needed to know about that.

"Well, I wouldn't say never," Will countered with a blushing smile. "Look at how this marriage has turned out."

"Yes, just look." Privately she thought that if anything proved her point, that did.

The final moments of the dance had them moving in intertwining circles and swinging rapidly from one partner to the next. When it ended, Leah was breathing hard and her cheeks were flushed.

"You're warm," observed Will, appearing more out of breath than she was. "I'd offer you some fresh air, but I don't think Rave would care for it if I went off alone with you. In fact, I know he wouldn't care for it at all."

"Why not?" she asked, intrigued. "Is he the possessive type?"

"I can't really say. Till now, he's never had anyone he cared enough about to be possessive of. Unless you count Charlotte Bonnaire, which I don't, because it was so long ago and Rave was so young, just barely twenty-one, and green as anything, especially compared to her, who had a good twelve years on him if she had a day. That's twelve that she owned up to. Privately, Colin and I always thought she'd shaved off a few years along the way. At any rate, that whole situation was such a bloody mess, begging your pardon, that I never put much credence in anything Rave said or did back then."

"Who's Charlotte?" asked Leah.

Will blinked rapidly. "What's that?"

"I asked who Charlotte was?"

"No one," he said, looking trapped. "I don't even know why I brought up her name. Oh, right, because you asked if Raven is possessive, and he's not, especially not with his things. He'd give you anything if you needed, the shirt off his back and all that. But this is different, isn't it? You're not a shirt, after all, you're his wife." His eyes brightened. "I've got it. How about a cold drink? There's no harm in that."

"None that I can see," agreed Leah, curbing the frustration that made her want to grab him and shake him until he told her everything about Charlotte Bonnaire.

A mysterious older woman and a randy, self-indulgent young nobleman. That certainly conjured up some scorching images in her mind. For once, she regretted the vivid fertility of her own imagination. She had known of Raven's reputation for philandering, of course, but apparently hordes of nameless women were easier for a wife—even a temporary wife—to overlook than two with names. One of whom he admitted to mauling publicly and the other had obviously played a significant part in his past.

She was still struggling to subdue her imagination as Will led her to an open space at the edge of the dance floor. "Wait here," he instructed. "I'll return straightaway with your drink."

"But . . ." Leah's protest faded as he bounded into the crowd, so eager to please that it did not occur to him that he was leaving her alone in a room full of strangers. Whispering, ogling strangers. Suddenly Leah felt a very long way from Baumborough and the assembly room dances, where music was provided by a single pianoforte and, on a good night, a servant with a talent for the fiddle. She felt a long way from everything that was familiar and safe.

She glanced around, desperately hoping to see a friendly face. Ironically, the only one she could envision was Raven's.

The devil you know, she told herself, fixing a smile in place in an attempt to appear confident and carefree, and doing her best *not* to look like an anxious, friendless wallflower, a sorry excuse for an adventuress who was in over her head and sorry as sin that she had ever had the bright idea to come—

"Leah?"

The stern female voice was instantly recognizable, having deep roots in both the unhappiest days of her life and some of her worst nightmares. Serves me right for wishing for a familiar face, thought Leah. Trying not to wince, she turned to greet the very last person she wished to deal with this evening, a woman whose dour expression perfectly expressed her outlook on life, a mean-spirited old crone with a heart as bad as her breath, an overbearing, wrinkled-up meddler without a kind or loyal bone in her body.

"Hello, Aunt Millicent. This is such a . . ." Wonderful? Nice? Pleasant? She'd rather smother herself than go that far. "Remarkable surprise."

"So," said her aunt, "you had the effrontery to come after all."

"If by *after all* you mean after your less than enthusiastic response to the news that I was planning to bring Christiana to town for the season, then yes, I suppose I did." She managed to maintain a civil tone in spite of her recollection of the curt reply to a letter she sorely regretted writing.

Not that she had expected an offer of help or hospitality, though her aunt and uncle, the present Earl and Countess of Aldwick, resided in the elegant—and expansive—London mansion that had once been home to her and Chrissie. She had contacted them only out of a sense of propriety. They were her closest family, after all. It would hardly do for them to hear from others that she and Chrissie were in town. And, to be completely truthful, she had hoped that the advance warning would enable her to avoid the unpleasant scene that was about to take place, judging by the pucker of her aunt's colorless lips.

"What do you hope to gain by coming here?" the older woman demanded.

"A pleasurable evening," Leah replied evasively. The last thing she wanted was for Raven to find her embroiled in a heated airing of the family's dirty laundry. "It is a marvelous ball, don't you agree? I don't think I've ever heard finer music for dancing."

"Don't be cheeky, girl. You know very well I was not referring to the ball, but your presence in London. What on earth can it serve but to dredge up a lot of ugliness and spoil my Jenny's season?"

Leah had not seen her cousin Jenny in years, but if she at all resembled the sullen, freckled monster she'd been at seven, her season would not hold much promise regardless of who was in town. She refrained from saying so, however, still intent on keeping the conversation cordial and ending it as soon as possible.

"I have no wish to spoil anything for anyone, Aunt Millicent. My only interest is in providing my sister with the same opportunity you are affording Jenny, a chance to meet a suitable young man and make a happy life for herself."

"Your sister's life is back in Baumborough." The powder-caked trenches that fifty years of scowling had etched in her cheeks deepened. "As is your own. I thought I had made the situation clear in my letter, but obviously I shall have to be more direct. No gentleman of consequence will marry the daughter of a whore. Let your sister seek a husband at home and be content, and you too, if you can find a man who'll tolerate your willfulness." She ran a contemptuous gaze over Leah. "You do not belong here."

It felt to Leah as if a dam had broken in her heart. Caution and civility gave way to the need to strike back for all the slights and insults that had been inflicted over the years on Chrissie and herself, and on their mother before that.

"On the contrary," she retorted. "I very much belong here, since this is my husband's home, and now mine as well, and it shall be Christiana's for as long as she desires."

Her aunt's eyes narrowed to slits. "Husband? What are you talking about?"

"It's true, Aunt. I am married, to a man who tolerates my willfulness every bit as well as he handles being married to the daughter of a whore."

The countess's ample chest heaved with anger. "You brag of this? As if your mother's legacy is something to be proud of?"

"Indeed, I am proud of my mother. She was not perfect by any means, but she was kind and loving . . . and she never sought to better herself at the expense of others," she declared pointedly.

"I suppose I should not be surprised to hear you take her part," said her aunt, her lip curled with distaste. "You have her look about you. You always did, even as a girl. Your father was wise to send you away to Baumborough and keep you there."

"The way you and my uncle kept me there even after his death?"

"For your own good. Who knows what further disgrace you might have brought on yourself and the rest of the family?"

"Disgrace? I was little more than a child when I was sent away, and Christiana only seven. Banished. Without friend or family—"

"You had your mother," her aunt spat.

"My mother died within a year of being betrayed by you, the sister-in-law she thought was her friend. Have you forgotten that?"

"Your mother was the one guilty of betrayal. She betrayed your father and dragged all our good names through the mud. And in the end it was she who chose to take her own life, leaving her children to fend for themselves. Have *you* forgotten that?"

"No. I shall never forget anything that happened back then."

"I'm pleased to hear that. Perhaps you will avoid making the same mistakes she did. Though I am a great believer that blood will tell. Why else would you have wed in secret? Without asking permission of your uncle?"

Leah gazed at her incredulously. "Did you honestly expect that I would ask permission from an uncle who cares so little for my happiness and well-being that for years our only contact has been through solicitors?"

The countess sniffed. "The Earl of Aldwick is a very busy man."

"And I am a busy woman—"

"Busy with what?" interrupted her aunt. "Those little books of yours?"

"Among other things," she countered, frustrated that this woman still had the power to hurt her. "I am far too busy to seek approval from those whose opinions do not matter, on decisions I am capable of making for myself."

The countess's round chin lifted in challenge. "Is that really the reason for your secrecy? Or were you simply reluctant to have us meet this new husband of yours?" Her eyes brightened with nasty anticipation. "Tell me, Leah, what sort of man would wed a woman whose own connections keep her at a distance?"

"This sort."

8

Raven was there, at her side, and Leah thought that if she lived to be a hundred and wrote a million "little books," she could never conjure up such a perfect scenario. She didn't even stop to wonder how much he had heard and what he must think of her. There would be time to deal with that later. At the moment she wanted only to savor the look of complete and utter shock on her aunt's face.

Ignoring the countess, Raven smiled at her, gently, adoringly, as if she were the answer to prayers he didn't dare to pray, and even though Leah knew it was all for show, she felt absurdly happy.

"I've missed you," he murmured, lifting her hand and running his lips lightly over the back of it. "Remind me never to let you out of my sight for so long again."

"It was only two dances," she replied.

"That's two too many, my love." He glanced at the

countess with a smile that flashed like a drawn saber in the light from the chandelier overhead. "I beg your pardon. I got carried away." Locking gazes with Leah, he added, "Again. Sweetheart, please do me the honor of introducing your friend."

"Of course . . . darling. May I present my aunt, the Countess of Aldwick?" She was aware of the flicker of surprise in his dark eyes, but kept her gaze riveted on her aunt as she continued. "Aunt, this is my husband, the Duke of Raven."

"I . . . I . . . ," her aunt stuttered.

"I'm pleased to make your acquaintance, madam," said Raven, bowing. "I've wondered where my wife gets her beauty and charm." The insolent curve of his lips said he wondered yet, but his manner was impeccable, leaving no doubt what sort of man Leah had married. "Aldwick, you say? I believe I've done business with your husband in the past. A shipping venture, if memory serves."

The countess nodded eagerly, a natural gift for ingratiation overcoming her shock. "Yes, yes, I'm sure you have. The earl has extensive holdings in shipping and transport."

But not nearly as extensive as the Duke of Raven's. Few men did, and that, as well as his rank, accounted for her aunt's sudden about-face. Leah could sense the wheels in her head spinning in search of a way to turn this development to her advantage.

Raven saved her the trouble.

"I shall have to consider renewing those dealings in light of our new *connection,*" he said. "I'm sure Leah will fill me in on all the pertinent details."

"Of course." Her aunt beamed shamelessly at her. "I was just scolding my dear niece for not informing us of her intent to wed, so that her uncle could see her off properly."

"I'm afraid the fault is entirely mine," he explained, reaching for Leah's hand once more. "I am not a patient man once I have found what I desire most. I refused to wait for banns and invitations and all that nonsense to make her my own. Besides, I was not ready to share her with others. I'm still not, so if you'll excuse us. Come with me," he said to Leah, in a voice that made her feel as though she was wrapped in black velvet.

"But your uncle . . ." The countess plucked at Leah's sleeve as they began to move away. She craned her neck to look around the room. "He's right here somewhere, and I know he'll want to extend his best wishes to you, Your Grace. To you both, that is."

"Some other time," murmured Raven, and her aunt simply smiled as if she'd been blessed instead of dismissed.

Ah, this was heady wine indeed.

"Perhaps we could call on you," she persisted.

"Send your card," instructed Raven. "Leah is intent on transforming Raven House as completely as she has me, and that will occupy a good portion of her time until her sister's arrival."

"Oh yes, dear little Christiana. We should love to see her too."

"And I'm sure you shall." He continued to ease Leah away, with the countess trailing. "You did mention hosting a soiree, didn't you darling?"

Leah nodded.

"A soiree?" exclaimed the countess. "At Raven House? How absolutely fabulous. Perhaps my Jenny and Christiana could both—"

"Perhaps," interrupted Raven, strategically turning his shoulder to block her advance. "Send a card."

Leah sighed with relief as they finally broke free and walked arm in arm through the ballroom. The gradual unclenching of her muscles made it clear how tense she had been. "Thank you," she said.

"My pleasure."

"I swear I detest that woman with every last fiber of my being."

"With good reason, I would say."

She went cold inside. "Why? How much did you hear?"

"Enough to decide that the only way I'd do business with your uncle again is to commission a sinking ship and put her on it."

Leah laughed.

"And enough to know you needed rescuing," he added.

Her smile turned pensive. "No one has ever come to my rescue before."

"Then we're even, because I've never before been inspired to rescue anyone. Damsels in distress are definitely not my weakness."

"Then why did you do it tonight?"

"The truth?" He studied her as if assessing whether or not she could take it.

"Of course."

"I wanted to sweeten you up and that seemed as good a way as any."

"Sweeten me up? Whatever for?"

"To get you into bed with me . . . in spite of our agreement."

Leah made an impatient sound. "Don't tease, Raven. What *really* made you do it?"

He stopped walking and shook his head, gazing at her with an odd, almost bewildered expression. "If you must know, it's because of this, this tiny V" —he ran a fingertip between her eyebrows—"that forms right here whenever you're worried or upset. I can't explain why, but just the sight of it makes me . . . weak . . . makes me contemplate doing things I wouldn't otherwise."

She gazed up at him, slightly breathless, until she remembered what a consummate actor he was.

"Oh, all right, don't tell me the truth if you don't want to," she groused. "It really doesn't matter. Whatever your reason for rescuing me, I am grateful to you. Now I just want to go home."

He took hold of her arm to prevent her from moving. "You mean run away? You disappoint me, Duchess. I didn't take you for a coward."

"I am not a coward," she said, indignant.

"Glad to hear it. Because a Devereau never runs. It's our family creed. Never retreat. Never surrender."

"I'm also not a Devereau." In response to his quirked brow, she added, "Not technically."

"You most certainly are, technically and every other way, save one, and we can debate that later, in private. You are my wife," he declared in a soft, implacable tone, "and a Devereau, and even if you do not fully understand the significance of that, I assure you that every one of the people staring at us so intently does."

Leah barely had to shift her gaze to see that he was right. They were being stared at. The music continued, but even the couples on the dance floor gazed steadily in the direction of the shadowy alcove where they stood, as if waiting to see what would happen next.

"Now I know I want to leave," she said, spinning on her heel.

He spun her back. "Too bad. I don't."

"What *do* you want to do?" Leah demanded hotly. "Stand here and let them all talk about us for the rest of the evening?"

"They shall talk about us for the rest of the evening—and then some—whether we stand here or not. Hypocrites that they are, they would simply prefer to do it behind our backs, and there is a unique thrill in denying them that opportunity."

"Odd, I don't feel thrilled," she retorted, her earlier gratitude wearing off.

"No?" He unhurriedly tucked a lock of hair behind her ear, managing to turn the small gesture into a lover's caress. The fact that the contact was intended for the benefit of their audience did not stop it from sending a shiver through her. "It must be a cultivated taste," he observed.

"And one I have no desire to acquire."

"You should have thought of that before you decided to remain married to a man like me."

"You promised to be good," she reminded him.

"I *am* being good. This evening's exhibition is all yours, Duchess. I'm simply going to teach you to use it to your advantage."

"And exactly how do I do that?" She was intrigued, but wary.

"Straighten my neckcloth."

"What?" she asked, incredulous.

"Just do it."

Hesitantly, she lifted her hands and adjusted his already impeccably arranged neckcloth.

"Not like that." He bent his head closer to hers with a seductive smile that would lead an observer to conclude he was saying something much more provocative. "Fuss with it and do it slowly. For God's sake, touch me like a wife, not a damn surgeon."

Leah forced herself to take her time smoothing the folds of his white silk neckcloth and tucking it into his waistcoat, letting her fingertips briefly trace the swirling pattern of the brocade.

"Better," he coached. "Confidence, that's the message I want you to convey. Sheer, utter confidence that I am yours and nothing anyone says will change that."

That was all well and good, she thought, but what about what *she* had to say? That might soon bring this whole foolhardy charade crashing down on her.

Giving the cloth a final pat, she looked at him skeptically. "That's it? Appearing confident and fussing with your neckcloth—*that* is your magic formula for undoing any damage done by my aunt's words?"

"Nothing can ever undo that," he returned carelessly.

"But—"

"Least of all, arguing or offering denials. No," he went on, one corner of his mouth curving into a devious smile, "malicious gossip is usually indelible. The only way to retaliate is to drive the scandalmongers mad by showing them that nothing they say or do troubles you in the least."

"As in never retreat."

"Never surrender. Shall we dance?" he invited, offering his arm.

As they passed through the crowd, he nodded at a number of gentlemen, who smiled and nodded in return. Several times he paused to make introductions. Leah was encouraged by everyone's polite, even solicitous response, but she was not fooled. They were bowing to an iron fist in a velvet glove. No doubt they believed, as she did, that Raven would not hesitate to remove the glove if necessary.

Before reaching the dance floor, they encountered Sir Arthur Gidding and his wife, whom she recalled had also been present at her unannounced arrival.

Sir Arthur gently poked his elbow in Raven's ribs and in a manly aside said, "I say, Raven, I'd soon be dismissing my valet if I were you, and letting my bride handle those duties."

Lady Meredith glanced at him sharply, unamused by the reference to Leah's performance a few moments earlier. "Tell me, Duchess, what did you think of this evening's entertainment?"

"I'm afraid we arrived too late to enjoy it," Leah replied.

"Consider yourself blessed." Lowering her voice and rolling her eyes, she added, "Lady Torrington's niece played the flute. Dreadfully. I detest the flute even when the musician is capable. I adore the pianoforte however and cannot wait to hear you play."

"I fear you will have a long wait, Lady Meredith. My musical gifts rival that of a common hedgehog. No, on second thought the hedgehog probably has a better ear."

With a low chuckle, Raven gave her arm an affectionate squeeze. "Don't be so modest, sweetheart."

"Yes, don't be modest," agreed Lady Meredith. "Seriously, when will you play for us?"

It took Leah a moment to reply, distracted as she was by the pressure Raven was exerting on her elbow. "I am serious. I resisted all of my governess's efforts to uncover some musical talent in me, though I was open to other lessons. I can ride, fence and shoot with the best of them. Perhaps you'll permit me to entertain you by shooting a cork from a wine bottle at thirty paces?"

Lady Meredith looked as if Leah had offered her a bite of lemon. "Governess? But Raven said you were taught to play by a master. In Rome."

Leah glanced at him, suddenly understanding the reason for his grip on her elbow. She felt a burst of panic, while his expression remained all innocence.

"Did I say Rome?" he asked. "I meant Scotland, of

course. The Duchess's country estate is so close to the border that if you miss her drive you'll be issued bagpipes and asked to don a kilt."

Sir Arthur laughed heartily. "That's a good one, Raven."

"Yes, most amusing." Lady Meredith's nose wrinkled slightly as her narrowed gaze sliced between Leah and Raven, as if she caught the scent of something rotten, but could not quite tell where it was coming from. "So you were taught to play in Scotland? Not Rome?"

"Did I say play?" Raven asked, shaking his head, his self-effacing smile beguiling in the extreme. "I meant to say ride. The Duchess was taught to ride in Scotland. By a master horseman. Sweetheart, why don't you tell Sir Arthur and Lady Meredith about the time you took first place for jumping at the Baumborough Fair . . . in a storm, no less?"

Leah turned her head slowly. First place? In a storm? He was mad to put her on the spot this way.

"Oh, please darling," she said, her smile privately wicked, "you know how I detest talking about myself. Besides, you tell it much better than I do."

His gaze locked with hers, his eyes bright. "I wouldn't dream of stealing your thunder, and you know that no one can surpass you when it comes to imitating the lead judge's lisp. I insist you do that part for us."

"Me? You are without question the master of the lisp. Don't tell me you haven't demonstrated it for your friends before this?"

She shifted her gaze to the other couple, but before she could say anything more, Raven's arm came around her in a spontaneous hug.

"Isn't she adorable when she's shy?" he asked the

others. "Gidding, help me convince the Duchess to share her story with you."

Naturally Sir Gidding picked up his cue and Leah was left no gracious alternative but to extricate Raven from the hole he'd dug himself. She hurriedly made up some nonsense about jumping hedges with thunder rumbling in the distance, which seemed to suffice.

"Thank you," he murmured when they finally escaped to the dance floor.

"One good rescue deserves another, I always say." She shot him a beseeching look. "But really . . . taught by a master? In Rome? Wasn't that going a bit overboard?"

"Not at all." He took her left hand in his as they circled each other. "Though I was concerned that I may have strained credibility a bit with my praise for your singing."

"You told people I could sing?" she asked, aghast.

"Like a nightingale, to be precise. Can you?" he asked nonchalantly.

"I can't carry a tune to save myself. For pity's sake, Raven, why couldn't you have boasted about some talent I actually possess?"

"Because," he reminded her in a dry tone, "I didn't know of any. You appeared so frail, so . . . delicate, how was I to guess you drive as hard a bargain as any Cheapside merchant and can shoot the cork from a bottle at twenty paces."

"Thirty."

"Thirty paces."

"Do you think Sir Arthur and his wife will mention our little . . . discrepancies?

"Without question. So it would appear we have to decide on future strategy. Do we continue to make this up as we go along, or devote some time to getting better acquainted?"

"We get better acquainted," she replied without hesitation.

Raven smiled *that* smile, that one that turned her spine to jelly. "I was hoping you'd say that."

"In the most cerebral sense of the word," she pointed out, trying to ignore the melting sensation inside. "In the meantime, we avoid any prolonged conversations with others."

"Impossible," he declared. "Remember the Devereau creed: Never retreat, never surrender."

"Never listen to reason is more like it. I find it curious that you diligently adhere to your ancestors' words, yet you're willing to let the family home go to ruin around you."

"I never said they were my ancestors' words," he said with that maddening casual air of his.

"Then whose—"

"Mine. Quite apropos, don't you think?"

"Eerily so." She regarded him with increasing suspicion. "And exactly when did you . . ."

"Tonight."

Leah sighed. "I should have known."

They danced and then there were more introductions, though they were careful not to be drawn into conversation. Will eventually appeared with a cup of warm punch and profuse apologies for taking so long, first to find the refreshments and then to find her.

At her hostess's invitation, Leah viewed the Torringtons' impressive collection of antiquities and then found herself in demand as a dance partner by a variety of gentlemen, from the young son of a viscount who clasped her with sweaty palms and gazed worshipfully at her the entire time, to an ancient Irish earl who seemed to know everything about everyone in the room and had her laughing out loud as they danced.

The evening was a success, in spite of its inauspicious beginnings. She had stepped into the lion's den, braved its bared teeth and snapping jaws, and survived. And through it all, Raven was by her side, or hovering close by, just the sight of him a surprising source of comfort and reassurance.

Of course, she knew full well that her success was entirely *because* of Raven, a man too rich, too powerful, too ruthless, to be trifled with. In a perfect world, she would have preferred to triumph on her own, but she'd learned a long time ago that this was far from a perfect world. For Chrissie's sake, she was willing to take social acceptance and respectability on any terms.

Then too, there was a degree of smug satisfaction in joining forces, however briefly, with a man who not only disdained the hypocrisy that had destroyed her mother and changed her own life forever, but toyed with it for his own amusement.

They returned alone to their carriage, Colin and Will having made other arrangements. Leah was exhausted, but content with her progress that evening, and so relaxed that she was caught completely off guard when Raven settled himself in the seat opposite her and leaned forward, no hint of either comfort or reassurance in his manner now.

"All right, Duchess," he growled, "time to get better acquainted. You can start by telling me exactly what the hell is going on."

"I'm not quite sure I understand what you mean."

"I'm quite sure you do."

Adrian watched as her back stiffened and her expression became shuttered. He'd approached this as he would any battle, on his own terms, hoping for a rout, but prepared for a siege. He settled against the velvet cushions and hitched one booted foot on the bench opposite, the bench where his full-of-surprises wife perched nervously.

Wounded innocent or skilled opportunist? Which was she? He was curious to find out.

She squirmed a bit as he continued to stare. "Very well," she said finally. "Since it appears you overheard more of what my aunt had to say than you led me to believe—"

"Please. I would hardly give credence to anything that spilled from that woman's mouth. No, my interest was aroused more by the intense scrutiny and whispers which followed wherever we went this evening."

"Come now, you had to expect that your marriage, especially one so sudden and unorthodox, would create a stir."

"A stir? Yes. An avalanche of innuendos from friends and foes alike is something entirely different."

"What did your friends tell you about me?"

"Nothing. Mostly because I refused to listen. I would prefer to hear the truth from you, *Duchess.*"

"Why?"

"To find out if I married a liar."

"God." She looked away for a second, as if his steady gaze was a sun too hot to stare at for long. "Are you always so direct?"

"Yes."

A small, rueful smile lifted one corner of her mouth. "Yes, you would be, wouldn't you? It is easy to be direct and forthright when you don't have to be afraid of the consequences."

"Are you afraid, Leah?"

Her small nod had a peculiar effect on him. He crossed his arms, resisting a bizarre urge to rescue her a second time. The first could be excused. He would no more allow someone to harass his wife than he would permit them to kick his dogs. It was a simple matter of possession. This was something different. The fact that he had no idea from whom or what he wanted to save her, did not quell his desire to gather her close and tell her she never had to be afraid again.

"What are you afraid of, Duchess?" When she slanted him a sideways look, his brows shot up. "Me?"

"I'm afraid of what you might do when you hear what I have to say. Oh, bother, why didn't I just come out with it at the start, before we struck our bargain?" She sighed heavily and lifted her chin to meet his gaze. "I will not blame you if you choose to end it here and now."

"Let's wait until I hear whatever it is before we go planning an immediate divorce, shall we?"

"Annulment," she corrected.

The very word was like a red flag waved at his pride. Instantly a wave of steely resistance rose up in him. Thinking *over my dead body,* he said, "Whatever. Come on, out with it."

She moistened her lips with a slow, utterly distracting movement of her tongue, then opened her mouth to speak and stopped.

"For God's sake, Leah, whatever you did cannot be that bad."

"Me? This is not about me. It concerns my family, my mother to be specific and her . . . disgrace. There. There's no other word for it."

"Disgraced in Baumborough. How very droll." He could not suppress a smug smile. "What happened, Leah? Did she invite the rector for tea and—"

She interrupted fiercely. "I didn't always live in Baumborough. I—we, my parents and sister and I lived here, in London, in the most handsome house in the city, with a huge, curving staircase and beds with lace canopies and closets as big as rooms to hold all my mother's beautiful gowns." She rested her head against the seat and gazed past him, seeming to lose her anger as swiftly as it had come.

"I remember hiding beneath her furs in the closet and listening to her laugh as she pretended she couldn't find me, her laughter coming closer and closer, and my heart pounding with anticipation, faster and faster, until she pounced and—" She caught herself and broke off with a self-conscious shrug.

"She used to laugh all the time in that house, and she read us stories and had tea with us whenever she was home and brought us back surprises from her little trips." She caught her bottom lip with her teeth. "Back then, I wanted to grow up to be exactly like her. Now all I do is worry that I have."

She glanced up at him apologetically. "I'm rambling on and you still don't know any more than you did a moment ago, do you?"

"Just tell me, Duchess," he urged in a soft voice. "Tell me what it is you're so afraid to say."

"My mother had lovers. A series of them, I suspect. That is why she spent so many afternoons and weekends away from home. She spent them with a lover."

"That's hardly a novel offense. More ladies of the *ton* than not take lovers, Leah."

"Do more than not have husbands who walk in and find them in bed with a lover? How many of their husbands get even by banishing them to the most far-off corner of the country possible? Their children with them? And never, ever allow them to come home?"

Adrian was suddenly without words to respond . . . and for the wrong reason. Leah's pain was visible, right there before him in her pale, trembling lips and the defensive, yet unmistakably defiant, set of her shoulders. It was a different pain, however, one buried in his own past, that had whipped him to silence. He'd spent years perfecting the art of holding at bay this particular pain and the bitter memories surrounding it. That talent failed him now. He could only imagine what it felt like to be a child sent away from the only home you knew. But he *knew*, with bone-chilling precision, he *knew* what it felt like to walk in and find the woman you love in bed with another man.

Quickly, desperately, he blanked the rest of the memory and forced his attention back to Leah.

"Sweet Jesus," he muttered, running his hand through his hair, feeling the dampness beaded on his brow, "I don't know what to say."

"There's nothing you can say," she replied in an even tone. One look at her told him what that composure was costing her.

"It is late." He leaned forward and reached for the hands clenched in her lap. "Perhaps it would be best to put this off until another—"

She pulled away from him. "No. I want you to hear everything. All of it. I want you to know who you've gotten yourself involved with. The daughter of a whore, in my aunt's words."

His anger was swift and instinctive. "I did not hear her say that. Had I—"

She silenced him with an impatient wave.

"Very well." He leaned back and folded his arms. "Let's hear the rest."

"After my father sent us away, my mother waited for him—her latest lover—to come for her. We all waited, my mother and Chrissie and me. Each morning we rose and got dressed up in our very best frocks, as if we were going to a fancy party, and we walked to the end of the drive, and waited. Most days we waited for hours, until Chrissie became impossibly bored or it started raining too hard to stay outdoors or my mother collapsed in one of her weeping fits.

"He never came, of course," she continued, sparing him having to ask. "Though right to the very end she insisted he would. Our Knight in Shining Armor, she called him, the man who was going to save us from my father's wrath and bring us back to London to live with him forever."

With one fingertip, she absently traced the closure at the neck of her velvet wrap. "We had been there almost a year when my mother drowned in the small pond on the property. There was never any proof that it was intentional, but it happened on her birthday, and I knew even back then that she had simply given up, believing that if he would not come on her birthday, he would never come for her."

Adrian hunched forward, drawn to her, and gave her leg a clumsy, ineffectual pat. Lord, he was useless at this. He knew a dozen ways to make a woman scream with pleasure and not a single one to comfort her.

"Hell, Leah, you were how old when all this happened? Fourteen? Hell. Surely your father must have—"

"Been delighted by her death, I imagine," she broke in, a new, harsh edge to her voice. "I cannot say with any certainty for I never saw the man again."

"You can't be serious? He couldn't just abandon you there? His own children?"

"His own *daughters*, you mean. He could and did. He remarried within a month, no doubt hoping to sire the son he longed for. He failed." In her tight smile Adrian at last saw a hint of the bitterness she had every right to feel. Betrayal at the hands of your father was another thing he understood all too well.

"Though now that I think of it," she continued, "perhaps a brother, even a half brother, might have proven a better ally than my uncle, who inherited instead."

"You have an ally now, one more powerful than your uncle, or your witch of an aunt, or anyone else who might seek to make you suffer for something you had no part in."

"Guilt by association is one of the *ton*'s most time-honored rules, is it not?"

"Rules are made to be broken."

"By you perhaps, but surely you can understand now why I am so intent on avoiding any impropriety that might reflect badly on my sister and destroy whatever chance she has for happiness."

"Nothing will. I promise you." He moved to the seat beside her and took her hand in his, firmly enough that she could not pull away again. "Trust me on this, Leah, as closet skeletons go, yours are not that appalling. Did you honestly think this was enough to cause me to go back on my word to you?"

"No," she replied. "I already know you well enough to realize that the threat of gossip would do more to provoke than deter you. I was more concerned that you would be angry that I didn't tell you right away, that I misled you."

"Why did you?"

She appeared sheepish. "I told myself I wasn't taking unfair advantage of you any more than you had me, but I think that, deep down, I wanted to tip the scales in my favor. I was desperate to have you go along with my plan. Then when I collided with that man on Bond Street and he called me Dava, I knew that if he could so easily mistake me for my mother, others would as well and —"

Adrian frowned. "What did you say?"

"I said the man who bumped into me earlier mistook me for my mother. All my life I've been told I favor her, but evidently the resemblance is even stronger than—"

"No." He shook his head impatiently, an icy premonition lodged square in his chest. "What did you say that man called you?"

"Dava. That was my mother's name."

"Sweet Jesus," he whispered. "The Incredible Dava."

She nodded ruefully. "You knew my mother?"

"We never met, but I certainly knew *of* her."

Her jaw tightened. "I've been told she was notorious back then."

"Perhaps. That's not what I meant. I knew of your mother because my father was her lover."

9

Leah looked stunned. She shook her head. "No, that's not possible. The man she planned to run away with was named Sheffield."

"I'm quite certain my father was not planning to run off with her," Raven said, his tone cynical. "He didn't have the guts. But I know for a fact they were involved with each other, and at length."

At the time he had been too involved in his own affairs to pay much attention to gossip. For him, the Incredible Dava had existed only as a taunt to throw in his father's face, a play for leverage.

"Good heavens." She shook her head, grappling with the revelation. "Well, there's enough irony in that to fill an ocean."

"Several," he concurred dryly.

He studied her, trying to ascertain whether her surprise was completely genuine. It was. If Leah was harboring a motive other than her idiotic, typically female obsession with seeing her sister wed, it did not have anything to do with the connection between his father and her mother. He found himself curiously relieved by that fact.

"Silly me," she said with a weary laugh. "I thought the reason Aunt Millicent looked so utterly stunned to meet you was simply because I had not only managed to wed, but had done so well for myself."

"You think she knew of the connection between your mother and my father?"

"I'm sure of it. Aunt Millicent was my mother's trusted confidante," she explained in a biting tone. "She was also the one who provided my father with information about her liaisons."

The carriage slowed as it approached Raven House. They rode in silence, both struggling to come to terms with this new complication.

"Hell," he muttered finally. "Bloody hell."

"I could not agree more."

"No wonder we caused such a damn furor. In terms of shock value, our union could not be more perfect if I'd orchestrated it myself."

"You did," she reminded him with a quelling look. "And I imagine there are any number of people who suspect that you did."

"And the rest all suspect you."

The suggestion seemed to startle her. "It will not be easy to convince them that at least one of us is not attempting to either exact revenge or relive the past."

"Why bother?" he retorted. "Remember what I said about denials being futile?"

She thought it over. "Why indeed? After all, what matters most for Chrissie's sake is that we are respectably married."

"And we surely are that," he murmured.

"For the time being."

"Of course, for the time being," he agreed. The driver opened the carriage door and she stepped over him with a rustle of silk and a scent of roses, leaving him wanting, and feeling a great deal more depressingly respectable than he did bloody married.

Leah leaned back and closed her eyes. It had been an exhausting evening and she was grateful for the comfortable overstuffed chair and the warm fire. Under Bridget's capable supervision, her chamber had been transformed. The furniture had been polished until it gleamed and the bedding aired; gone was the clutter and any trace of mustiness.

The result was a spacious haven, with more charm than she'd believed possible on first sight. The pale roses of the black Persian rug were echoed in the soft peach tones of the walls and satin bed coverings, making the entire room glow prettily in the candlelight.

At the moment, what she was most grateful for, however, was the bucket of warm water Bridget had fetched for her to soak her tired, aching feet. They were not accustomed to attending balls that went on into the wee hours of the morning. She sighed and wiggled her toes in the cooling water.

She heard the door open and close.

"Bridget? I'm glad you're back," she said without opening her eyes. "Will you please see if there is any hot water left in the kettle? My feet still feel as if they've been trampled by a herd of elephants."

She heard the scrape of metal and then felt the glorious swirl of heat around her feet and ankles as water was slowly added to the bucket.

"Ahh, thank you," she murmured, sighing with pleasure. "That feels heavenly."

"Any time, Duchess," said a voice that was deep and male and definitely not Bridget's.

She opened her eyes.

Raven stood before her, swinging the empty kettle from one finger and smiling insolently as his gaze roamed over her, from her unbound hair and the robe she had tossed on over her white nightgown and neglected to fasten, to her submerged feet.

Lord, how humiliating, was all she could think.

"You do have a knack for turning up when I least expect you," she grumbled.

"I don't recall any complaints when I miraculously appeared to rescue you from your aunt's clutches."

"Perhaps because I was dressed at the time."

"I like you better this way." His voice was pitched caressingly low, and his blue eyes gleamed wickedly.

Refusing to blush, she pulled the hem of her nightgown down to cover her legs, managing in her haste to thrust most of it into the bucket. The sopping fabric molded transparently to her shins and ankles.

"Don't bother," advised her husband. Ridding himself of the kettle, he dragged a chair closer, giving every indication he meant to linger. "I've already seen it all."

"By *it all,* I assume you mean you've seen my feet?" She did her best to sound unruffled, in spite of the excruciating awareness that she was in utter disarray while he—curse his black heart—was as impeccably attired as when they arrived at the ball.

"Feet *and* ankles. Let's not forget those enticing, shapely ankles. I know I shan't."

"How fascinating," she drawled.

"Your ankles? I'm not sure I would go as far as to call them fascinating at this point. Perhaps if I took a closer look . . ."

She rolled her eyes. "I was referring to the fact that you find the mere sight of my bare feet and ankles so enticing. It's hardly the sort of reaction I would expect of a man with your reputation."

"My reputation for what?"

"Why, as a connoisseur of femininity, of course. While I was freshening up in Lady Torrington's powder room, I chanced to overhear one *lady* holding forth to another that you are generally acknowledged to be the most skillful and adventurous lover in all of London, perhaps all of England, or even the entire world."

He gave a negligent shrug as he straddled the chair in the fashion he seemed to prefer. "I don't know about the entire world."

"Don't be so modest."

"Don't you believe everything you overhear in powder rooms."

She smiled sweetly. "I didn't."

He laughed. "Very shrewd of you. Far wiser to settle such matters for yourself . . . and we both know how very fond you are of settling matters for yourself." He bowed his head with exaggerated grace. "I am at your service, Duchess. When would you like to get started?"

"Never." She wished she sounded more certain, and that her heart would stop doing that funny little skip whenever he let his gaze dip below her shoulders.

"Is that enticing pout intended to discourage me?"

"Yes." Just the same, she took the precaution of pressing her lips tightly together.

He shook his head and sighed deeply. "You have a great deal to learn about men, I'm afraid."

He was afraid? She was the one who felt as if she were picking her way along the edge of a very steep cliff. Blindfolded. She hardly needed to be reminded of all that she did not know about men.

"Is that so?" she challenged, hoping the quick arching of her brows gave the impression that she was terribly amused by him, and not that she had a nervous tic.

"Yes." Leaning forward, he rested his chin atop his folded arms. "Take old Prince Nevar, for example."

"What?" She glanced at the writing desk in the corner and her eyes narrowed accusingly. "You read my manuscript?"

"I couldn't resist," he confessed, looking not especially contrite.

"When? When could you possibly have read it?"

"The first time?"

"How many times . . ." She stopped and lowered her voice. "Yes, the first time."

"The night you were ill. I couldn't sleep. Your bag was right there in plain view." He flashed a lopsided grin that Leah would wager had gotten him out of any number of tight spots with women.

"I cannot believe you went rummaging through the personal belongings of a complete stranger."

"You weren't a stranger," he reminded her. "You were my wife."

"Oh, please."

"You're right," he conceded, still smiling. "It was a scurrilous thing to do and I beg your forgiveness. But surely you can understand how once I started reading Olivia and Nevar's story, I was captivated and had to see how it would turn out."

"Not even I know that yet," she snapped, refusing to let him see that she was in any way flattered by his interest.

"When will you know?"

"Not until I finish writing it, which may not be for months since it's not due at my publishers until the end of the year."

"Publisher?" He regarded her with astonishment, and new interest. "Do you mean to say you've sold your story? Before you've even finished writing it?"

"That's right, and six others before it, all written under the pen name Lee Alexander. I don't expect you to recognize the name," she added. "They're children's books."

"I shouldn't be surprised that you are published. You're a very talented writer, Leah."

"Thank you," she said, her feelings of irritation doing battle with the sheer pleasure of his compliment.

"But you made a serious wrong turn in that last bit you wrote."

Irritation won.

"You don't say?" she drawled. "And you base this on how many years of literary critical analysis?"

"I base it on a lifetime of being a man. There is no way on earth Nevar would let Leah—or any other woman—see him without his mask."

He was referring to the scene she'd written only that morning, which meant he must have invaded her chamber before he'd come looking for her.

"He didn't *let* her see him," she informed him. "Olivia stole into his room, in much the same sneaky way you stole into my chamber, I imagine, and hid, with the express purpose of seeing something which was none of her business."

He ignored the thinly veiled jabs. "I understand. But don't you see that could never happen, because Nevar is nowhere near as naive as you are? He would make damn sure he was alone before he took off his mask. I know that for a fact."

"Can't you see that it's *because* he has come to trust Olivia not to violate his privacy, that on some level he's not even aware of, he feels confident taking it off?"

"No man who's reached the age of reason ever trusts any woman that much."

"That's the point. He's sick of the life he is living. He *wants* to trust her. Desperately."

"What he wants—desperately—is to bed her."

"That's ridiculous. This is a fairy tale, written for children."

"Nevar is not a child, and if ever he did find himself alone in his chamber with the woman he desires more than his next breath, whose very scent haunts him night and day, he would not turn away from her for any reason."

"I never wrote anything about her scent."

He shrugged. "I'm reading between the lines."

"My point exactly. This is *your* interpretation of his motives, but you've neglected one critical fact—Nevar is noble."

"Nevar is randy."

The conversation was absurd, not to mention totally inappropriate. It was also the first time Leah had ever discussed her work so intensely with anyone. Chrissie always expressed interest in how a book was coming along and her young readers wrote her letters telling her how much they enjoyed a particular story and her publisher provided editorial input. But this was the first time anyone had ever displayed such interest in the actual work itself, as if what she did was important enough to argue about. Leah found it exhilarating.

"And another thing," he was saying, "no man ever lets a woman know where he's most vulnerable. Sweet Jesus, that's tantamount to handing her a weapon to use against him."

"All right then," she asked impulsively, "what do *you* think Nevar would have done?"

The query seemed to take him as much by surprise

as it did Leah. After a few seconds of silence, he shrugged and stretched. "I'll have to give it more thought, and my brain is not at its best at this hour."

"Mine either," she said, feeling both relieved and disappointed by the signs that he was preparing to leave. "And my water has grown cold. Would you mind ringing for Bridget on your way out?"

"I sent Bridget to bed." He stood and casually reached for the towel warming by the fire. Crouching before her, he held it spread open and regarded her expectantly. "Come on," he urged when she sat there as if made of stone. "Let's have them."

"No, really, there's no need—"

"There is every need. I cannot permit my duchess to dry her own feet."

He moved the towel closer.

Leah instinctively reached to pull together the front of her robe.

"Leave it." It wasn't a request, but an order. If she had stopped to think, she would have cinched the robe on principle alone, but she didn't think. She simply dropped her hands to her lap. "There's no need to get your robe wet as well," he said.

"Of course not," she murmured.

Of course not. He was only being helpful. She was simply being sensible. There was no need to get her robe wet, just as there was no need for her palms to be damp and her stomach to be taking flight and for shivers to be racing up and down her spine, but that's precisely what was happening.

She lifted one foot from the water and placed it on the towel in his hands. Raven wrapped the thick cloth around it gently, and as efficiently as if drying a lady's feet were a commonplace occurrence in his life. Given his infamy, perhaps it was.

"Lift your night dress," he directed.

She stiffened. "Really . . ."

"Yes. Really. I won't have you dripping all over what I've just dried."

That made sense too. Everything he said made such perfect sense. So why did she feel as if the world was suddenly spinning one way and she another?

"That's better," he said when she had reluctantly inched the wet nightdress midway to her knees. "I'll have the other foot now."

As she lifted it from the water, he slid the bucket aside and moved closer, enfolding both her feet in the towel and patting and rubbing them. She'd had no idea her toes were so sensitive or that the soles of her feet could tingle.

Raven did not hurry, and with each lingering stroke, Leah felt her immunity to him dissolving and drifting away, replaced by a combination of dreamy somnolence and raw excitement.

So much for keeping him at a safe distance.

At last he tossed aside the towel, stood, and without warning, lifted her in his arms.

"What are you doing?" she demanded in a husky, stranger's voice.

"Carrying you to bed."

"You could have simply fetched my slippers."

"I could have." He smiled down at her, a roguish smile that reminded Leah of his nickname and how he had earned it.

Another heartbeat and she was on the bed, flat on her back, her and Raven's arms and legs such a tangle she didn't know where to begin sorting out.

"First I discover I am wed to the daughter of an infamous beauty, then that she is also a successful authoress." His voice alone, deep and rough, spun a mood of sensual awareness that held her motionless.

"What other surprises do you have in store for me, Duchess?"

"None," she replied, her breathing shaky. "I am really quite ordinary. Tiresome, even. Really, I've heard it said many times."

He laughed softly and ran his lips across her throat, a meandering drizzle of a caress. "As a connoisseur of femininity, I must disagree. Strenuously." He touched the tip of his tongue to the hollow above her collarbone and Leah trembled inside. "I think you harbor all sorts of secret delights, Leah, love. Secrets even you have yet to discover. I think that beneath the protests and the denials, you are a gloriously passionate woman. I want that passion, Leah, all of it. I want to be your lover."

Nothing he said could have frightened her more.

His fingers were threaded in her hair, holding her head still as his mouth claimed hers in a kiss that was slow and deep. If she'd had any lingering uncertainty as to his intent, it ended there.

"Raven," she said as soon as she could draw breath to speak. She meant to sound firm and was startled by the small sound that emerged from her throat. She tried again. "Raven."

Without lifting his head, he nibbled at the corners of her lips, then trailed his hot, damp mouth down the side of her neck. She felt the edge of his teeth on her skin, the sensation sharp and thrilling. Then the pressure turned softer and more diffuse, as if he were . . . Oh my God, he was. He was definitely licking her, her neck and her nightdress and through it, her breast. A torrent of unknown pleasure gushed inside her.

Leah gasped and tried to hold herself absolutely still, but that only served to heighten the effect of his caresses. "Raven."

"Adrian." He lifted his head just enough to speak, just enough for her to see his tongue drag lazily across the turgid peak of one breast, intensifying her pleasure, and her panic.

"Raven . . ."

"Adrian," he murmured again. "My name is Adrian and I would prefer you use it when I am making love to you."

His words, dripping with self-assurance, were her lifeline and she grabbed it.

Placing her hands against the solid wall of his shoulders, she pushed hard. "You are *not* making love to me."

He lifted his head and smiled at her. "If you say so, Duchess."

"Yes, I do say so." Leah was incensed now and not feeling in the least lethargic. "And you, curse your scoundrel's soul, are going to listen."

She felt his chuckle as much as heard it, a rough vibration against her breast. He was *laughing* at her, dismissing her wishes as if they meant nothing, as if she were a powerless child all over again.

A frantic glance around turned up a crystal vase on the bedside table. She seized it and brought it down hard, aiming for his back. Unfortunately he reared back and she connected with his head instead. The vase was too heavy to shatter, but it made contact with a solid thud and he went limp.

He lay on top of her, silent and motionless.

"Oh, my God," Leah whispered, struggling to free herself and going up on her knees beside him. "Oh my God, oh my God, oh my God. Raven . . . please . . ." She tried without success to turn him over. "Raven, please, don't be dead," she pleaded, shaking him. "Are you dead?"

She yelped and pulled away as he suddenly rolled

to his back, rubbed the back of his head and glared at her. "No, I am not dead. Though it would serve you bloody right if I were." He muttered something that sounded like *cursed hellcat* as he gingerly felt the back of his head. "What the blazes did you hit me with, anyway?"

"A vase." She gave him an awkward, apologetic smile. "A very small vase."

"It didn't feel small. If you were not interested in my attentions, why didn't you simply ask me to stop?"

"I did."

"I never once heard you utter the word stop. That would have done it, I assure you. I am not in the habit of forcing women."

"Of course not." Her conciliatory mood faded quickly now that she was certain he was all right. "Your style is to trick them."

His expression grew fierce. "Are you suggesting that I need to trick a woman to get her into my bed?"

She shrugged. "I have only my own experience to guide me."

He was off the bed as if she had set fire to it. He stalked across the room. Leah braced herself, wary, but not so wary she failed to notice—with some glee—that he now appeared nearly as rumpled as she was. And every bit as physically aroused, though he could not hide it nearly as well, she observed, noting the thickness at the front of his snug breeches, a sight so novel and intriguing that she had difficulty looking away.

He took note of her attention and one corner of his mouth lifted suggestively as he pointed a finger at her. "I did not trick you this evening. I told you at the ball of my intent to bed you."

"You were teasing."

"Was I?" He smiled and managed to look even

more menacing. "Let me assure you, madam, I am not teasing now."

"But you are attempting to turn an innocent situation to your lecherous advantage."

He made an impatient gesture. "That's a different proposition entirely."

"And you definitely tricked me into marrying you."

"That was an aberration, a drunken aberration, for which I am paying dearly."

She gave a noncommittal shrug.

"It's true, blast you. I have no more need to trick women than I have to force them."

"Then just how did you acquire your randy reputation?"

"I seduce them . . . as I will seduce you." He arched one dark brow. "What? You don't believe I can?"

"I am far from an authority on the subject, though I associate seduction with tender glances and poetic compliments and gallantry. But if you insist you have a gift in that area, I suppose I will have to accept your word on it."

"I never said I had a *gift* for it," he corrected. "The word gift implies a natural talent. On the contrary, this is an acquired skill. I long ago reduced a love affair to its four basic stages and mastered each one."

"My, that is romantic," Leah purred, fluttering her lashes.

"You might not think so now, but you will. And soon. We have already passed stage one, *Selection*, and are ready to move on to stage two. *Seduction*."

She feigned a yawn. "Fine. Be certain to wake me when we get there."

"Perhaps you won't want to wake when we get there," he said softly, walking slowly toward her. "Perhaps you'll enjoy being charmed into doing everything—and anything—I desire for you to do. You may find you like relinquishing control to me, becoming a slave to my passion . . . and your own. There is a definite allure to losing yourself in a world of sensual lassitude, a world without rules or limits or consequences."

He stopped directly in front of her, his still roused body only inches away from where she knelt at the edge of the mattress. The dark heat of his gaze made it hard for her to concentrate on resisting the pull of his deep voice.

"There is no such world," she told him, hoping to sound as if she knew what she was talking about.

He laughed softly. "Oh, but there is. And I intend to show it to you, my beauty. From the start, I have desired you. But tonight, dear lady, you have managed to transform yourself into a challenge of the first order." He lifted her chin a fraction. "And I make it a point never to resist a challenge."

"I won't cooperate," she insisted.

"You don't have to." He tilted his head to the side and brought his lips close to hers, so close Leah was certain the finest parchment would not have fit between them. She waited for him to touch her, to try to kiss her the way he had kissed her before, so that she could demonstrate exactly how uncooperative she intended to be.

But he did not kiss her. His mouth never actually touched her at any time as it slowly, slowly passed over her mouth and cheeks and the ultra sensitive skin beneath her uplifted chin. Mysteriously, the act of not touching her was more disturbing to her senses than kissing her would have been. His hot breath penetrated her nightgown and she felt her breasts tighten in response.

"In fact," he said, his gravelly whisper a different

sort of caress, "I would prefer you not cooperate. That will add to my excitement, and to my pleasure when we finally move on to stage three." He tucked her hair behind her ear and leaned close to whisper. "Complete . . . and total . . . *surrender.*"

Surrender. With the word still swirling inside her head, he straightened abruptly and smiled at her. "Sweet dreams, Duchess."

Surrender? He was fooling himself. She would never surrender. Ever. Even if she wanted to, which she did not, she had Chrissie's future to consider. The promise of a speedy annulment was the only thing she had to offer Raven to keep him in line. Without it, she would be completely at his mercy.

Pulling off the wet nightdress, she hurled it at the closed connecting door before donning a dry one.

The blackguard. Surely he could see that annulment was the best solution—the *only* solution—for them both. He'd made it clear he did not desire her to be a wife to him any more than she desired to be one. Of course, he would not be the first person who ever put lust ahead of common sense. There was also his propensity to act on impulse and damn the consequences to consider.

Not that she feared he would break their agreement by forcing her to mate with him. That was definitely not his style. Already she understood Raven well enough to know that this game was not about staking his claim, but about surrender. Hers.

Selection. Seduction. Surrender.

What nonsense.

Just the same, she wished it had occurred to her to ask what the fourth stage might be.

Adrian grimaced as he passed his reflection. He was a mess. His clothes were damp and rumpled, his hair in disarray, and there was a lump the size of a turkey egg at the back of his head.

And the woman responsible had been in his life for only two days. What would he look like after two weeks? Two months?

Whatever the cost, there was no turning back now. Even if he had not boasted to his friends, even if her damn annulment did not threaten his very ability to hold his head up in public, even if he did not want her more than he could recall wanting any woman in years. Tonight she had thrown down the gauntlet, he'd picked it up and that, by God, was that.

Any concern he might have had that he was taking undue advantage by sabotaging their agreement was gone. Leah had no trouble making her position known. His throbbing skull was proof of that. And she'd been forewarned. What could be more fair than that? He'd told her outright of his intent. As she had told him outright of hers.

He planned to bed her and she intended to fight him every step of the way.

Crossing the room, he yanked the cord to summon Thorne. The servant appeared, still tying his robe.

"Yes, Y'Grace?" He didn't bother to conceal the yawn that distorted his grizzled features.

"Thorne, I want you to wake me for breakfast tomorrow."

"Yes, Y'Grace. At the usual hour?"

Adrian's jaw clenched in exasperation. "Is three in the afternoon the time you would normally wake someone for breakfast?"

Thorne hesitated, eyeing his master as if this might well be a trick question.

"Well, is it?" demanded Adrian.

"Not normally, I wouldn't say."

"Nor would I." Adrian waited impatiently. "Well?"

"Well what?"

"Well, what time do normal people rise for breakfast?"

"I believe it varies, Y'Grace. The Duchess, she requested her breakfast at nine, if that helps."

"Nine?" Adrian looked at his watch and grimaced. "All right, dammit, wake me for nine. And do not, under any circumstances, allow me to go back to sleep."

Nine o'clock in the bloody morning, Adrian fumed as he waved off Thorne's offer to fetch his valet and instead stripped off his clothes and boots himself. He couldn't remember the last time he had been awake at that hour. It couldn't be healthy to be walking about in all that damp morning air. It certainly was not fashionable. How was a man expected to function with so few hours sleep, much less attempt to seduce his own wife?

He fell on the bed and punched his pillow.

But seduce her he would. It was only a question of how soon. He had yet to meet a woman he could not have if he desired her badly enough.

Except for Charlotte nagged a small voice inside, which he quickly silenced. Charlotte had not been just any woman, and he had been young and inexperienced. He had learned much since then.

He rubbed the spot on his head that still hurt. Of course, his usual approach was obviously going to require some fine-tuning where Leah was concerned. He would have to take things slowly and lower her defenses one small surrender at a time. If she wanted poetry and tender glances, by God, she would have them.

Nine o'clock. That left him only six hours to sleep *and* come up with some suitably revolting poetic tidbits with which to sweeten her morning tea. God help him.

He grinned suddenly, struck by the irony of plotting a seduction while lying, of all places, in the legendary Raven wedding bed. His father must be rolling in his grave, he thought with satisfaction. After all, tradition had it that this bed was reserved for the *duty* of love, for fulfilling obligations and siring heirs. For Raven men, pleasure resided in other places, and in other beds.

Until now.

10

Three consecutive mornings, Adrian dragged himself out of bed to breakfast with his wife, only to find that she had already gone off to do whatever it was she spent her days doing. He had every right to ask what that was, of course, but he refused. Instead, each morning he rose a half hour earlier, and so, apparently, did she.

She was avoiding him. He was convinced of it. Staying away all day and only returning home in time to dress for another evening out and about. Not surprisingly, his new bride was quite in demand by society. The curiosity factor at work, he thought cynically. And, thanks to his advice, she was rapidly mastering the art of turning all that attention, favorable and otherwise, to her advantage.

She seemed resolved not to decline a single invitation. And so their evenings were a whirl of theater and opera appearances, bracketed by tedious dinner parties before and pointless gatherings after. All in the distasteful interest of greasing her sister's slide into matrimony. There was nothing forcing him to accompany her, but how the blazes was he to seduce a woman he never set eyes on?

Besides, to add to his confusion, he found himself actually enjoying time spent with a woman *outside* of bed.

So while her mission, lining up prospective prey, appeared to be progressing nicely, his own had yet to make it out of the starting gate. The fact that she so obviously did not trust herself alone with him should have fortified him. Instead, Adrian felt as if Leah treated him like an afterthought, a damn prop, about as indispensable as one of the beaded reticules that completed each of her outfits.

Like a husband.

But no more, he thought fiercely, as he made his way downstairs at the ungodly hour of eight in the morning. He was tired, frustrated and blurry-eyed, but he was determined that she was not going to escape today. Somehow, some way, he was going to get her attention.

At the foot of the stairs, in the exact spot where his morning paper ought to be, was a pot of daffodils. One more seemingly inconsequential inroad on his household and his life. Adrian scowled, then grinned suddenly, and plucked the tallest of the bright yellow blooms.

It was too soon for daffodils, of course, but these bulbs, he'd been told, had been sheltered and coddled and forced into early bloom in a sunny patch out by the stables. His initial response had been to snort and wonder aloud if his groomsman's preoccupation with daffodils explained why the stables were such a disaster.

Now he gazed at the blooms in a new, self-serving light. What, he asked himself as he impulsively clamped the stem between his front teeth, could be more insipidly romantic than greeting his lady love with a fresh flower?

He was so busy congratulating himself on his creativity that he paid no heed to the sounds emanating from the dining room until he had already crossed the threshold. Then it was too late. He stopped in his tracks, trapped, the daffodil dangling idiotically between his teeth for the benefit of his wife and his two closest friends.

Will and Colin recovered quickly and let loose with loud gusts of laughter. Leah simply gazed at him from the far end of the table, her eyes bright with a blend of sympathy and amusement. Not at all the response he had been hoping for.

What a sight he must make. The aloof and haughty Duke of Raven, munching on a daffodil and making a total ass of himself. For a woman, no less. He had sworn never to be in this position again, but evidently he was as big a fool as ever. He felt a burning urge to turn on his heel and walk out. It started deep in his gut and rose, like bile, until it was an effort just to breathe.

Pride alone demanded he carry through to the bitter, humiliating cnd. For the same reason he had once, as an underclassman, played an entire game of rugby with a dozen raw eggs running down his back, he nonchalantly ambled the length of the dining room and dropped the damn flower from his teeth to his open palm and offered it to Leah.

"For you," he murmured . . . and waited for her to toss the bloom in his face and make his mortification complete.

He told himself he would not care. But he was a

damn liar. He did care. More than he wanted to, much more than was wise.

"Thank you, Adrian. It's lovely." She accepted the daffodil, and the kiss he pressed on the back of her hand, with equal grace.

She was dressed in a shade of yellow that was softer and more delicate than daffodil, and the sunlight pouring in the window behind her spun a hundred different shades of burgundy and gold across her hair. At that moment, he had no doubt she was the most beautiful woman he had ever seen, and if they had been alone, he might have told her so.

Turning to Thorne, she said, "Will you please bring me a vase? Daffodils cannot live long without water."

He moved to his place at the head of the table on a wave of relief. She had saved him. And she had called him by his given name for the first time. That could only be construed as progress.

As soon as he was seated he felt more like himself.

"Forgive my tardiness," he said, with a heavy undercurrent of sarcasm. "I had no idea we were hosting a breakfast party."

"Tardy?" retorted Colin. "I don't recall ever before seeing you upright before noon, and usually not for a good while after."

"Colin came by to drop off a book of poetry he has recommended," Leah told him.

He quirked a brow at his friend. "Poetry? At this hour? I'd no idea you were such a devotee."

"Even I have a cultural side, you know," Colin muttered.

"These are epic poems," explained Leah. "We were discussing my work and Colin thought I might find them inspiring in terms of theme."

Adrian couldn't help glaring at her in disbelief. "You discussed Olivia and Nevar with *him*?"

"Actually we talked about my earlier books," she replied.

He had a discomfiting sense that she was trying not to smile.

"Who are Olivia and Nevar?" asked Colin.

"None of your business," snapped Adrian. "And since when are you an early riser? Either of you?"

"I suggested they come early and keep me company for breakfast, since I'm seldom here to receive calls later in the day."

"Really?" Adrian reached for the cup of bitter chocolate Thorne had poured for him. "I was not aware your schedule was so full these days."

"Almost too full."

Almost? he thought.

"I once feared that I would have trouble keeping Christiana entertained when she finally gets here, but already I am struggling to keep up with all the invitations and requests from people who want to pay calls." She indicated the silver salver piled high with engraved calling cards and invitations. "And more arrive each hour. Fortunately, Will has offered to help me sort through them all."

Adrian glanced sideways at Will as a footman placed before him a plate piled high with eggs, toast and ham. "How very . . . noble of you, Rector. And nowhere near as obvious a ruse for spending time with another man's wife as a book of poems."

"Adrian," scolded Leah. "What a horribly uncharitable thing to say in response to such generosity."

"Perhaps if you knew these two—" Adrian broke off, heeding the small inner voice warning him that he was about to take a giant step off the path to successful seduction. "You're right, of course," he said, attempting to look chastened. "Horribly uncharitable.

And after all my two old friends have done for me of late."

He smiled warmly at them and received looks of outright suspicion in return. They knew him well.

"I can't think what got into me. Forgive my appalling lack of sensitivity to your feelings," he went on, laying it on so thick both men's jaws dropped. Reaching for the plate of sweet rolls, he offered them with a smile. "More sweet rolls, gentlemen? Will, I know these are your particular favorite."

"Well, perhaps just one," said Will, helping himself to two.

"Actually," Adrian went on, after pressing a roll on Colin as well, "I am particularly glad to find you here, Colin. It saves me a trip to your office later."

"My office? What would bring you there?"

"I seem to recall your mentioning that you had acquired a gallery in Soho."

"That's right," said Colin. "Talk about useless winnings. I should have pressed young Wickerson for his interest in the carriage works at Tingsley instead. At least there's some use to them."

"It so happens I have use for a piece of property in that area and your gallery will fit the bill perfectly. That is," he added, buttering a piece of toast, "if you're interested in relieving yourself of it."

"Interested? I'd give it away for the sum of the taxes."

"Then we've a deal. Send the tax bill with the deed and I'll take care of it."

Leaving Colin looking startled by the speed with which he'd been taken, he turned his attention to Leah. "I assume you have plans for the day?"

"Yes, I've arranged to visit my publisher's office and I have to stop by the millinery shop to check on several new bonnets I ordered for Christiana. Not that she was in need of any," she added, with a small shake of her head. "You shall see what I mean when she arrives with trunk after trunk of every bit of frippery imaginable."

The men laughed appreciatively.

"A lady can never have too much frippery," Will assured her.

Easy knowing *he* wouldn't be lugging in the chit's trunks, mused Adrian.

"When do you expect your sister?" inquired Colin.

"I don't know for sure. Adrian was kind enough to send a carriage for her the day after I arrived in London. I expect word any time now that she is on her way."

Her animated tone revealed how much she anticipated her sister's arrival. One more thing to distract her and occupy her time, he thought, wishing he'd told the driver to take the long way back from Baumborough.

"As eager as I am to have her here, however, I am glad for this time to prepare the house and plan her schedule. Which reminds me," she continued, "I also have to stop at the stationer's to order calling cards for her. I'd assumed I could simply add her name to my own, but I've received individual cards from several unmarried ladies, so that must be the current trend. I want Chrissie's first season in London to be perfect to the last detail."

"It shall be if we have anything to do with it," Colin promised before Adrian could get a word out. "Between us, Will and I know everyone worth knowing."

"We'll take her to the theater," Will offered. "My sisters have a box."

"And to Astley's," said Colin. "That is, if she enjoys that sort of thing?"

"I'm sure she will. Chrissie is eager to experience

everything that London has to offer. This is a dream come true for her."

She met Adrian's gaze across the table, her eyes sparkling as if she were the one who was eighteen years old and about to embark on the adventure of her life.

"Well," she said, a bit self-consciously in the face of his probing stare. "If I'm to accomplish all I have planned, I should be off."

All three men hastened to their feet as she stood.

Adrian tossed his napkin beside his untouched plate. "I'll go with you." When she glanced at him in surprise, he added, "It so happens I have business at the stationer's myself."

The stationery shop was located just off Chancery Lane. The small bell above the door jangled as they made their way back out. Leah preceded Adrian up the narrow stairs to the sidewalk and, surveying the afternoon sky, gloomily predicted another rainy evening ahead.

"I wouldn't be surprised," he concurred, with a quick glance at the clouds. "This is England, after all."

"Well, it can rain all it pleases for the time being, but I here and now request a perfect, sunny day for Christiana's arrival, and you are my witness. I want the whole city to sparkle and glow before her, just the way it did for me. Also," she continued in the same lighthearted vein, "I forbid any rain to fall along her route. I shan't have her delayed by mudholes and washouts."

She met his gaze and paused in the act of adjusting the black feather that adorned her hat at a rakish angle. "What is it?" she asked. "Why are you staring at me that way?"

"Because you're beautiful, the most amazingly

beautiful and perfect woman I have ever known. And if there is a God in heaven, I have no doubt he will be as powerless to ignore any wish of yours as I am to take my eyes off you. Which means the sun will shine on your sister every step of the way between Baumborough and here."

"I was only joking." She knew she had been right to avoid being alone with him for as long as she had, and very, very foolish to have broken that self-imposed rule today. It was not only the distracting things he said, it was the way he looked at her when he said them, and the way her foolish heart was only too eager to respond. Adrian was a mighty adversary, but far more than conquest, she feared insurrection within.

"I want to thank you for your advice on the wording on Christiana's cards," she said, eager to make her escape.

He gave a lazy bow. "I was happy to oblige. Though I am sure I am not as knowledgeable about the subtleties of calling cards as Will, who actually pays attention to the ridiculous things."

She sensed the same undercurrent in his voice she had at breakfast, when he questioned her about discussing her work with Colin. Was it possible he was jealous of her growing closeness with his friends? She wasn't sure. And because shc was never entirely sure when he was playacting and when he was not, she had to be extra vigilant around him. An exhausting effort, as she had learned over the past several hours.

"Your advice was impeccable . . . as was your performance with Mr. Pickering," she added, in reference to their earlier visit to her publisher on nearby Fleet Street. "I'm sure he thinks I have the most loyal and supportive husband in existence."

"Who says it was a performance?"

"Was it?" She turned to meet his gaze squarely.

A mistake, she realized at once. Never make direct eye contact with a predator. How many times had she said that to Chrissie when they encountered a strange dog on one of their walks? Their gazes remained locked, as passersby detoured around them and the first scattered drops began to fall from the sky and their breathing seemed to come in unison.

"I think I shall abstain from answering," he said at last, "on the grounds that I'm damned if I do and damned if I don't."

"How so?" she countered, filled with a strange excitement, the way she might be if observing a wild animal through a cage door she was not sure was locked.

"If I say I was pretending, you will—mistakenly—conclude that I do not greatly admire you and your talent. If I deny it, and tell you I meant every word, every fawning glance in your direction, you won't believe me anyway and will conclude that you have even more reason to distrust me in the future."

"You have a point," she conceded with a small smile. "I wouldn't answer me either. And now, I must let you go."

"Why?"

She blinked, startled. "Why? Because I'm sure you have many more serious matters to attend to than accompanying me to a millinery shop. Don't you?"

"No. As luck would have it, my entire day—and night—are free. I intend to do nothing but fulfill your every desire." He let that hang provocatively in the air, his smile as intimate as a touch. Then, with another of those small, insouciant bows of his, he added, "Where to, Duchess?"

It was still sprinkling an hour later when they emerged from the preeminent millinery shop at Pall Mall. Leah had gone there with the intention of changing the color of the ribbon on one of the bonnets she had ordered and adding flowered trim to the other. She left not certain if the straw bonnet was to have the daisies and the felt the poppy-red ribbon or the other way around.

She was not at all confused over Adrian's purpose in spending the day with her, however. He was launching an unabashed, all-out campaign to charm his way past her defenses. And to her delight and distress, he was winning.

"Wait here." He positioned her under the shop awning. "I'll send for the carriage."

"Please don't," she said. "It's only a short distance and if we stay beneath the overhangs, we'll hardly get wet at all." The truth was that she was in no hurry to be alone with him in the close confines of a warm carriage. "And we can window-shop while we're at it."

Looking as if he'd been asked to crawl the entire distance, he bowed to her wishes and gallantly steered her to the drier path close to the buildings. They'd gone only a few steps when the display in the bow window of a silversmith caught her attention. Pieces of brightly colored glass were arranged on a mirrored tray, along with a stand holding an engraved silver cylinder.

"Look, a kaleidoscope," she exclaimed.

He seemed surprised she recognized it. "Have you seen one before?"

Leah nodded. "The Brewsters at home are cousins of Sir David Brewster. He built his first kaleidoscope some years ago, from cardboard and bits of glass and mirror, though he's only recently obtained a patent for his work. He left one of his early efforts with Kit

Brewster when he came to visit last year and for weeks after we all wore a path to her door to take a turn with it." She laughed, recalling it. "We nearly wore Kit and the kaleidoscope out in the bargain."

She glanced sideways at him. "Have you ever looked through one?"

He nodded. "Last year. At a scientific exhibition in Rome."

"What did you think?"

"I thought it was very entertaining."

"I thought it was like breathing color," she said softly, gazing dreamily at the one on display. "Sir David is a most accomplished gentleman. Can you imagine creating anything so absolutely amazing out of ordinary bits and pieces?"

"No, I cannot, but you should have no trouble imagining it." When she glanced at him quizzically, he added, "You do that very thing all the time in your books."

"It's not the same," she protested.

"Not the same, perhaps, but every bit as impressive, and equally phenomenal to those of us who lack your gift for creating something fascinating and compelling where nothing existed before."

Leah kept her gaze carefully focused on the kaleidoscope, while she committed his compliment to memory. The things he said about her eyes and her hair were flattering, but she had no doubt he'd spoken odes to numerous other eyes and other hair before hers. But this, God help her, this she believed was real. The day suddenly seemed bright and warm, and everything inside her hummed with pleasure. "That's very kind of you to say."

"Kindness has no part in it," he retorted with a trace of impatience. "It happens to be the truth. Now, were you thinking of going inside to examine this model more closely?"

"Actually, I was thinking what a wonderful marriage gift it would make." From the corner of her eye she saw him start to grin and realized how easily her comment could be mistaken for a hint. Hurriedly, she explained, "For Chrissie to give to her bridegroom, I meant."

With a quick motion, he flipped up the collar of his coat and hunched his shoulders. There was no mistaking the strained patience in his tone this time. "Does it not occur to you, madam, that having had her calling cards, bonnets and bridegroom all pre-selected on her behalf, that your sister just might prefer to pick out his damn gift for herself?"

Leah colored fiercely. "An excellent point, sir. I shall mention the kaleidoscope and leave the decision to her."

She turned to resume walking, briskly. He offered her his arm with stiff formality. She accepted it in the same manner. She was very eager to reach the carriage now, confident the icy wall between them would not be thawed before they reached home.

They'd gone about a block in total silence when two boys scampered from an alley, directly into their path, forcing them to a sudden halt.

"Give it here, I said," shouted the smaller of the two boys, reaching around the other to grab whatever it was he was crouched over so protectively. They looked clean and cared for, Leah noted, though their coats and breeches had seen better days.

"I won't," cried the other boy. "It's mine."

"Is not."

"Is so."

With that, the bigger boy swung out a hand, catching the other square in the face and sending him flying backward onto the sidewalk.

"Enough," Adrian said firmly, hauling the boy back to his feet and taking hold of both by the back of their collars. "Are you all right?" he asked the child who'd been knocked on his posterior.

"I . . . I think so," he replied, wiping the back of his hand across his eyes.

"What does your friend here have that you want so badly?" Adrian asked the boy.

"He's not my friend," both boys cried in unison.

Now that she had a good look at them, Leah realized that one boy was quite a bit bigger than the other, and probably a year or two older.

The older one, whom she guessed to be about ten, said, "He's my brother."

"I see." Adrian looked from one to the other. "That still does not answer my question. What did you just slip into your pocket?" he asked the bigger of the two.

He stared at his feet. "Nothing."

"Fine. Let's have a look at nothing," said Adrian. "Now, son."

Reluctantly, the boy withdrew a sugar biscuit from his pocket.

"Where did you get that?" Adrian asked him.

"From the pastry shop over on Bartlett." He indicated the direction with his shoulder.

"Did you steal it?"

"No," he cried, his eyes widening fearfully. "The man gave it to me for carrying his empty flour barrels."

"I carried one too," his younger brother chimed in. "He said to share."

Leah rolled her eyes at the sheer idiocy of giving one biscuit to two hungry boys. "I think sharing it is a good idea," she said. "Why don't you give your brother half?"

"I tried to," he told her, "but he don't want me to break it."

" 'Cause he'll give me the small half," argued his brother. "He always does."

"Then how about if we let the little fellow here break it?" suggested Adrian.

The older boy shook his head frantically, as Leah had known he would. "No, sir, then he'll give me the small half to get back for all those other times."

Adrian grit his teeth.

"I have an idea," Leah said, hoping to defuse things before he dropped them both on their bottoms. She looked first at the older boy. "Why don't you break the biscuit into two equal pieces, and then we'll have your brother here take his choice? How does that sound?"

Neither boy looked thrilled by the proposal, but it was too reasonable to protest and so the deed was done. After which, Adrian gave them each coin enough to buy a week's worth of sugar biscuits.

"You are a soft touch, Your Grace," she remarked as they disappeared into the alley.

He shrugged uncomfortably. "And you are nothing short of a modern-day Solomon. That was brilliant."

"Yes, it was. Unfortunately I cannot take credit for it," she confessed. "My friend Sophie has five children under the age of ten and I have seen her resolve their differences hundreds of times. The *one cuts, one chooses method*, as she refers to it, is one of my particular favorites."

"I'll bear it in mind the next time Will and Colin lock horns. Though frankly, I doubt it would work quite so neatly with a woman."

"I think this time I shall abstain from comment."

She smiled, the awkwardness of a few moments ago gone.

"Tell me, Leah," he said, "have you never wanted children of your own? You seem so natural around them."

"Have I ever wanted them? I suppose. There was a time when I blithely assumed that a happy marriage and a full nursery would be my future. Of course, that was a time when I assumed a great many things about life and the people around me, people I both loved and trusted."

There was a note of regret in her voice. The answer to his question was bringing her close to places inside herself that she had closed and locked long ago and she quickly pulled back.

"But, as you know, my life took a different turn from the one for which I had been groomed. And, my writing aside, I am a diehard realist. I long ago accepted my fate and decided to look forward to being a doting aunt to Christiana's brood."

"Does she want children?"

"Well, of course, she does," she answered. "She will make a wonderful mother. Personally, I hope she has at least a half dozen, so there will be plenty of birthdays on which to spoil them, and always one or two the right age for me to whisk off on holiday." Seeing the dubious look on his face, she added, "True, it will not be quite the same as having a family of my own, but it is more than I have now."

"I can hardly argue with that logic, I suppose."

They came to the corner. When he tried to steer her to the right, Leah resisted.

"The carriage is that way," she reminded him, pointing left.

"But my favorite tearoom is that way." He pointed, nudging her to the right. "You're chilled, I can feel it through your sleeve. You can do with a cup of chocolate, and I have a sudden yen to sit with my bride in the front window of Beresford's."

In the end, it was a table in the far back corner of the popular establishment where they were seated, having been led there at Adrian's request by the owner himself, a short, dapper little man with a thin mustache. He hurried from the back room to greet Adrian and personally take their order.

"I thought you had a sudden yen to sit in the front window," she ventured, after the man had returned with two steaming mugs of chocolate and disappeared.

He leaned back, his blue eyes glinting. "It passed. My yen at this moment is to have you entirely to myself."

"Are you frequently given to such fits of whimsy?"

"Only lately."

More nonsense. More tummy flutters. More of that awful-wonderful shivery feeling along her spine.

She was having serious second thoughts about being there, ensconced in a private corner of his favorite tearoom, where the air was saturated with rich aromas and the tiny table brought his long legs into much too close contact with her own.

"I've heard wonderful things about your latest venture," she remarked, hoping to steer conversation to a safe, neutral subject.

"Have you indeed?" He wore a look of cautious interest.

"Yes. The London House of Birds is on everyone's tongue and it doesn't even exist yet. When do you expect it will open?"

"Not for months. These things take time."

"Of course. Personally, I wouldn't know how to begin organizing an aviary."

"Nor would I." When she looked askance, he smiled. "I'm not planning an aviary. I'm planning a brothel."

For an instant, one horrible instant, Leah could swear he was telling the truth. But that was impossible. A brothel, of all things. The very fact that it was so outrageous was, of course, what made it perfect for his brand of cynical humor.

She shook her head and shot him the most disapproving look she could muster. "Tell me, do you ever overlook an opportunity to shock?"

"No. Never."

So much for safe, neutral subjects. They sipped their chocolate in silence, with her glancing around at the other patrons and his gaze never wavering.

"You're staring again," she said softly.

"You're right. I am."

She took another sip, trying to pretend it did not bother her. She was licking the froth from her top lip when she saw how the sight mesmerized him.

He grinned. "Shall I apologize?"

"That depends. Are you sorry?"

"No more sorry than I am for having opened my eyes this morning or for drawing my next breath. Gazing at you is that vital to my existence."

Leah leaned back in her chair. "Does this approach usually work with the women you pursue?"

"I don't pursue women."

"Of course, how sillly of me. They pursue you," she said, with a little shake of her head.

"You misinterpreted my words. I meant only that, until now, the only sort of women who interested me did not require pursuit. I knew where to find them when I wanted them, and they were always there, waiting and willing."

"I see." She felt torn between the lady's code of

honor, which required her to huff and change the subject immediately, and the curiosity that had been gnawing at her since the Torringtons' ball. Curiosity won. "Does that include Charlotte?"

He went still, though his expression remained relaxed, even playful. "Who?"

"Charlotte Bonnaire. I believe that was her name."

"Now where did you hear about Charlotte Bonnaire? No, let me guess. My faithful friend Colin told you about her?"

"Actually it was Will," she admitted.

"The good rector strikes again," he said lightly. "And what, exactly, did he tell you about her?"

"Exactly nothing. He really is much more loyal than you give him credit for being. He only mentioned her name in passing when I expressed interest in the women in your infamous past."

"Then he didn't tell you that we were to be married?"

Leah felt a soft thud in the pit of her stomach. "No. He didn't. What happened . . . or shouldn't I ask?"

"Of course you should ask. How else will you find out what you want to know about my infamous past? The fact is, she left me standing at the altar."

"No."

"Yes. And all because, as my brides go, she lacked the one crucial attribute that drew me to you." He leaned closer, then kept her waiting a few seconds before adding, "She was conscious."

He flashed his pirate's grin, yet Leah sensed that he was not at all pleased by the discussion.

"At times like this, I'm never sure whether to believe you or not," she told him.

"Good," he said, his voice deepening. "That means

I shall have to increase my efforts to convince you of my undying devotion and fascination."

Lord help her if his efforts became any more enthusiastic. Leah reached for her spoon and stirred her chocolate.

She looked up.

He was still staring.

"All right, enough." She let the spoon clatter to the saucer and offered him a resigned smile. "You've proven your point. You are a master of the art of seduction. I'm sure you have cut a wide and successful swath through the ladies of the *ton*—errant brides aside—and if I were not so absolutely determined not to be seduced, I myself might possibly, perhaps, in some small way, fall victim to your charms. But I am. Determined that is. So you can stop now."

He leaned forward until she felt caged in her chair by his closeness. "What if I told you I cannot?"

"Cannot stop?"

"Cannot stop . . . cannot help myself . . . cannot control this feeling inside me."

"I would say you are going beyond the pale with this silly game. Far beyond."

"What if I told you that it is no longer a game?"

She waited for him to smile or add something scandalous, but he did neither. He simply continued to gaze at her as if she were the most fascinating sight he had ever encountered.

"I would still ask that you cease and desist," she said finally. "It is unnerving to be stared at so . . . forcefully."

Immediately a look of concern replaced his look of ardor. Leah trusted neither.

"There must be some room for compromise," he ventured. "Some way to resolve this to our mutual satisfaction . . ." He brightened. "I have it. If I had a likeness of you, I could gaze at it to my heart's content without making you feel . . . overpowered."

"A likeness?" She eyed him cautiously. "Are you asking for a miniature?"

"A miniature won't do. It must be a full portrait. I'm asking your permission to paint a portrait of you."

Her eyes widened with astonishment. "You paint?"

"Not overly well," he replied, with uncharacteristic modestly. "But, at least in this instance, with great passion."

Leah debated whether or not to believe him, finally deciding that such a claim was too easily verified for him to risk lying about it. "I'm impressed," she said. "Not to mention astonished. I took you for a consummate rake who slept all day and played all night, with no care for anything more substantial than your whims of the moment. Apparently I was wrong."

"I accept your apology." He reached for her hand and pressed his lips to the inside of her wrist. "Does this mean you will sit for me?"

Leah hesitated, going weak inside as the damp heat of his breath passed through her glove.

"Please, Leah," he urged. "Let this be *your* wedding gift to me."

He was up to something. She knew he was. She just did not know what, and it was not in her nature to refuse such a direct plea. Especially not when his tongue was making forays between the tiny pearl buttons that ran along the inside of her forearm, drawing all sorts of untoward attention from the ladies at the next table and making her head spin.

Subvert and conquer. That was his tactic and it was working. She knew what this low, deep vibration inside boded and a part of her brain screamed *run.* But another part wanted to feel this way for as long as possible, until she was hanging directly over the snapping jaws of disaster.

"All right, I'll do it." With a sigh, she withdrew her hand. "Though I'm not so green as to discount the distinct possibility that I shall live to regret it."

11

When they arrived back at Raven House, Adrian accompanied her as far as the front door.

"I've remembered some business that requires my attention today, after all," he told her. "I shall return in plenty of time to accompany you to the Hoddletops' dinner party."

"Please do not rush your business for my sake. I could meet you there, if you prefer."

"I definitely do not prefer," he said, a glint of pure, primal possessiveness in his eyes. "Wait for me."

Run, ordered the same small voice inside.

"Very well," said Leah. "I shall wait."

As soon as she entered the house, Thorne approached.

"Have you had a chance to speak to the others?" she asked, before he could utter a word.

He bobbed his head. "I did."

"And are they agreeable to giving my plan a try?"

"They say it can't hurt."

Coming from Thorne, it was a ringing endorsement, and she smiled happily.

"If" he added, "it's all approved by the Duke."

"Of course, it's approved by the Duke," she assured him, reasoning that Adrian had told her to do as she pleased with the house as long as she stayed out of his way. Not only would this not be getting in his way, in the long run it would improve his life immensely. "Do you think for a moment that I would rearrange the entire household staff if he did not approve?"

Thorne eyed her in wary silence for a few seconds. The two of them had forged a grudging respect that night in the kitchen and she was counting on his support to pull this off.

"I suppose there's approval and then there's approval," he said finally. "I suspect His Grace won't waste any time letting us know his feelings." With a creaky bow, he turned to go, then stopped and handed her the calling card he was holding. "I nearly forgot the gentleman waiting for you in the drawing room. Holt's his name."

Leah peered at the Honorable Michael Holt's card and her brow wrinkled. "Are you sure he asked to see me and not the Duke?"

"Sure as—" He caught himself. "Very sure, Y'Grace. He looks harmless enough."

He followed Leah up the stairs to the drawing room. As she approached the door, he drew her attention to the tortoise-shell-framed mirror hanging above a mahogany inlaid chest.

"It's off again," he said, though she could not see where it was so. "Been meaning to rehang it for a while now. I'll just be right outside the door here, seeing to it."

Understanding dawned. *Right outside the door*

meant he would be only a few steps away if she needed him.

Leah touched his arm. "Thank you, Thorne. I appreciate your diligence."

Michael Holt stood by the window overlooking the garden. He turned as she entered and Leah's breath hitched with surprise as she recognized the man she had collided with on Bond Street several days earlier.

"Thank you for seeing me, Your Grace." He crossed the room and bowed deeply over the hand she offered him.

"Have we been introduced?" she inquired, her expression guarded.

"We have," he replied with a gentle smile, "though you obviously do not recall it. I apologize for my impudence in coming to see you this way. I only dare because of the connection between us. I am your cousin, thrice removed, and I am proud to say that I was also a close friend of your mother's."

"That could mean any number of things," Leah said, trying in vain to recall his face from her childhood.

"It means only that we had shared interests, and that she trusted me."

"And were you worthy of her trust?" she asked bluntly.

To his credit, he replied the same way. "I was. Though I was unable to save her in the end. None of us who loved her were, as you surely know better than anyone."

Leah crossed the room and turned to view his tall, solid frame, swept-back silver hair and strong features from another angle. It had been ten years. People change.

"If we are connected as you say, why do I not have any recollection of you at all?"

"Probably because my visits to your home were so few. We are related on your father's side." The slight twist of his mouth showed disapproval. "But from childhood the only thing he and I shared was a marked lack of affinity. It was Dava who was like a sister to me."

"Why have you come to see me?" she asked.

"Why?" He gave a humorless laugh and ran his palm over his hair. "For any number of reasons." His expression softened with undisguised affection, encouraging Leah to trust him. "To see you again. To see if my first impression could possibly be right. And to apologize for what must have been a very disturbing encounter the other day. I know it disturbed me," he added ruefully. "Sent me straight to my club for fortification, you did, madam."

Leah smiled. "I am told I favor my mother."

"Favor her? In the coarse, but very accurate words of my poor Irish granny, she could have spit you out."

She laughed outright at that. "Your granny may be Irish, but I know some out by the Scottish border with the same gift for a colorful turn of phrase."

"You have her laugh, as well," he said quietly. "Did you know that?"

She shook her head, not wanting to try to speak past the sudden lump in her throat.

"And you move the same, with your head always up, as if you cannot wait to see what life has waiting for you around the next bend. "But enough of that," he said, with a broad sweep of his arm. "I did not come here to put tears in your eyes."

"They are not unhappy tears, sir. It is just so strange to hear someone talk about my mother to me. Except for commenting on our likeness, no one ever does." She folded her arms, feeling cold. "Sometimes it's as if she wasn't even real."

Michael Holt nodded as if he understood. "She was real, all right. All too real, perhaps. That is another reason I came. I've no idea what you've been told about your mother or how much you know about what happened back then, but I feel it's safe to say I knew her as well as anyone. If you have questions, perhaps I can answer them. Or if you ever just want to know more about what she was like, I am at your disposal."

"Thank you, I would like that very much. Perhaps you'll come to dinner some evening?"

He clenched and unclenched his fists by his side. "I will if you like, but it may prove awkward. At the risk of severely overstepping my bounds, Your Grace, may I say that I have heard talk that your marriage was of a rather . . . impulsive nature. And I . . ." He hesitated, then his heavy silver brows came together in a fierce frown. "The devil take it, have me tossed out on my ear, if you will. I bit my tongue once and lived to regret it, I won't make the same mistake with you. How much do you know about your husband?"

"I know his father was once my mother's lover," she replied, taking him by surprise.

He nodded grimly. "And do you know what they call him, this duke of yours?"

"He's called the Wicked Lord Raven."

"Aye, and he comes from a long line of the same. I don't pretend to know what his game is in marrying Dava's daughter, but I will not rest until I find out. In the meantime, I would have you be always on your guard, my dear."

"Thank you for the warning. There are many who would not have had the courage to come here today. That you did is, I think, proof of your regard for my mother."

A pleased smile spread across his face.

"In return," she continued, "I hope I can ease your mind by telling you that Raven is not his father." Before he could voice the concern that flashed in his eyes, she added, "And I am definitely not my mother."

It was long after the Hoddletops' dinner party had ended when Adrian made his way up the narrow wooden staircase to Thorne's tiny chamber. Holding a candle in one hand, he used the other to shake the older man to a semi-awake state.

"Forgive the hour, Thorne," he whispered. "There is something I require you to do for me first thing tomorrow."

Thorne squinted up at him. "Wake you for breakfast again?"

"Yes, that too, I suppose," Adrian muttered. "But after that, I need you to visit an artists' supply shop." He took a scrap of paper from his pocket and handed it to him. "Here, I've located a likely one. Go there and purchase everything necessary to stock a studio. Paint, brushes, canvas, an easel . . . Several would be even better, and one of those wooden things with a hole for the thumb. The word escapes me."

"Palette," supplied Thorne.

"Exactly. You never fail to amaze me, Thorne. A few of those as well, along with anything else a serious painter might require. I'll also need a chair for the Duchess to sit on. No, no, make it a chaise. Preferably a velvet chaise." He smiled, mentally refining his strategy. "Red velvet."

Thorne yawned.

"Will you remember all that?" Adrian asked him.

"Paint, brushes, canvas, several easels, palettes,

painterly bric-a-brac, and a red velvet chaise for the Duchess. Will that be all?"

"Yes. No. See if you can't pick up a few works in progress. For atmosphere. Have everything sent at once . . . and discreetly, do you understand? Have the room at the top of the stairs cleaned and aired and have it all arranged in there."

"It could take several days," Thorne warned him. "Especially the red velvet part."

"Just get it done as quickly as possible. And without the Duchess knowing about it."

"I see. It's to be a surprise then?"

"A surprise?" Adrian winced to think of Leah's reaction should she discover the truth, that he had not held a paint brush since he was in shortpants, and had been none too adept with one even then. "Not if my luck holds."

"I feel silly," said Leah, as they climbed the narrow staircase to Adrian's studio for her first sitting.

"Why? Beautiful women pose for artists all the time."

"I know that, but I do not think of myself as beautiful and—"

"You should."

"And it is still difficult for me to think of you as an artist, rather than as . . ."

At her hesitation, he stopped, forcing her to do the same on the step below. "As what? Your husband? Confidante? Lover?"

"Nemesis."

His wry expression reflected no surprise. The exchange was typical of his tireless efforts to charm the drawers off her and her own secret, mutinous, increasingly strong inclination to raise the white flag and let him.

He was her husband, after all, by law if not by choice. He was interested. She was curious. All right, she was a bit more than curious. She was tempted. Very tempted. The more time she spent with Adrian, the more shocking and unthinkable things seemed quite natural.

He opened the door and stepped aside for her to enter. She let loose a cry of pure delight.

"Adrian, it's wonderful. So bright and airy and spacious." She did a complete turn, taking in the tall windows that let in the late afternoon sun and the paint-splattered cloth covering the wood floor at the center of the room. Canvases in various states of completion leaned against the far wall, brushes and jars of paint covered a well-worn worktable, and in the air there was the scent of the oil of clove in which brushes were soaking.

"This is a fine place to work," she said. "I envy you. I vow that the moment I get back home I am going to strip my writing room to the bare walls, toss out the clutter and make room for the creative energy I sense here."

He looked around as if seeing the room for the first time. "I suppose we should get started."

"Of course. There's little enough light left," she observed. "I'm curious that you choose to paint so late in the day. Most artists prefer the morning light."

"Not I. I do a great deal of work with shadows."

"But aren't shadows accomplished . . ." She shrugged, abandoning her question on technique, when he turned his back to her. He busied himself at his worktable, shifting around brushes and examining jars of richly colored oil paint as if looking for something in particular. Watching how thoroughly he became engrossed in his preparations, she felt contrite for ever having suspected that this might be just one more ruse.

He reached for a palette, opened a jar of white paint and poured a generous amount, so generous in fact that paint ran over the palette's edge and dripped onto the floorcloth.

"Damn," he muttered.

"Can I help?" she offered.

He waved her off and reached for the jar of black paint.

She leaned closer.

He turned his head, the sudden motion setting her back on her heels.

"Now you're the one who is staring at me." Irritation was evident in his tone and the downward slant of his mouth.

"I'm sorry. Does it bother you?"

"Frankly, yes. I'm not used to having others around when I work."

Hmm, temperamental, she thought.

"I see. Do you usually paint still lifes then?" she inquired, glancing toward the canvases leaning against the wall. "Do you mind if I have a look?"

He was prevented from answering by the sound of footsteps on the stairs. Colin strolled into the room with Will close behind.

"Good morning, Duchess, Rave," Colin said, glancing around. "What the devil is all this?"

"What does it look like?" snapped Raven, clearly annoyed by the interruption.

"Is this the first time you've seen the studio?" Leah inquired, smiling to offset Raven's curtness.

"As a matter of fact it is," replied Colin. "I had no idea you were an artist, Duchess."

"Nor did I," echoed Will, his expression injured. "You never mentioned you painted as well as wrote."

"I don't," she said, puzzled. "This is Raven's studio."

"Raven's?" Colin furrowed his brow. "What does Raven need a studio for?"

Raven spoke for himself, his tone emphatic as he turned to face his friends, putting his back to Leah. "For my work, of course. My painting."

"Your painting? Oh, your painting." Colin nodded vigorously. "Of course. I thought you had given all that up. Didn't you, Will?" He poked Will with his elbow.

"Yes, I did." Will grinned at Raven. "It's nice to see you haven't lost your gift."

Colin gave Leah a conspiratorial look. "Did he tell you he was a child protegé?"

"That's enough," Raven warned.

Colin sighed. "So modest, never wanting anyone to talk about his talent. It's no wonder it completely slipped our minds that he had any."

"I'm so sorry you can't stay longer," Raven said, moving to the door and holding it open.

Smiling, Colin strolled in the opposite direction and began looking through the canvases leaning against the wall. "Some of your work?" he asked. "Very . . . ecclesiastical, Rave."

"What are you talking about?"

He, Leah, and Will gathered to peer over Colin's shoulder at the paintings. The first canvas was simply a sketch of a crucifix with a few brushstrokes here and there. The others, mostly unfinished paintings, were all similar in subject matter, but displayed a wide variety of styles.

Raven's jaw tightened the way Leah noticed it tended to when things were not to his liking.

"Yes, well," he said when they had reached the last canvas. "Surely you've heard that all artists go through phases. These represent my early God-fearing phase. Very early," he added, turning the outermost canvas face in. "Actually I ordered them tossed out long ago. I shall have to have a word with Thorne about it. And now, gentlemen," he added, this time dragging Colin and Will with him to the door, "good day."

His friends made disgruntled noises and then could be heard laughing as they made their way down the stairs. Leah, already skeptical, was even more so after seeing their reaction.

"You really *can* paint?" she inquired, as he returned to pouring paint onto his palette.

"Of course I can paint." He glanced up with a wry expression. "Do you really think that anyone in his right mind would go to all this bother as a joke?"

Leah looked around the studio. There was no denying it had a well-used air. "I suppose not."

But there was one sure way to find out, she thought. She would let him work for a while and then insist on seeing his progress.

"Are you ready for me?" she asked.

"Soon."

He now had paint dripping from jars onto the table, the floor and himself. Leah, trying not to stare, resisted the urge to wipe up after him.

"I hope what I'm wearing is appropriate," she said, fingering the skirt of the simple ivory organza dress. "You said you wanted a wedding portrait and this is something I might have worn."

"Mmm," he said, tossing aside brushes and other tools with abandon. At last he turned to her, dripping palette in hand.

"Do you need a rag?" she asked, gently, lest she upset his concentration.

"A rag?"

"Yes, to wipe the excess paint. I don't see any. Where do you keep them?"

"I . . ." He looked around, frowning. "Actually I don't use rags."

"No rags?"

"No rags. I prefer to let creativity take its natural course without any interference whatsoever."

"That's very . . ." She made a gesture with one hand. "Very creative of you." Temperamental *and* eccentric.

Adrian looked at her dress as if seeing it for the first time and his lip curled with disapproval.

"What is it?" Leah asked, grasping the folds of her skirt. "Is something wrong?"

"It's all wrong. The dress, the hair . . . even the shoes."

Leah touched her hair where it was pinned on top of her head in back and looked down at her satin slippers. "In what way? Am I overdressed?"

"Overdressed," he repeated. "That's precisely the word I was searching for."

"But you said you wanted this to be reminiscent of a wedding."

"I said I wanted it to be reminiscent of *our* wedding," he corrected.

"Oh." Leah struggled not to snap at him. How in the world was she supposed to dress to remind him of *their* wedding when she had been all but unconscious during it?

"But don't worry." His tone turned reassuring. Silky, even. "I took the precaution of selecting the perfect dress for you to wear. It's hanging behind the screen there." He pointed to the wicker privacy screen in the corner. "If you'd care to slip it on, we can get started."

Leah stepped behind the screen and immediately stepped back out.

"This," she told him, swinging the sheer white lace garment she had found hanging by one of its absurdly narrow straps, "is not a dress."

"It's not?" asked Adrian, all furrowed brow and concerned innocence. "What is it then?"

"It's a nightdre—"

His dark brows arched—like devil's horns, she thought. "Night what?" he prompted.

"Nightdress," she said, snapping now and his concentration be damned. "You understand perfectly well what I meant."

"Obviously it's you who does not understand what *I* meant when I said I wanted this painting, which is to be my only lasting reminder of you, to be a memento of our wedding night."

"We had no wedding night, you conniving blackguard. For all intents and purposes we had no wedding. This is all a game . . . and don't you try to deny it. A game you want very badly to win, and to do so, you are trying to make me forget that it's a game. But it will not work."

"Are you certain of that, Leah?" he asked quietly.

"Absolutely, positively certain."

In that same deep, maddeningly calm tone, he said, "Then why are you so afraid to put on the nightdress and honor your promise to sit for me?"

"Honor?" She shook the nightdress at him. "You dare to talk to *me* of honor?"

He unfurled his dark angel's smile and leaned back against the table. "I'd dare anything. You, of all people, should know that."

She told herself she ought to toss the harlot's nightdress in his face and walk out. She ought to put an end to this sensual fencing match between them. She ought to do as she had vowed and refuse to cooperate in his game.

So what if he went away thinking that he had triumphed and had, in some small, meaningless way, broken her? She wouldn't have to endure his smug gloating for too long. Soon Christiana would be there and Leah had every confidence that, with a little guidance, her sister would be happily betrothed before the season was half over. In fact, the less time she was forced to waste on senseless games, the more she would have to devote to Chrissie and the entire situation would be resolved that much sooner.

In the meantime, what did she care what this arrogant, unprincipled scoundrel thought of her?

"All right," she heard herself say, "I'll put on the damn dress, and I'll honor my word to sit for you. If only to prove to you once and for all how totally hopeless your silly little seduction campaign is. I have a few *S* words of my own, you see—strength, stamina, and self-control."

He smiled and made a little scooting motion with his hand. "The dress," he prodded.

Leah made an exasperated sound through clenched teeth and disappeared behind the screen.

"You'll find matching stockings and slippers back there as well," he called after her.

It was worse than she'd first thought, Leah realized even before she had finished shimmying the flimsy garment over her hips. Much worse.

The fabric was as insubstantial as smoke and molded itself to her body. The deep scoop neckline was secured in front by ten tiny, satin rosettes. On her left side, the filmy skirt fell to the floor, but on the right the material was gathered just below the hip in a larger rosette. Leah looked for some way to undo it without ruining the dress, but it was hopeless.

Intent on concealing as much as she could, she reached for the stockings. They too were sheer white lace and ended mid-thigh. Coupled with the slippers he provided, silly things trimmed with soft white fur, they left her feeling more exposed than she would have with no stockings at all. Which, she had no doubt, was her husband's calculated intent. Well, it was not going to work.

In the limited space behind the screen, she practiced walking while maintaining her modesty. Difficult, but possible if she took small steps and kept her hands by her sides to keep the frothy skirt from swishing.

Tossing back her shoulders and anchoring the hip rosette firmly in place, she stepped from behind the screen, looked him in the eye and said, "Let's get this over with, shall we?"

Adrian's jaw dropped and he sucked in air. Oh, he masked his loss of composure quickly enough, sweeping her with that lazy, arrogant look of his. But not so quickly Leah did not see the effect she was having on him. Behind that cocky air of self-assurance, the man was reeling. His strategy had backfired. He was utterly dazzled by the sight of her in this dress he had chosen.

My my, this *was* an interesting development.

He always managed to radiate an aura of controlled desire, but no one's control was absolute.

Let him try to hide his vulnerability. Let him deny it even. It was as real as the sweat on her palms, and in some subtle way she did not yet fully comprehend, it shifted the balance of power between them.

She smiled at him, thinking it was worth dressing up like a tart to have finally discovered a chink in Adrian's armor.

"Where do you want me?" she asked, and again

saw him flinch. The power was going to her head. This, she decided, was much more fun than playing the delicate maiden. "By the window?" she suggested, knowing full well how the light would enhance the effect of the nightdress.

He stared at her with the determined but wary look of a lion tamer. Leah let her lashes drift slowly downward.

"No," he said. "I want you there, on the chaise."

He held out his hand to her and even though it meant releasing her hold on the rosette, she took it and let him lead her to the heavily tufted chaise he had positioned in front of his easel.

"I gave a great deal of thought to the choice of what color to dress you in," he said, watching with thinly veiled amusement as she lowered herself onto the chaise and discovered that the nightdress had not been designed with sitting in mind.

"That's right," he coached, his touch quick and light on her shoulder, her hand, the back of her knee. "Lean all the way back, legs up, bent a little, not quite so much. There." He straightened and studied her thoughtfully, moved her skirt a fraction of an inch and nodded.

"Yes, I was right to choose the white. I had some concern the color might wash you away, that your skin might be too pale. But it's not. You are perfectly, ethereally luminous." He trailed his fingertips under her jaw, his touch infinitely careful, as if she might be damaged if he exerted too much pressure. "I was certain that white would be the most dramatic choice against the red velvet, providing the perfect symbol of a bride's transformation on her wedding night, purity giving way to passion."

He slipped one narrow strap off her shoulder, tilted his head to consider the effect and once again nodded approval. "Yes, the contrast is quite stark, almost . . . shocking."

Leaning over her, he opened the first few rosettes at her bodice, as casually as if he were flicking a piece of lint from his lapel.

She tried not to think about how much of the upper swell of her bosom he had exposed. She had come too far to go all lily-livered now. Besides, the nightdress left so little to the imagination as it was, any further disgrace could only be a matter of degree. She was determined to see this through to the end, no matter what.

He frowned, opened one more rosette and smiled with alarming satisfaction. "Perfect."

Next, he moved around behind her and she felt his hands on her hair, dislodging pins and loosening the careful coil that had taken Bridget an hour to assemble.

"I hope you don't mind," he said, when it was too late for her to say if she did. "This is too structured, too fussy for what I have in mind."

"If I agreed to this dress," she observed in a dry tone, "I'm hardly likely to balk at letting down my hair."

"How inordinately rational of you."

Using his fingers as a comb, he gently went about freeing all the twists and tangles in her hair, working with excruciating patience until it hung loosely around her shoulders.

Still standing behind her, he carefully repositioned one tendril in front of her shoulder so that it curled across her breast. Judging by his smile, the effect pleased him greatly. Then he undid yet another rosette, and the warm pressure of his fingertips between her breasts caused a sharp, sweet thrill. "Perfect."

"You said that a moment ago," she pointed out,

irritated, mostly with her own subversive response to him.

"Can I help it if you defy the age-old wisdom that says you cannot improve on perfection?" He moved to stand beside the chaise once again, his speculative stare making Leah feel like a lump of clay about to be molded into shape. He appeared to have recovered nicely from his initial shock. Now it was she who was overwhelmed.

While she was changing, he had removed his coat and waistcoat and loosened his neckcloth so that he was clad only in snug black trousers and boots, his white shirt open at the throat. She had a vague feeling that she was safer when he was all buckled and buttoned and looking the perfect gentleman. But she liked best the rakish, pirate image he now presented because she knew it was closer to the truth, and there was so precious little she could count on being true or genuine between them.

He stood with his arms folded, his eyelids lowered slightly, like an appraiser assessing the value of a rare find and determined not to overlook the tiniest detail. A lock of dark hair tumbled across his forehead and she took note of the black whiskers shadowing his jaw and upper lip. But it was his mouth, soft and contemplative, that wreaked the most havoc on her poor, scrambled senses.

"The pose is good," he pronounced at last. "Now for your expression."

"Shall I smile?"

"God, no. A smile denotes happiness and satisfaction. It's much too soon for either. What I want from you is a look of anticipation . . . of longing . . . of excitement. The ceremony is over," he told her in a deep, mesmerizing tone. "You're alone in your chamber, waiting for your husband to come to you. You've sat for a moment to reflect on the day past, and to speculate about the unknown pleasures of the night ahead."

Leah gave a small nod, her mouth suddenly too dry to speak. His gaze roamed slowly over her body. She tried to lessen its power by closing her eyes, but felt it still, heating her, awakening sensations too quickly and in too many places for her to control.

"You're waiting. Restless. You kick off your shoes."

Her eyes flew open as she felt him pulling off her slippers. He tossed them to the bottom of the chaise, as if she had kicked them there.

"You take a sip of wine." From out of nowhere it seemed, he produced a glass of wine and handed it to her, waiting for her to take a sip. The wine eased the dryness in her mouth, but added to her headiness.

"You let your imagination wander . . . the way you know your lover's hands and mouth will soon be wandering over your body, touching you in ways and places where no man has ever touched you before . . . places no other man but this one will ever touch . . . or gaze upon . . . or possess."

The restlessness inside her intensified. Heaven help her. He'd barely touched her, had only *spoken* about it, and her resistance was crumbling like a house of cards. The flickering urge to run away was quickly swamped by a much more powerful and elemental desire to stay.

She *wanted* him to touch her, she realized, and immediately, as if privy to her thoughts, he did.

"Your head falls back," he said and his hand was on her throat, his thumb stroking her cheek as he eased her head back onto the chaise. She let him, at the same time turning her face into his hand to prolong the caress.

"You hear his footsteps outside your door. Your

eyes close. Your heart pounds. Your mind races. You're thinking . . . any moment . . . any moment he will come to me . . ."

Yes, Leah thought, yes, yes, yes.

"You wet your lips." She felt his thumb slide across her bottom lip and tasted oil of clove and was too far gone to wonder how he had managed it.

His thumb stroked now in the opposite direction, sliding deeper into her mouth. Her tongue moved of its own volition, seeking more of the spicy essence, seeking him . . .

"You're warm." He was whispering now, his rough, hushed tone like a bow drawn across her tightly wound nerves. "On fire almost. For him. Your beautiful body is flushed . . . everywhere. And there is a faint sheen, a glow of expectation . . . here." He ran his oiled fingertips across her forehead. "And here." A single fingertip trailed fire from her chin to her breastbone. "And here." He brushed the tops of her breasts, first one, then the other. She felt branded, as by fire, and the yearning inside grew sharp and focused.

In that instant, she knew exactly what she wanted. Thoughts of tomorrow and the price she might pay for it were only a soft haze at the edges of her mind. She wanted this. She wanted it now, and she wanted it to never end.

Without thinking, she arched her back, lifting herself to him, like an offering to the gods.

"Ahh," murmured the achingly beautiful god looming over her in the growing darkness. "I was right about this gown. It was made for you, made to caress your luscious thighs and hips and breasts." He spoke slowly, worshiping at each of those places with his touch. "The only question is, shall I take it off, or will you?"

12

There was no mistaking the intent, or the hunger, in Adrian's dark gaze. Leah had imagined this moment at least a hundred times, and had rehearsed numerous clever ways to extricate herself with her virtue and self-respect intact. But she had not planned on mutiny. She had not prepared for the possibility that the rest of her might not want to be extricated.

Now she gazed up at her husband, her own eyes luminous with barely leashed desire, and said, "I think if it is to come off, you shall have to be the one to do it. My bones and muscles have all melted inside me."

It was clearly not the response he had expected.

"Are you sure, Leah?" he asked quietly, while his palm molded the curve of her shoulder and stroked the length of her arm and added irresistible new dimensions to the yearning within her. "Are you sure you want this?"

At that moment, with his touch on her fiery and

clever and possessive, wanting him was the only thing in the world she *was* sure of.

"Yes, very much." She wished he would stop asking questions and stop looking at her as if she were an intriguing riddle. After all, there was no doubt this was what *he* wanted, what he had wanted all along. Why didn't he simply take her, for pity's sake?

"I want to know what happens next," she told him, pushing aside thoughts of tomorrow, of everything that existed outside of that room. "I want to know what happens when my most dilatory bridegroom finally decides to grace me with his presence."

His beautiful mouth curved into a slow, knowing smile. All trace of hesitancy disappeared, from his gaze and from the fingers that slid beneath the straps of her gown and deftly peeled them off her shoulders.

"Dilatory? Not at all. Shrewd is more like it. He dallied, you see, in order to heighten your anticipation." One fingertip trailed idly along her throat and traced the upper swell of her breast. "He is a most exacting lover. He wants you eager . . . and ripe . . . and ready for him."

"I think it worked." Her breathing strained as she watched those strong, skillful fingers reach for the few rosettes still securing her bodice. "Is he pleased with what he sees when he opens the door?"

"He is most definitely pleased." His voice was pitched low, a rough counterpoint to the lightness of his touch as he released the final rosette. The rapid rise and fall of her full breasts parted the fabric, and the quick brush of his fingertips swept it aside, exposing her breasts to his ardent gaze. "He is quite speechless actually, unable to even attempt to capture what he feels in words, so he must resort to letting his hands . . . and mouth . . . and body . . . convey his utter, unmitigated devotion."

As he finished speaking, he moved onto the chaise beside her, half-covering her with his body, claiming her mouth with his, touching her everywhere at once, it seemed to Leah. She was drowning in him, in his heat and the erotic power of his touch, and in the need she felt simmering in him, just beneath the surface. Novice though she was, she recognized that need in him as the natural complement to the longing that burned at her very core. And she knew that once joined, the two would comprise a force that would be impossible to turn back.

He ran his hand over her slowly, following the movement with his gaze.

"Sweet Jesus, you're beautiful," he murmured. "I thought I could do this slowly. I can't. I can't wait . . . I want to see all of you. Now, Leah."

His tone was staccato and thrillingly rough, as he dragged the filmy white lace over her hips and along her legs. Leah was torn between an instinctive urge to cover herself and a shocking new desire to have him see her. All of her. *You're beautiful,* he'd said, and the way he was looking at her now, she felt beautiful. And strong. And cherished.

He gathered the gown in one hand and tossed it aside, leaving her clad only in those ridiculous sheer white stockings that ended mid-thigh, and suddenly they did not seem quite so ridiculous. The dark gleam in his eyes when he lifted his head to look at her assured her that the sight pleased him mightily. And for reasons she was beyond explaining, that pleased Leah.

Propping his head on one hand, he continued to gaze at her, lazily now, his impatience checked for the moment, as if he had the rest of his life to study each and every fascinating inch of her and just how he might decide to use it.

When she thought she would die if he didn't touch her, he reached with his free hand to cup her breast, lifting it so that its fullness overflowed his palm. His thumb brushed back and forth across the tip, arousing it to a tight peak, and pleasure moved through her in waves.

He repeated the delicious torment on her other breast, then slid his palm lower, coasting over the slight swell of her stomach and fanning to both sides in turn to mold the fullness of her hips and shape of her thigh.

With a rough groan, he levered himself up and began tugging impatiently at the buttons of his white shirt.

"I want to feel you against me," he told her, his deep voice cutting through the air, which had become heavy with expectancy. "I want your skin against mine."

Just the thought of it made Leah's pulse race. It had barely steadied when, still holding her gaze, he stripped off his shirt and dropped it on the floor. It was the first time she had seen him without it and when she looked at him it almost hurt to breathe. Adrian fully clothed was perfection. Adrian bare-chested was a gift from the gods. His arms and shoulders were leanly muscled, his skin smooth and several shades darker than her own. The glow from the lowering sun highlighted the ridges of muscle and bone.

She longed to touch him, to run her fingers over him and trace that fascinating line of dark hair that tapered and disappeared beneath the waistband of his trousers.

"Do it," he urged, moving closer so he was within easy reach.

Her eyes widened in surprise. "How . . . ?"

He laughed softly. "Because I can read your mind.

Touch me, Leah. I know you want to." He took her by the wrists and drew her hands to his chest. "Touch me the way I want to touch you. Everywhere."

Leah closed her eyes and allowed him to press her palms against him. He was warm and hard, the feel of him totally new and unfamiliar. Even the texture of his skin was a seductive surprise, so very different from her own. Not rough, exactly, but not smooth either. He felt firm and resilient and gloriously male.

She moved her thumbs and encountered that dark arrow of hair at the center of his chest. With her eyes still closed, she stroked back and forth across it, discovering that even that felt extraordinary, the strands crisp and short and slightly curling.

She felt his heart beating, and learned the way his chest rose and fell with each deep breath. Unconsciously she matched her breathing to his, lulled by its strong, regular cadence.

Growing braver, she turned her hands so her fingers pointed inward and played them up and down his chest, down a few inches, then up, then down, venturing lower each time. When her thumbs finally brushed the band at the top of his trousers, she heard him suck in a sharp breath and felt his muscles beneath her fingertips contract.

Muscles were wonderful. Men were wonderful, she thought, feeling heady and womanly and alive.

When at last she opened her eyes, the strained indulgence in his made her wonder how long she had dallied in her unhurried exploration of his body. He looked the way she felt, as if he had been waiting for this his entire life and could not bear to wait a single moment longer.

When she moved her hands away he caught them and pressed his palms against hers, their fingers lacing together. Pushing her arms over her head, he pinned them there as his weight pressed her into the pillows piled behind her.

"Let's see now," he whispered against her lips. "Where shall I kiss you first? Here?" He brushed her mouth with his. "Or here?" His lips slid along her neck and hovered just above her breast. "Or . . ."

He hesitated, letting the moment and her anticipation spin out deliciously. Leah felt his breath on her flesh and that slight contact alone was enough to make the tips of her breasts tighten.

He responded with a soft, teasing laugh. "Or shall I kiss you in one of the other hundred or so other places I have in mind?"

"My choice?" she asked, breathing hard.

"Of course."

"Could you name them for me, please?"

"I believe someone already has named them," he replied, his dry humor familiar and reassuring. "But I'd be happy to show them to you if you like."

"I'd like." She arched her neck as he touched his tongue to the soft indentation beneath her ear. "Oh, yes I like that very much."

"So do I," he said, not lifting his head. "How about this?" His teeth closed gently on the tendon between her neck and shoulder and the entire upper half of her body erupted in goose bumps. "Yes, I rather thought you would like that," he murmured, not needing a reply. "And this."

He brought his mouth to hers and kissed her, hard, using his lips and tongue and teeth until she was twisting beneath him. He groaned when she swirled her tongue around his, and grunted sharply when she pressed deeper, imitating his rhythmic thrusts. When at last he lifted his head to string hot, damp kisses along her throat and chest, they were both breathless.

Releasing her hands, he caressed her leg as far

down as her knee, then back up and down the other, teasing her sensitive inner thighs while the secret place in between grew hot and wet and frenzied. Leah shifted her legs and arched her back, but nothing could slow the sharp, mounting urge centered there, in her woman's place.

"Please," she whispered, and Adrian bent his head to her breast and suckled her. The thrill his avid mouth sent spiking through her was heavenly, but not enough. Leah wasn't sure exactly what she wanted, only that she wanted more.

"Please," she breathed again, and his hand swept between her thighs, a fleeting shadow stroke that she clamped her legs together to try to hold.

His laughter was a low-pitched rasp that danced across her breasts.

"There," he said as he brought his hand back to the place that wept for him.

This time his touch was firm and sure. She felt his fingers separating the delicate folds, opening her, finding new and sharper points of pleasure, each one more unbearably intense than the last. The sensations were exciting and frightening at the same time, pain and pleasure at once.

Leah knew now what she wanted. She wanted this. She didn't care about safety or propriety or tomorrow. She wanted *this.* She wanted it from Adrian, her husband.

He pushed one finger inside her and she bucked against the strange, unfamiliar pressure.

He licked her nipple and caught it lightly between his teeth and whispered something low and wicked.

Two fingers. She felt aching and full. A new urgency swept through her, obliterating pleasure and pain and control, commanding all of her energy and desire, and focusing it on feeding the wild, twisting, rushing need deep inside her.

She whimpered and closed her eyes and pushed against his hand, knowing intuitively that in some primal sense, at that instant in time, he alone held the key to her existence.

"That's it," he urged, his mouth at her throat as he rolled her to her side so that her back was pressed to his chest, his arm circling her hips, his hand hot and busy between her thighs. "Push. Rub against me. You know how . . . you know what you want . . ."

"I don't" she whimpered, feeling a raw thread of frustration entwining with the pleasure his fingers were bestowing. "I don't."

"You do," he whispered, making delicious circles just inside her with his thumb. "Your body knows. That's it. Use my hand. Do it hard. Harder. Make it feel good, Leah. That's what this is all about."

As he spoke, his hips moved against her from behind. She felt surrounded by his strength and masculinity. His hard man's part pushed against the back of her thighs, as if demanding entrance. An impossibility, since he still wore his trousers, but she felt the pulsating heat of his desire for her right through the fine wool and that thread of frustration inside her snapped.

Time stopped. The world froze. White hot pleasure gushed and swamped her. Ecstacy. Leah first cried out, then she just cried, her tears flowing silently. She wept with amazement, with relief, and with sheer joy.

Adrian was startled to taste tears when he hurriedly pushed her onto her back and kissed her mouth. Only a woman would think to cry at one of life's most pleasurable milestones, he thought.

It was his last coherent thought for a while.

He had been afraid that he wouldn't last. His lust

for her was so great, he'd feared it would drag him under and it would be over before he'd succeeded in satisfying her, much less gotten his damn trousers open. Even at the risk of his own disappointment and humiliation, however, he had been determined to pleasure Leah fully.

It seemed to him that her first time ought to be memorable for more than pain and a few spots of blood. He'd wanted Leah to know the thrill of release, before she felt the full impact of a man's complete possession.

And this would be full, and furious, and fast. He was already at fever pitch when he pressed her thighs wide open with his own and guided the throbbing tip of his erection to the place his fingers had stroked and teased to hot, slick readiness.

The playfulness that had marked their mood earlier was gone.

Leah looked up at him, unsmiling, her eyes dark and watchful.

He swallowed hard, knowing he was about to hurt her and knowing the only thing that could stop him now was her.

"The first time can be rough," he warned her.

"I know," she said.

He entered her with one hard, fast thrust. He felt her virgin's membrane give way, felt her quake beneath him. But there were no more tears and no plea for him to stop.

Instead she clutched his shoulders, desperation in her grasp. He closed his eyes and forced himself to remain still for a few seconds, wanting to let her tender flesh adjust to the invasion.

Withdrawing slowly, he told himself he would continue to go slowly if it killed him. He threw his head back and clenched his teeth together. God, it would kill him. She felt amazing. Hotter, tighter, wetter than anything he had ever felt before.

On the downstroke, her arms came around him and she bent her knees. It was like sliding deep into heaven.

He was most certainly dying.

He didn't care.

His vow to go slowly lasted for three full strokes. Maybe four. After that the stroking was finished and he was thrusting, hard, fast, grinding against her and forcing her legs farther apart to accommodate his need to sink all the way in and lose himself in her.

"Please," he moaned, with pleasure, with hunger. "Please."

"Like this?" Her voice soft and eager, she lifted her legs higher, holding him inside her with delicate tremors that sent him spiraling to the very edge of his control.

Adrian grunted and grasped her thighs, pushing them higher still, until her long legs were locked around his waist. His heart pounding, he reared back and looked down at the place where their bodies were joined and he was stunned by the erotic intimacy of the sight, and by an unprecedented sense of wholeness, of completion. It was as though they were alone at the center of the universe, as if their coming together had been destined by forces from within and without, all driving them toward what he did not know.

God, he was hallucinating. He must be, if he was mixing philosophy and sex. Evidently, he'd wanted her even more desperately than he'd realized. He had never felt so feverish . . . or so alive.

If he had not been delirious, he never would have done what he did next, something he avoided doing whenever he was making love to a woman. He looked into Leah's eyes, and the undisguised passion he saw there did him in. He had a sense that he was seeing all the way to her soul and, even more alarming, that she could see all the way to his. The shock nearly made him forget the one taboo he could not afford to violate.

Plummeting over the edge, rushing into the darkness of fulfillment, only at the very last instant did he remember to withdraw and spill his seed safely outside her body.

Release. And not a second too soon.

Sanity returned slowly. His breathing slowed. His head cleared. The fire blazing in his veins subsided and his first rational thought was that he had won.

He'd done it. He had seduced his wife, put an end to any further nonsense about an annulment, and proved . . .

Adrian frowned and peeled a long chestnut curl from his damp neck. He'd proved whatever it was he'd set out to prove, that's what he had proved. And splendidly, if he did say so himself. Leah looked all dazed and drowsy, and he himself felt uninspired to move anytime soon. Perhaps not for weeks, he thought. Months even. That's how long it would take for him to begin to fulfill the fantasies that even now were teasing the edges of his mind.

Sweet Jesus, he wanted her again. Right away. And that, most definitely, was not part of his careful plan.

He tried to ignore the gentle movement of her hands on his back and the effect her touch was having on his pulse. It was useless. He felt himself start to harden against her thigh, saw the wonder and delight in her eyes, and knew that far from being over, the game was only beginning.

Never had victory been so fleeting.

Taking her was *supposed* to have quenched the lust

that had been riding him hard ever since she'd arrived. Consummating their marriage was *supposed* to bind her to him forever, providing a hedge against every other conniving female in the world, and put him firmly back in control of his own life. Instead, he felt more under her spell now than when she'd stepped from behind that damn screen and sucked the breath from his lungs.

Which explained everything, he told himself, reaching for her in spite of the gut instinct warning him to walk away.

He couldn't leave her. Not yet. Just as he could not get it through his thick skull that nothing with Leah would ever be the way it was *supposed* to be.

Leah's stomach growled. And no wonder, she thought, shielding her sleepy eyes from the late morning sun that spilled across her rumpled bed. She'd missed dinner last evening and had slept well past her usual breakfast hour.

She stretched, wincing to discover she was sore in some very surprising places. Deliciously sore.

So this is what the morning after felt like, she mused with a contented smile. Hungry, sore, alone . . . and not a bit sorry. Well, perhaps she was a bit sorry to find herself alone, but that was all. What was done was done, she told herself cheerfully, knowing she would not undo it if she could.

Last night had been a wonderful surprise, far surpassing her feeble daydreams of romantic wedding nights, surpassing anything she could ever have dreamed or imagined or anticipated. She might have attributed her amazement to lack of experience alone, but Adrian had obviously been every bit as overwhelmed as she was by the passion that had exploded between them.

"I never knew it was like this," she had whispered to him after he had carried her to her chamber and made slow, perfect love to her all over again.

He'd tightened his arm around her as she lay with her head on his chest, and brushed her hair with his lips. "It never is."

It never is. So said the man with more than enough experience to know. But it *had been* like that last night, for both of them. Not that she was silly enough to fancy herself in love with the man, or naive enough to expect him to fall in love with her simply because they had gone to bed together.

They might be husband and wife legally, but last night had been strictly about pleasure, something that mature, sophisticated people shared all the time. Her husband had wanted a memento of their wedding night and he had gotten one.

Sighing, she held up her left hand and studied the heavy signet ring on her third finger, recalling the first time she had awakened and seen it there. That night had changed her life forever, and it would seem last night had done the same.

"With this ring," she murmured, tracing the crest engraved in gold and feeling more married than she had at any time since she'd been wearing it.

It was time to think about what would happen next. Any day now Christiana would arrive. That much remained unchanged. She was no less determined to see her sister properly wed. But what then? What effect would last night have on their agreement? What became of schemers turned lovers, when an annulment was no longer a possibility, and a marriage that wasn't supposed to be one was suddenly all too real?

Unfortunately, she had no suitably sophisticated answers. Apparently neither did the Wicked Lord

Raven, she thought wryly, or she would not have found herself alone in her bed that morning. The jaded libertine who never lost his head or his heart, and who could walk away from any woman without a backward glance, had not walked away this time. He'd run.

But it was too late. For better or worse, they were in this together forever now, and together they would have to find a way to deal with it.

Of course, she was something of a master at playing the hand she was dealt. Adrian did not have the same advantage. He had never been forced to compromise or adapt or make the best of a situation that was not to his liking.

Until now.

Luckily for him, he had her to help him through it. Somehow, some way, she was going to make him see that in spite of what he'd been telling himself for years, having a warm, willing wife in his bed was not the worst fate that could befall a man.

13

Stepping from her room into the master chamber was like moving from day into night. The mahogany furnishings were dark and imposing, and the Raven colors of midnight blue and deep gold dominated. The tightly closed draperies kept out any hint of sunlight, making it difficult to see. Leah waited for her eyes to adjust before tiptoeing across the room, a naughty smile shaping her mouth as she envisioned Adrian's response when he woke and found her in his bed.

"What the hell do you think you're doing?"

His gravelly voice stopped her in her tracks. It was not quite the welcome she had anticipated and it took willpower not to bolt.

"I wanted to surprise you," she told him.

"You succeeded," he retorted, still without opening his eyes or lifting his head from the pillow. "Now please leave."

She decided she didn't like his tone, and she definitely did not like being treated like an intruder on this, of all mornings.

"Why?" she demanded.

His eyes opened and his head jerked up. "Why? I order you to leave and you stand there and ask me why?"

"Yes. And you needn't look so indignant. I'm not one of the servants."

"Obviously. Servants are paid to mind their manners."

"I hardly think it ill-mannered for a wife to want to share her husband's bed," she snapped. "Especially when he seemed not at all averse to sharing hers last night."

"Last night is over. Besides, you cannot share this bed." He yawned as if the entire matter was boring beyond endurance. "Not this morning. Not ever."

Stung by his indifference, she refused to heed a very prudent urge to retreat, slam the door behind her and say to hell with him.

"Why not?" she persisted.

"Because it's cursed, that's why." He rolled to his side and yanked the covers nearly over his head. "Now will you get the hell out?"

"No." She folded her arms across her chest. "Cursed how?"

Muttering under his breath, he flung the covers aside. For a second Leah wondered if he was about to remove her forcibly, but he merely punched the pillows into a mound at his back and sat up.

He was naked and bleary eyed, with black whiskers shadowing his jaw, his dark hair tousled and a red crease along one cheek where it had been pressed to the pillow. He looked awful. And irresistibly male. To her horror, Leah's desire to slip into bed beside him was greater than ever.

"You want to know about the curse? I'll tell you . . . since you're obviously determined not to give me any peace until I do. In fact, you ought to know the truth. Then maybe you will come to your senses and leave me alone.

"This," he indicated with a dramatic sweep of one arm, "is the eighth wonder of the world, otherwise known as the Raven Wedding Bed. My father was fanatically proud of this bed. He slept in it from the day he wed my mother until the day he died. All my life I was told that this bed would become mine on the day I married, and that I was not to sleep in it until then." An edge of cynical amusement crept into his tone. "But as usual, I had other ideas. I slept here the night my father died, and countless nights since."

"To honor your father?" she asked hesitantly.

He laughed. "No. To spite him." His sardonic smile emphasized the bitterness etched in the tense lines around his eyes and mouth.

"Legend has it," he went on, "that when the master of the house takes his bride for the first time in this bed, a son is conceived. Sounds preposterous, I know, but it has proven true for six generations, so who am I to argue?"

"I'd hardly call that a curse," she exclaimed, bewildered by his attitude. "In fact, most people would consider it a blessing."

"Not I." His clipped retort lashed across the distance between them. "Though I can see how you would easily make that mistake. After all, most men of rank dedicate their lives to producing a male heir. I've devoted mine to *not* producing one."

"Why on earth would you do a thing like that?"

"Justice. If I die without male issue, the Raven title and holdings pass to my distant cousin, Wilbur the Beneficent, to borrow my father's name for him. Suffice it to say that proper, pious old Wilbur represents everything my father despised."

"And that is your notion of justice?"

He shrugged. "Not by a long shot. But it will have to do."

"Why do you hate your father so much?" She moved closer until his hard stare froze her in place a few steps from the bed.

"What makes you think I hate him?" he countered, his gaze completely shuttering. "Haven't I modeled my life after him? I make money, wield power and influence, and do exactly what pleases me no matter the cost to anyone else." He smiled cruelly. "You, madam, are living proof of my dedication to that particular family tradition."

She refused to be sidetracked by his taunt. "If you think to shock me, you don't. I understand only too well how it is possible to feel blinding rage toward your own father, someone you ought to love and trust above all others. But I also know the price you pay by holding on to that kind of bitterness, and how it can ruin your life if you don't put it behind you. I'm sure whatever your father did to make you feel such resentment—"

"You're mistaken. I feel nothing toward my father other than a burning desire not to inflict him on future generations. He won only half the battle, you see. He got the son he always wanted. I am, without question, the latest in a long line of Wicked Lord Ravens. I'm also the last."

"You're serious about this," she said, her voice quietly incredulous. "I thought your predilection for recklessness and debauchery was all about sowing wild oats and refusing to accept responsibility, but it's much more than that. *This* is the real reason you went to such lengths to avoid marriage."

He nodded, his expression dark and smug. "Now you understand why your little surprise this morning went awry, and why I will never take you in this cursed bed."

"But . . ." She paused, frowning, half-formed thoughts streaking back and forth in her head. "Then why did you make love to me at all?"

"Don't be obtuse."

"Don't you be." His nonchalance infuriated her. "I may have grown up in the country, but I'm worldly enough to know that your stupid bed is not the only place an heir might be conceived."

"Not quite worldly enough, apparently," he remarked, his lips a thin, disparaging curve. "I withdrew before I climaxed, Duchess. That means I spilled my seed elsewhere. Coitus interruptus is the technical term. I shall take your lack of notice as a compliment. The technique is something I've become quite good at over the years."

Leah's face warmed with comprehension, then with shame and resentment. *The technique is something I've become quite good at over the years.* How easily he lumped her with all the other female bodies he had used for his own pleasure and left behind.

She'd known that he had set out to seduce her, and for the most self-serving reasons, but she had foolishly believed that something had changed when they came together, that he had been swept up by the passion between them just as she had been. And tucked away in a corner of her heart had been a fragile hope it might lead to something more.

Now he was lounging there, casually boasting that, far from being carried away, he had coolly calculated the matter from start to finish.

It was as if he was deliberately trying to provoke her . . . as if he wanted to hurt and humiliate her

. . . to make sure she understood that last night had meant nothing to him. And he had succeeded. But Leah swore she'd walk through hell before she'd let him see her cry.

She tossed back her hair as silly, half-formed dreams of happily-ever-after gave way to a deep, pressing ache.

"Thank you for the impromptu science lesson," she said, her voice blessedly steady. "You certainly did think of everything last evening. Everything except for one small detail, that is."

"What small detail is that?" The amused indulgence in his tone made Leah regret that there was not a heavy crystal vase handy now. She contented herself with flashing a smug little smile of her own.

"The annulment," she said. "There are no longer any grounds for one. You may have managed to avoid getting an heir last night, but you most definitely acquired a wife." Her smile broadened. "I believe the technical term for it is 'till death do us part.' "

"Fine." He rose from the bed, naked and magnificent and not at all self conscious, and reached for his trousers.

Leah watched suspiciously as he stepped into them. "What do you mean *fine*?"

"I mean fine. There will be no annulment. Till death do us part . . . figuratively speaking, of course."

"Why aren't you angry?" she demanded.

"Why should I be?"

"We had an agreement," she reminded him, marshalling her own thoughts.

"I have no intention of reneging on our agreement. We shall continue to display our marital contentment in public until we've turned every stomach in London. He added, smirking, "And I will see your sister wed to the man of *your* dreams if I have to parade before you every eligible male alive to do it."

"And then?" Her hands fell to her sides, fists tightly clenched.

He shrugged. "Then you will return home to write about beautiful princesses and the stupid, noble men who love them, and I shall get on with my life here. Where the hell is my shirt?"

He crossed to his wardrobe.

Leah followed, wary, her emotions caught in a crosscurrent of relief and dismay. "What exactly are you proposing?"

"*I'm* not proposing anything." He yanked open the wardrobe door and rummaged through the stack of identical white linen shirts. "I'm merely picking up where you left off by coming here."

"But our original agreement was for an annulment."

"For God's sake, Leah." He grabbed a shirt and slammed the wardrobe door so hard, she jumped. "There was never any possibility of an annulment."

"What are you talking about? Of course there was the possibility. We *agreed.*"

He pinned her with his sardonic gaze. "Did you really believe, even in your wildest little virgin's dreams, that I would play the part of the besotted bridegroom and then permit you to announce to the world that I had failed to bed you? Even I have some pride."

Shock and anger raged through her. "What I believed was that when you gave me your word, you meant it."

"I also gave you my word that I would seduce you," he reminded her, shoving his arms into the sleeves of the shirt. "And I kept it. Don't look so horrified, Duchess. Life's not a fairy tale, and I'm no goddamn prince. You would have found that out for yourself sooner or later. I simply spared you the trouble."

"Thank you, but I believe I would have preferred to be kept in suspense at least until I had the chance to present you to my sister."

Oh God. Christiana. Leah felt a fresh emotion—panic—add to the clamoring inside. Her chest was rising and falling painfully. She could not imagine how she was going to pull herself together and go on pretending to be happily married for another moment, much less the entire length of Christiana's stay. Just the thought of smiling through endless balls and soirees with her deceitful, manipulative *husband* by her side, made her skin crawl. The man was beyond contemptible. He was a . . . a devil. If he thought that he could keep her there under false pretenses, use her for his own sordid amusement, blithely destroying whatever slim chance she might have had of someday marrying a decent man, and then send her away without a second thought . . .

She went cold inside.

He intended to send her away. He'd intended it all along. It made perfect sense when you considered that an absent wife was nearly as much protection as a dead one.

It was as if a dark shadow had moved over her, stretching from deep in her past to her most whimsical fantasies of the future. His message was clear. She wasn't needed or wanted there, and what she thought or felt about it did not matter.

Or so he thought.

It was true that experience was the best teacher. This was a heartache she recognized all too well. She knew exactly how to deal with this kind of pain, how to draw strength from it, how to contain it, and let it out to do its damage only when she was all alone, in the deepest hours of the night.

"Let me be certain I understand you," she said, her voice stiff and polite. "We are to continue as if last night never happened."

For just an instant his insouciant air seemed to falter. "If you prefer it that way. Personally, I have no objection to sharing a bed with you from time to time, provided it is not that one."

She ignored that last remark. "And Christiana will still be welcome to stay here?"

"Of course."

"And once she is wed, you will expect me to leave Raven House and return home."

"That's right."

"Wrong," she snapped. "I am not going anywhere, *Your Grace*. I will not be banished to the ends of the earth like some tired old nag that has served its purpose. No one, not you, not the King himself, no man, is ever going to send me away again."

"Sweet Jesus, Leah, no one is *sending* you anywhere."

"Good, then we understand each other." She turned to leave.

"You'll simply be going home, as agreed."

She turned back to slant him an incredulous look. "Oh, so the terms of our agreement matter when they suit your purposes?"

"All right, forget the damn agreement," he said, flushing and running his fingers through his hair. "This is what you said you wanted."

"I've changed my mind."

"But I thought you preferred life in Baumborough," he argued.

"So did I," she countered airily, "but it turns out I prefer it here. Whomever Chrissie marries, she will doubtless settle closer to London than Baumborough. Living here, I'll be able to see her and her children more often."

He paled. "Her *children*? You cannot seriously expect us to continue living under the same roof . . . permanently?"

"Of course not," she assured him, her smile silky. "Once Chrissie is wed, I shall naturally require a house of my own."

"In London?" he demanded loudly.

"Of course, in London. I do recall your offering me precisely that. A cozy little setup of my own, I believe is how you put it. It does not have to be anything grand," she hastened to add. "Certainly nothing on the scale of Raven House. A simple townhouse anywhere in Mayfair will suffice. With a carriage house, of course. And a garden would be especially lovely."

"You're mad." His face was no longer pale, but a more satisfying shade of red. "I cannot possibly set up my own wife as if she were my damn mistress."

"Of course you can. You can do anything you dare, remember? Don't look so horrified," she admonished, taunting him with his own words as she moved toward the door. "You got what you wanted, after all."

"And what is that?" he demanded, following.

"You seduced your own wife, a feat of great duplicity." She paused to eye him sardonically. "I'm assuming now that the entire portrait escapade was simply one more trick?" His stony silence told her all she needed to know. She sighed. "As I was saying, a feat of great duplicity and little impact, signifying nothing."

She reached for the brass knob.

"Signifying nothing?" he echoed harshly. "What the hell does that mean?"

"Exactly that. If you preclude the possibility of either love or children, then really, what's the point?"

"Pleasure," he asserted, catching her arm firmly. "Don't even try to deny that I gave you pleasure last night."

"I wouldn't dream of it. It was a very pleasant experience." She watched with relish as that faint praise ruffled his demeanor.

"Pleasant?" he growled.

"*Very* pleasant. I just do not believe it would be enough to satisfy me for a lifetime."

As she turned the knob, his hand slid down the silk sleeve of her robe and clamped over hers. "Too bad, Duchess. Because it is enough for me. It has to be."

"Why?" He was so close she could see flecks of gold in his blue eyes. "Why are you so afraid of love?"

He jerked his hand away as if she'd caught fire. "I am not *afraid* of love. I simply don't believe in it."

"Oh, please." She rolled her eyes. "Lie to yourself if it suits you, but I have no patience for it."

He chuckled, as if he found her patently ridiculous, but even in the shadows she could see the tension in him. "After everything else I've said to you this morning, why the hell would I bother to lie about something like this?"

"Because it's easier . . . or so you believe." She opened the door, and paused. "Once, while I was entertaining my friend's little boy for a few hours, he fell and cut his knee badly. He came running to me, sobbing, with his little hand clamped over his knee. Blood was running down his leg and it was obvious how much it hurt, but he would not take away his hand and let me see the wound. He was afraid to look, and even more afraid that if he let me touch him, it would hurt worse.

"I think you're like that little boy," she told him.

"You've been hurt badly, and you've convinced yourself that it is less painful to cover it up than face the truth squarely and heal."

"And what is the truth, Leah?" His eyes had darkened dangerously, sending a warning she heeded only insofar as she tightened her grip on the knob.

"That I do not know . . . exactly. But if you twisted my arm and stuck hot coals between my toes, I would have to say that it has something to do with Charlotte Bonnaire."

She moved quickly, closing the door behind her with a bang.

Seconds later there was a second, louder bang, as Adrian flung it open and it hit the wall.

He stood in the doorway, looking like a man with his self-control on a very short leash, and glared at her. "That is the second time you have thrown that woman's name at me."

He moved closer.

Leah stood her ground.

"You think you have me all figured out, don't you?" he asked in a soft, menacing voice. "Charlotte broke my heart and I'm still licking my wounds. It's as simple as that."

"Not at all," she replied. "Truthfully, I do not think there is anything simple about it. I believe you are the most complicated mess I've ever encountered."

"And you want to help me, is that it?" He didn't wait for her reply. Grabbing her hand, he drew her inexorably closer. "Let's do it, Duchess, let's look at my wounds together. That is what you want, isn't it? For me to bare my soul to you, so you can reclaim it from the devil and turn me into something worth hanging on to?"

She was shaking her head, trying to move away, but if he registered her desire to be free, he ignored it.

"I'll be a good little boy and show you where it hurts. Then you can kiss it and make it better."

"*I* cannot make anything better. You have to do that for yourself."

"But you can help. I know you can. What's more, I know how badly you want to. You lied when you said you were not a romantic. Only a dyed-in-the-wool romantic would believe a beautiful princess could fall in love with a hideously scarred man."

She refused to be goaded. "I know the difference between fantasy and reality."

"God, I hope not. If you're going to approach this realistically, I'm doomed. I was counting on you to produce a fairy godmother for me, or at the very least a spell of some sort. Actually, when you come right down to it, I'm so far gone, I need a bloody miracle, Duchess."

"Let me go."

"No. What's the matter, Leah? Changed your mind about helping? Don't you deal in lost causes?"

"I would never refuse to help anyone who truly wanted my help, but you obviously are not in the right frame of mind at the moment to even discuss it."

"Wrong. I am in exactly the right frame of mind. And it's the first time in ten years I have been." He eyed her mockingly. "I want to tell you things I've never told anyone. You're not going to turn me away and let me go on bleeding, are you, Duchess?"

Leah considered her options and didn't like any of them. She had no illusions that this was anything but another game to him, but if this was the first time he'd been willing to talk, even for the wrong reasons, it couldn't hurt to listen. Besides, who knew how he'd respond to being rebuffed? The last thing she wanted was for Christiana to arrive and find her in a state of open warfare with her new husband.

"If you want to talk, I will, of course, be glad to listen."

His smile was taut and derisive. "I knew you would. And just for the record, Charlotte did not break my heart so much as she ripped it from my chest and stomped on it."

He released her hand abruptly, looking startled that he had said even that much, as if the desire to unburden himself had been a threat he never had any real intention of following through on and he didn't know where to go from there.

Leah wouldn't have been surprised if he walked out. Instead he stalked to the fireplace and put his shoulder against the mantel. When he met her gaze he looked like himself again, haughty and invincible, and all she could think about was the pain locked behind all that pride, and wonder at what cost.

"Charlotte was not subtle, you see, but she was thorough to a fault. While she was at it, she paid a back-alley butcher to rip my unborn child from her womb and dispose of it as well."

Leah drew a deep, shuddering breath.

"She did this against your wishes?"

"Against my wishes?" he echoed savagely. "She did it behind my back. Do you think I would have allowed it if I had known?"

She shook her head. "No, I don't. I hardly know what to say. I surely understand now why you object to having her name brought up. What she did was unbelievably cruel. And this was a woman you once thought to marry?"

"I had every intention of marrying her, even before she told me about the baby." He shoved his hands in his pockets, his composure fraying. "Against my father's direct and very specific wishes, I might add."

"So he did not approve of her?"

"Approve?" He smiled sardonically. "He considered her a scheming opportunist, unfit to bear his grandson, and threatened to disown me."

"But you went ahead anyway? You must have loved her very much."

He nodded, and Leah felt a small twinge, which she knew was absurd.

"I was young and ignorant. I saw how my father and his friends lived, how they treated their wives, the women they were supposed to love, and decided I would never become that kind of hypocrite. I wanted something different, something more." His mouth curved slightly. "What I wanted was all-consuming passion."

"And did you find it?"

"I thought so. Charlotte was also a master of illusion. She was older than I, older than all the silly, suitable little flirts my parents were forever arranging for me to meet. She was experienced, a widow, and when it came to passion, she knew exactly what I wanted and how to give it to me."

"I see."

"Do you?" He looked doubtful. "I would have done anything for her," he went on, in a voice that held a very revealing tremor. "I would have battled dragons, waged wars, waited forever." He gave a short, ugly laugh. "Hell, it felt like forever the day I waited at the altar for her. I was telling the truth about that as well."

"She just left you standing there? No message? No word of explanation?"

"Oh, there was a message, eventually. A note from my father, summoning me to Charlotte's apartment. I ran all the way there, wondering the whole time who could have told him about what was supposed to have been a secret ceremony, wondering even more what the hell he was doing at Charlotte's. His style would have been to halt the ceremony by marching down the center aisle and dragging me away."

"There was no answer when I knocked, so I did what anyone would do, what he had known I would do. I used my key and walked in . . . all the way into the bedchamber, where my father and my soon-to-be-bride were having a rousing old time in bed together."

Leah's legs nearly buckled, she was so shocked. She hadn't known what to expect, but definitely not *that.*

His father, his own father. What a horrid, unspeakable blow it must have been. She understood what that kind of sudden, absolute betrayal felt like. Even now she could smell it and taste it and she remembered how, at the most unexpected moments, the bitterness could suddenly rise up and make you gag.

And she knew that nothing anyone said or did could make it go away until you were ready to let go of it. Still, she longed to take him in her arms and comfort him.

"Adrian, I'm so very sorry. I cannot imagine anything worse."

"Can't you?" He laughed disparagingly. "What I did next was worse by far." He hesitated and seemed to withdraw to some place deep inside himself.

"I crawled," he said, in a voice she had to strain to hear. "I crawled and I begged her not to leave me. I still thought I was holding the trump card, you see—the baby. The baby no one knew about but us. The baby she was carrying even as she lay naked beneath my father. *My* baby. Still I wanted her, and I wanted our child. You have to marry me, I said to her when nothing else I said had swayed her, you're carrying my baby. And she said . . ."

He clutched his forehead with both palms, his eyes

tightly shut. He swept them with the heels of his hands before lifting his head again. "She said to me, as I stood there like an idiot in my fine wedding clothes, she said, not anymore. Not anymore I'm not."

He made a sound, not quite a laugh or a curse. It was a sound Leah could imagine coming from a drowning man.

The urge to touch him was overwhelming, but she was afraid, afraid to approach, afraid to say the wrong thing, afraid to say nothing.

"And that," he said before she had made up her mind which fear was strongest, "was the day I became my father's son in earnest. Oh, it took a few stiff drinks to clear my senses and make me realize it was all for the best. But my father did what he set out to do. He proved to me that Charlotte was not the woman I thought she was, and that I was not the man I wanted to be."

He waved off her effort to protest.

"Needless to say, I embraced my birthright. I proved to him that I could outdrink, outgamble, and outwhoremonger anyone. And I promised myself that I would never again allow anyone to have that kind of power over me. I would never again let myself need anything enough to beg for it. I vowed I would never even let myself want something unless I knew the price up front, and was willing to pay it."

"Oh Adrian, I can only imagine how enraged you must have felt . . . and how helpless. What I cannot imagine is why any woman would do such a thing. If she was carrying your child and you were willing to marry her in spite of your father's threats, why—"

"Sweet Jesus, Leah, you are even more naive than I was. She did it because she was for sale, and I was not the high bidder. My father was."

She shook her head stubbornly. "That can't be

right. I can perhaps understand how your father might pay her to break your betrothal, but the other . . . Surely he would not have paid her to—"

"Kill my child? His own grandchild? Yes, he paid for it all," he said baldly. "Couldn't risk any troublesome bastards cropping up when I finally came to my senses and married a woman who *could* produce a suitable heir. And he paid through the nose, if I know Charlotte at all. How did she put it when I asked her why she did it? Oh, yes. She said she was sorry—sorry, mind you, as if she had stepped on my toe while dancing—but that she had to look to her own best interests. Life was short, she told me, and expensive."

"My God. What kind of woman—"

"What kind?" he interrupted harshly. "A woman like every other woman in the world when she's found someone willing to meet her price. For women like Charlotte, the price is measured in pounds and shillings. For women like my mother and all those countless other wives who smile and look the other way, the price is steeper, measured in titles and prestige and position. That's one more lesson my father taught me—every woman has her price."

He cupped her chin and tipped her face up to his, his gaze hard and flat. "And I refuse to pay yours."

14

Adrian glanced up from the papers he had been staring at for over an hour and stared out the window instead. He was holding a list, compiled by Cyril Gates, of details he must attend to before plans for the House of Birds could progress. The venture, which had once promised to be so entertaining, seemed only tedious today. As did everything else he touched. Everything that was not Leah.

He tossed the list aside and leaned back in his chair. Through the open window came the sound of a shovel working the earth.

What the devil was she having planted now? he wondered, and where? Between the fountain and the new shrubbery, he'd have sworn there wasn't sufficient space remaining for a blade of grass. By leaning forward, he could easily have seen for himself what was being done, but he didn't bother. The garden was a vexing reminder of the changes taking place all around him. If she had her way, she would leave her mark on everything in the place, including him.

A knock sounded on the library door, and he called "Enter" without bothering to turn his chair around.

"Your Grace, a messenger has arrived from Baumborough. He says it is urgent he speak to you right away."

That did bring him around. The only thing he was expecting from Baumborough was the delivery of one troublesome, no doubt senseless, sister-in-law. She would have to be, to permit a gooey-eyed romantic like Leah to oversee the most significant and misguided occurrence of her life.

"Send him in," he ordered, then glanced sharply at the figure in the doorway. "Phelps?" His eyes narrowed as he took in the man's immaculate, well-cut blue and gold jacket and pantaloons. White stockings and black boots as highly polished as any he'd seen outside of a military review completed the outfit. "What are you doing in that getup?"

"The Duchess arranged for new livery for the entire staff," Phelps replied, squaring his shoulders with obvious pride.

Adrian's lip curled. "A bit overdressed for the stables, aren't you? And why are you in here announcing messengers?"

"It's part of my new duties," he explained.

"New duties?" A quiver of suspicion worked its way along Adrian's spine. "Where is Thorne?"

"In the kitchen."

"What in God's name is he doing there?"

"He relieved Snake, so he could take over the garden from Mannington, who is now in charge of the stables. And I," he concluded, with a precise bow, "am the new major domo. At your service, Your Grace."

"Lucky me," drawled Adrian. "And just whose brainstorm was this?"

Phelps looked puzzled. "Why, yours, sir. The Duchess assured us you had evaluated our individual . . ."

He didn't bother to listen to the rest. There was no need. If his manservant was cooking, the cook gardening and the groundsman running the stables, who else but his conniving Duchess could possibly be behind it? He had a mind to order them all back where they belonged, but he refused to give her the satisfaction of knowing she could get to him in any way.

He had endured betrayal, bayonet wounds, and treks across bloody battlefields, and he would, by God, endure her. It's not as if it would last forever. As soon as he had the sister out of his home, he would find a way to make Leah see it was in her best interest to leave. And not simply to remove herself to a townhouse right under his nose, where she would be a constant reminder of all he could never have, an ever-present temptation that he was not at all sure he could resist.

When the time came, he would make her see that she belonged back home in Baumborough. Meanwhile, let her turn the house inside out, install cupids outside his window and serve dinner on the roof if she pleased. Let her change every last wall hanging and floorboard in the place. She would not change him.

"Don't just stand there," he barked at Phelps. "If you're going to be major domo, get to it. Send the man in."

Seconds later, a young man looking bedraggled and road-weary hurried into the room. Adrian recognized him as one of the footmen who had gone along with the carriage. Clutching his cap to his chest, he bowed hastily.

"Your Grace, I am just back from Baumborough with news for you."

"Has Lady Christiana been detained?"

"Not exactly, sir. She won't be coming at all. She's eloped."

"Eloped?" Adrian jerked to his feet. Sweet Jesus, eloped. "Are you certain?"

"Yes, Your Grace. When we first got there, there was all manner of confusion in the household, but no one was letting on why. I don't think they could believe the young miss had just upped and offed that way, and for certain they did not want any outsiders knowing what she was up to."

"Then how do you know she eloped?"

"Quigley finally had it up to here with their runaround," he said, referring to the driver and indicating a spot high on his neck. "He had a sharp word or two with the woman in charge, making it plain Your Grace would hold her personally responsible for any more delay, and she coughed up the whole truth, how the girl and this fellow had sneaked off together in the dead of night. A bunch of men from town went off to Gretna Green after them, but it was no use.

"She left this behind though." He turned his hat over and pulled a paper from inside the brim. "For the Duchess."

Adrian took the folded note and glanced at it. It was addressed to Leah and sealed with the initials *CS*. Christiana Stretton.

"Eloped." He shook his head at the sheer irony of it. "Do we know whom she eloped with?"

"A fellow by the name of St. Leger. He's the nephew of a neighbor, not a bad chap, according to the locals. Raises sheep, they say."

Sheep. He snorted. So much for Little Miss Fussy's search for a debonair, well-connected bridegroom for her sister. Someone ought to have a word with her about the best-laid plans.

He glanced up sharply. "There's no chance you're mistaken? Or that there might still be time to stop them?"

The messenger shook his head. "None at all, sir."

"Good. That is to say, good job in relaying the news with such haste." He clapped the young man on the shoulder. "Now go have yourself a hot meal and a bath."

While I, he gloated silently, celebrate with a good cigar.

It appeared he was going to have his way much sooner than he'd anticipated. There would be nothing to hold Leah there now. In fact, he decided, cutting the cigar tip, it would not surprise him if she chose to be on her way home at once upon hearing the news. God forbid the young couple begin their married life together without her there to choose their bedclothes for them and tell them which side of the bed to climb out of in the morning.

This was perfect. The coup de grâce. He had played her game, more or less by the rules, and he had won. Winner take all, that was his new motto.

He flicked a match, imagining Leah's reaction to the news. He could see it now. She would be stunned. And furious. And brokenhearted.

The image that suddenly floated before him was like a steel fist in his gut. He shook the match out and dropped the cigar onto the desk unlit. Bloody hell. All he could see was the look on her face that morning. He'd hurt her, he knew. It had not been intentional, but it had been necessary. Inevitable, in fact. Just the same, the sight of tears in her eyes had battered his heart.

Had just one of those pooled tears made its way

down her cheek, he would have been done in, but she had not allowed any to spill. She was too proud. And too stubborn. He prayed that same fierce will would protect her now. How many disappointing blows could she be expected to take before her spirit was crushed? Before her smile was extinguished for good?

Her sister's note lay where he had tossed it. Seeing it, he felt a sudden flash of anger at this thoughtless chit he'd never even met, an ungrateful girl with so little regard for her sister's feelings and the sacrifices she'd made on her behalf. Had she no care that it was for her sake Leah had made the trip to London in the first place?

With a twinge of remorse, he acknowledged that it was also for her sake that Leah had gone along with his botched scheme, putting herself in the untenable position of being a wife to a man who did not want one. He no longer took pleasure in any of it, or felt any satisfaction, only weariness and relief that it would all soon be over. For both of them.

One thing he was most definitely not looking forward to was telling Leah the truth, that her most cherished hopes and dreams had been shattered. What the hell was she thinking, pinning all her hopes and dreams on someone else?

She would deny it, of course, but that's what she had done. A fool could see that the whole scenario—the perfect London season, disgustingly proper bridegroom, a passel of brats, and happily ever after—was the product of her overzealous imagination. The fact that her sister had eloped, with a farmer no less, suggested she'd had her sights set in a different direction all along.

It was Leah who longed for romance and a church filled with flowers and a noble prince to sweep her off her feet with promises of forever after. What's more, she deserved it. And, thanks to him, she would never have any of those things.

"Would it help to talk about it?"

Leah turned abruptly. "Michael. You startled me."

She and her distant cousin were standing in the garden of Trevor Place, the magnificent brick mansion that had been her childhood home. Returning there for the first time in ten years was proving to be more emotional than she had anticipated. Curiosity had prompted her to accept her aunt's invitation to tea. When Michael had appeared at Raven House to escort her, she had, in the wake of her disastrous confrontation with Adrian that morning, nearly canceled.

"My apologies for startling you," Michael said. "I was simply worried when I saw you slip off alone and thought I would check to be sure you were all right."

"I'm fine." She did her best to form a smile.

"Perhaps, but you still have not answered my question. Would it help to talk about it?"

"About what?"

"Whatever has stolen your smile this afternoon."

His comment was a relief. Since he had noticed her unhappiness, she felt no obligation to go on trying to hide it from him. "I suppose finding myself here again, after so many years of missing everything about this place, has me feeling a bit melancholy."

"At the risk of being disagreeable, might I be allowed to point out that you were melancholy before we arrived?"

"You're much too observant," she told him drily.

"Only because I am so concerned about you," he replied. "Are you certain it's only the surroundings that have you on edge?"

She hesitated only briefly. Without Christiana or any of her friends from home to confide in, she needed someone with whom she could talk candidly, and it was already easy to envision Michael becoming that person. Though they had spoken only on occasions when their paths crossed socially and during his brief visits to Raven House, she felt safe and comfortable around him.

"No, it is more than that. Oh, being here stirs memories to be sure, both good and bad, but that is all they are—memories." She lifted her gaze to the window of what had once been her chamber. "Like the toys I once played with and the lessons I learned here, my connection to this house is a thing of the past."

"And it is the future that worries you now, is that right?"

"Did I say I was worried?"

"You didn't have to."

She slanted him a rueful glance. "You're right. Again. I wish I had taken your first warning more seriously."

"Why?" he asked sharply. "Has Raven done something—"

She shook her head. Raven had done something all right; he had stopped her foolish heart dead in its tracks by making it clear that she would never mean anything more to him than a convenient shield to hide behind. She could hardly indict him for it however; she had been given ample warning as to what sort of man he was, by his reputation, by Michael, and by Adrian himself.

"It is not so much what he has done," she told Michael, "as what he *is*. Oh, you were so right to tell me to be on guard. I have learned the hard way that Adrian is much more like his father than I wanted to believe." Her gaze fell to the flagstones beneath her feet. "And, though it shames me to admit it, I am as much like my mother as I feared."

"What do you mean by saying such a thing?"

"Only that the similarities are so obvious I was a fool to ignore them." She glanced cautiously at the French doors leading from the drawing room, where a dozen or so guests were gathered for tea.

"The circumstances surrounding my marriage to Adrian are . . . unusual, and complicated," she revealed, "far too complicated to go into here. But you may take my word for it that he intentionally misled me, just as his father probably misled and used my mother. Raven men are of a breed interested in women for one thing and one thing only.

"It is my misfortune to share my mother's weakness in that regard," she continued, with a mixture of anger and regret. She would not be saying so much if she wasn't so upset or had no need to unburden herself. "In spite of your warning and all my own good intentions, I fell victim to a man's wicked, practiced charm just as she did."

"Now see here," exclaimed Michael, his silver brows gathered in a perplexed frown. "You're suggesting that your mother was a . . ." He colored profusely. "And a victim besides? Dava? That's preposterous."

Leah was indignant. "How can you doubt that she was victimized? By my father, by Adrian's, by Sheffield, and God knows how many other men."

"Hold your tongue, young lady. I will not listen to you speak of your mother that way, in spite of the fact that the whole debacle made victims of you and your sister. If Dava had a weakness, it was her irrepressibly romantic nature."

"You're very charitable," she countered, her expression brittle. "I have heard her described less delicately."

"Than you heard wrong," he snapped. "No doubt much of it from the Countess of Slander in there." He jerked his head toward the house, where her Aunt Millicent was holding court. "She was always jealous of Dava, and with cause, I can't deny that. Your mother was everything Millicent was not, and could never hope to be. She was beautiful and sensual and so exuberant she could brighten your whole day with a look and a word . . . the same way you can, dear Leah."

"That is exactly how I remember her," Leah conceded, a tremor in her soft voice. "But there must have been another side of her, the side that drew her to seek attention from men, the wrong kind of attention."

"No, no." He shook his head forcefully. "There were any number of men who paid attention to your mother, that is true enough, but she did not *seek* them out in the manner you are implying. Men pay attention to women like Dava. It has been that way since Adam bit the apple, my dear girl. The most natural thing in the world."

"Perhaps. But in turn she—"

"She smiled," he interrupted, his own mouth curling upward. "She glowed, she sparkled like the fabulous jewel that she was. Again, all very natural. Why, I've seen you do the same when men pay court to you, and when they trip over their own tongues trying to impress you."

"They don't."

He laughed. "They do. I've noticed. Your husband notices as well. He glowers. Have you not seen him, lurking at the edge of the dance floor whenever he is forced to relinquish you to another man's arms? To be truthful, it is the sentiment behind all that glowering that gives me hope there might be more to the man than I once thought."

"You misread his sentiment," she said glumly. "If he is glowering, it is most likely at me."

He gave a sympathetic chuckle. "Poor child, you do have a lot to learn. In that way, at least, you are different from your mother. Dava had a highly refined sense of her own power, and she was not above wielding it to get what she wanted."

"But she didn't get what she wanted," Leah protested. "She ended up being banished."

"Banished?" He cocked an eyebrow. "I suppose some may have seen it that way. Your father was rightfully enraged when he discovered her with another man. He told her to leave, if that's what she wanted, and Dava went."

"Because she had no choice."

"Because she wanted to leave. Trust me, it would have taken more than an order from old Aldwick to drive Dava away if she did not wish to go."

Leah was more confused than ever. She tried to reconcile what Michael was saying with truths she had accepted—and chafed under—for years. "The fact is he didn't want her here anymore. Or us either. Because she was flagrant in her unfaithfulness. And because she had failed to give him a son."

He looked aghast. "Who told you all this?"

She shrugged. Who had told her? "It's all mostly bits and pieces. Some things Mother told me, some I overheard at the time, servants' gossip . . . and Aunt Millicent spoke with me at length the day we left."

"Oh, I'm sure she did." He sounded disgusted. "You were little more than a child at the time," he reminded her gently. "Confused and hurt, devastated to be leaving the only home you knew. Isn't it possible you may have confused or misinterpreted some of what you heard?"

"I did not confuse or misinterpret my father's actions," she said hotly. "They speak for themselves. What he did proved he did not love my mother or us."

Michael's gaze grew anguished in response to the undisguised heartache in her voice. "You're wrong. I am certainly no apologist for your father, but I believe he did love you and Christiana. It was simply easier for him to be free of any reminders of his greatest, most public failure."

"If that is supposed to make me feel less resentful for the years he left us in exile, without so much as a word or a visit, it does not."

"Of course it doesn't," he agreed. "But you have proven you are strong enough to rise above it. As for your mother, I partially agree with you. Your father never loved her the way she needed to be loved. That kind of passion was just not in him."

"Then why did he marry her in the first place?"

He gave a philosophical shrug. "He saw her and was dazzled, and like every other man who fell under her spell, he wanted to possess her. I suspect it was not until he had won her that he realized he had taken hold of fire . . . a fire much hotter than he knew how to control.

"But Raven knew," he went on, "your father-in-law, I mean. During the time they were together, he knew exactly how to handle all those lovely flames that made Dava the woman she was. Now those two would have made a fine match, but it was too late, of course. By the time they met, they were both already wed to others."

"So he used her," declared Leah, the accusation against the father simmering with the full heat of her anger at the son.

"He *loved* her," Michael corrected. "Quite desperately, as I recall."

"Then why was she running away with another man?"

"Because Dava wanted a new life, a different life from the frivolous, duplicitous one she was leading here." His eyes misted. "She planned to take her girls and sail for America to make a fresh start, so you could all live a life that was simple but happy. That was her dream and she was brave enough and reckless enough to risk everything to make it come true."

"And Raven was not," concluded Leah.

"Let's just say he was not a man to be ruled by his heart, and he was wise enough to understand that she was and wished her only the best."

"Ha! Knowing his son as I do, I doubt the man was capable of considering anyone else's feelings but his own."

"You're wrong," Michael said quietly.

"How can you be so sure?"

"Because I knew Dava. And," he added, reaching into his coat pocket, "Because had he not loved her and cared about her welfare, he would never have given her this to take with her."

He carefully loosened the cord securing a black velvet pouch and poured into his hand a single strand of diamonds set in platinum, from which hung a ruby the size of a robin's egg, surrounded by more diamonds.

Leah caught her breath. She had never seen anything like it, so simple and spectacular at once. "Is it real?"

Michael laughed. "Oh, it is very real. It's called the Sun and Stars, and it was a gift from Charles II to one of your husband's more infamous ancestors, payment for services rendered, according to the legend. The nature of those services is probably best left to the imagination."

Leah was hardly listening. Awestruck, she ran her fingertip over the brilliant gem. Touching it produced an eerie feeling inside her, a sense of connection with the past, with her mother, and beyond.

"Take it," he urged. "It's yours."

"Mine?" she exclaimed, drawing her hand away as if the stone were as hot as its namesake.

"I can't think of anyone with better claim to it. It's been in your husband's family for generations, and then was given without strings to your mother."

Still unable to take her eyes off it, she asked, "How do you happen to have it in your possession?"

"A few weeks before her death, Dava had it delivered to me, with a note asking that I personally and discreetly return it to the Duke. At the time, I simply thought she had decided she did not want any reminders of the past." His sigh held a heavy edge of self-recrimination. "Since then I've come to believe that she was close to giving up, accepting that Sheffield was not going to come and that her dream was doomed, and did not want this to fall into the wrong hands once she was . . ." His shoulders slumped. "If only . . ."

He broke off and Leah found herself patting his arm to comfort him. "You could not have known."

"I did try to return it to Raven, as she requested, but for weeks the man was constantly unavailable. I heard from others he was embroiled in serious problems involving his son . . . that would be your husband," he said, as if putting that piece into the puzzle for the first time. "I don't know what the problem was."

Leah nodded, but said nothing. She knew. It was ten years ago that her mother had died, and ten years ago that Adrian had walked in and found his father with the woman he loved. No wonder the duke had been *unavailable.* He was busy arranging for the sacrifice of his unborn grandchild and destroying his son's life.

"After her death, I lost interest in giving it back to him. Out of spite, perhaps, telling myself that if he had handled things differently she might still be alive. Foolish, really. I tucked this away in my safe, not quite certain what I would do with it.

"Then I saw you," he said, his smile wistful, "and Dava in you, and I knew that when the moment was right, I would return the Sun and Stars to its rightful owner. Your mother never had the chance to wear it, but it is said to bring the wearer love and luck. May it always be so for you," he whispered, pressing it into her trembling hands.

"Leah? Where *have* you disappeared to?"

At the sound of her aunt's shrill voice, Leah groaned and hastily wiped the back of her hand across her eyes, where tears had welled for what seemed the hundredth time that day.

Michael quickly stood between her and the door to the house, while she hurriedly dropped the pouch with the necklace inside into her reticule.

"Take a moment to pull yourself together," he urged. "I'll occupy the dragon."

Leah was grateful to be left alone, though she was certain it was going to take far longer than a moment to sort through everything Michael had told her. Listening had been painful, but heartening as well. If he was right, her mother had not been the victim of her own impulsive passion, but rather she had made a brave, albeit reckless, grasp for love and happiness. And she had failed.

Leah sighed wistfully. She could never condone

what her mother had done. Too many innocent people had suffered as a result. But she at last felt she understood her better, and that brought its own kind of peace.

Perhaps she and her mother were alike after all, she mused, no longer finding the notion a cause for concern. Adrian had accused her of being a romantic. Michael had described her mother as irrepressibly so. Suddenly, it was very easy to imagine her mother as the heroine in one of her stories. Olivia, for one. Beautiful, headstrong, reckless Olivia, willing to risk everything in her quest for true love.

A shiver of awareness ran along her spine as it occurred to her how accurately that described yet another person. Adrian too had been willing to risk everything, defy his father and forsake his birthright, to be with the woman he loved. Or rather, the woman he *thought* he loved.

Granted, it was bizarre to think of the Wicked Lord Raven as an irrepressible romantic, and he would no doubt recoil at the very suggestion. But the more she mulled it over, the more convinced she was that her husband and her mother had a great deal in common. Both of them had loved unwisely and too well. Both had seen their daring hopes for love destroyed.

And something else—both of them were loved by her.

The realization that she had fallen in love with Adrian came like an avalanche. It washed over her, first with shock, then with a profuse sense of inevitability and rightness. She was meant to love him. Destined for it. All the curious twists and turns in their respective paths that had finally landed them together had to be proof of that. She had tried so hard to hide from the truth. Now the wall she had built for her own protection vanished, and all the feelings and longings she had been denying even to herself poured forth.

For the first time since Adrian had stalked from her chamber that morning, she allowed herself to truly think about his revelation. It occurred to her that the reason he had worked so hard to keep her from seeing past his anger to what was in his heart, was because his heart was still vulnerable. That was why he lived inside a shell of an existence, trusting no one, loving no one, and making certain no one got close enough to love him.

Hope grew inside her. She had been unable to save her mother, but she had every intention of saving Adrian from himself, whether he liked it or not.

"Leah, my dear, where *are* you dashing off to now? Not planning a French leave, I hope," joked her aunt.

A hasty, unannounced departure was precisely what Leah had planned. She had come directly from the garden to the center hall, in search of Michael.

"I swear, I have not seen you for longer than a few moments all afternoon," the countess added.

"I'm sorry, Aunt Millicent," she said, still looking around for Michael. "But—"

"No need to be sorry." Her aunt took her firmly by the hand and led her into the drawing room. "Now that my other guests have all gone, we can settle in for a nice long, cozy chat. More tea?"

Leah felt trapped. She did not want more tea, or more silly little sandwiches or biscuits with chocolate. And she most definitely did not want to settle in for a chat, cozy or otherwise. All she wanted was to go to Adrian. Right that instant.

"Actually," she said, resisting her aunt's efforts to nudge her into a chair, "I must leave."

"You can't," exclaimed the countess, then attempted to soften the sharp command with a coy smile. "That is to say, my dear Duchess, that I have so been looking forward to speaking privately with you, and now we have our chance."

"Another time, perhaps. I have a sudden headache." It was *almost* true. She would surely have a headache if she had to endure a private tête-à-tête with this woman who suddenly seemed more like an octopus than a dragon.

"How awful. Perhaps you ought to lie down. I'll ring for—"

Leah clutched the small bell as her aunt lifted it from the table. "No. Really. It's not that severe. Yet. I simply want to make it home before it gets worse."

"Since you're determined to leave," her aunt snapped, "I'll just have to speak my piece now, before Michael returns and calls for his carriage."

"About what?" Leah inquired warily.

Her aunt plucked at the white lace trim on her cap, then knit her fingers together in a tight ball at her waist. "Actually, it's a request I have to make of you. I want to ask you to intercede with your husband on your uncle's behalf. The earl has submitted a business proposal for his consideration and he—"

"I'm sorry, Aunt, but I do not involve myself in my husband's business dealings. I would urge you to do the same. Now, if you would be so kind . . ."

"We are ruined. Busted," her aunt announced baldly.

Leah stared at her, wondering if she had heard right.

"I thought that would get your attention."

"How is that possible?" she demanded. "The Aldwick estates are among the most extensive—"

"That's the problem. The estates *are* extensive and elaborate and *expensive.* The upkeep alone has drained every last penny we possess." She glanced around and lowered her voice to a whisper. "We are quite out at the heels, do you understand?"

"I do not recall money ever before being a problem. What of the income from the estates?"

"Income, ha." She shook her head. "It's dwindled steadily over the years. With your mother and you girls gone, your father seemed to lose interest, and it never quite picked up. Your uncle tries, Lord knows, but he doesn't have the gift for turning an easy sovereign, as some do." She sniffed. "The only venture of his that ever proved a plum was his shipbuilding arrangement with Raven. *That's* what he's proposed again this time. It's sure to be a money-maker for all involved, *if* you could get the Duke to reverse his decision."

"You mean to say he's already turned my uncle down?" she asked, amazed at the woman's audacity.

Her aunt waved her hand. "A preliminary decision, that's all it was. Surely, if you were to approach him . . ."

"As I said, I do not involve myself in matters of business."

"What about matters of family?" Her aunt pinned her with an accusing gaze. "Do you involve yourself in those, *Your Grace*?"

Leah looked away with a small, incredulous laugh. This really was unbelievable, that Aunt Millicent, of all people, should be lecturing her on family loyalty. It was beyond laughable, it was absurd.

"Not that you have anything to worry about, in the situation you landed yourself in," the countess continued. "But think of your sister."

She quickly brought her gaze around. "Christiana's inheritance is not in any way tied to the estates."

"No," her aunt conceded, "but just think of the

scandal if word of our situation gets out, as it surely will if something is not done . . . and soon."

Leah shrugged. "I hardly think the unfortunate circumstances of relations she has not seen in a decade will adversely affect Christiana's prospects, especially when she has the full backing and support of the Duke of Raven."

Her aunt squirmed, as if Leah's statement had settled like a burn under her chemise. "You may be right. But my Jenny cannot claim the same advantage."

"Jenny is not my concern." She felt a twinge of conscience, which she tried to conceal by fixing her aunt with a stare worthy of a duchess.

"You don't mean that," the other woman protested, touching Leah's arm lightly, though her own gaze remained beady and intent. "You were never a selfish girl, or a mean-spirited one."

"Selfish?" Leah exclaimed. "Mean-spirited? You dare use those words to me after the treatment my sister and I have received at your hands all these years? You dare to ask me for a favor, when each and every time I wrote to you with a request, for permission to visit for the holidays or even a simple word of encouragement when I let it be known we would be in town this season, you turned me down cold? This has nothing to do with being selfish or mean-spirited," she declared, raising her hand in her fervor to make her point, "and everything to do with . . ."

The word froze on her tongue.

Justice. Adrian's brand of justice, the kind that annihilated everything in its path, guilty and innocent alike, and left the landscape so barren that nothing could survive in its wake.

She had been intending to rush home to Adrian, to nurture whatever tenderness was left in him and help him heal the deeply buried wound that when poked, caused him to lash out the way he had that morning. How could she ask him to put aside the pain and the injustices of the past, if she was not willing to do the same?

Her aunt had taken advantage of her silence to resume her appeal. She was wasting her time. There was no argument and no amount of reasoning that could bend Leah to her will. Her days of being bullied were over. It was completely her decision whether to let go of the past, or carry it with her forever. Just as it was her decision whether to remain in London or return to an empty house in Baumborough, whether to be a wife to Adrian or retreat inside a shell of her own.

"I cannot make any promises," she said, cutting the other woman off mid-sentence. "But I shall speak to Raven on my uncle's behalf."

15

Something was different. Adrian sensed it the second the front door closed behind him. He stood still and listened to the silence. He glanced around Raven House's marble entrance hall. Everything appeared as usual, only a little brighter. He had never realized the crystal chandelier overhead had quite so many facets, all of them now twinkling like clusters of diamonds.

Not different, missing. That was it. Something was missing. He took another, closer look around. Dust, he thought triumphantly. There wasn't any, anywhere. Not on the floors or furnishings or glass lamps, of which there seemed to be so many more than he recalled, all of them aglow. That soft gray film, which had served to tone down color and texture and make everything just a little easier on the eye, was gone.

He sniffed the air and discovered it was different too. How was he expected to deal with a woman who could change the very air a man breathed? he thought irritably.

Lemon oil. That was the scent, he decided, thinking it very likely also accounted for the blinding glare coming off the carved walnut banister. Hovering just beneath the lemon oil was another scent, this one spicy and very appealing. His mouth watered. Whatever it was, it definitely was not mutton, and by his calculations, tonight was mutton night. What the hell was going on?

He started to call for Thorne and then remembered that Thorne had been reassigned to the kitchen. The head groom was now the manservant in charge of the household. Or rather, the *major domo,* he thought, with a sneer. He opened his mouth to bellow for Phelps.

"Yes, Your Grace?" came the response before he had made a sound.

Adrian gave a jerk. "Damnation, man, where the hell did you appear from?"

"There, sir." Phelps indicated a spot by the stairs. "I heard the door close and came to stand at the ready until you called for me."

"But I didn't call."

"I anticipated your intent, Your Grace."

"Well, don't," snapped Adrian. "It gives me the damn shudders. I'll call when I want you." Thorne had never appeared until he was summoned, he thought with new fondness for the old coot, and sometimes not even then.

Phelps bowed his head. "As you wish, sir. Though the most expedient means of summoning assistance would be to use the bells." He indicated the brocade bellpull nearby.

"It would indeed, except that fully half the bells do not function properly."

"They do now, Your Grace."

Adrian bit back an oath. "How very . . . efficient. Has the Duchess returned?"

"Yes, sir. She is in her chamber. She left word to request you kindly join her there as soon as you arrive home."

He glanced up to the place where the wide staircase curved into the darkness above. Recalling the mood of their last encounter, he decided he would prefer to meet her on neutral territory.

"Please inform the Duchess that I would have her join me for dinner," he said.

"Madam has already arranged for dinner to be served in her chamber," Phelps informed him.

Ah, still pouting, he thought.

"Dinner for two," the servant added.

Then again, maybe she wasn't pouting. Even so, he had hardly expected to be invited back to her chamber until hell had frozen over, and even then not for an intimate dinner for two. What in blazes was the woman up to now?

There were three of them in the room, he realized as soon as he was welcomed inside the chamber by Leah herself. Him, the Duchess and The Bed. The covers had been turned back to reveal a lacy nest, which seemed to dominate the room. Certainly it was dominating his thoughts, and, the longer he thought about it, the more he came to understand that there were three of them there *only* if you did not count the gown she was wearing.

Clearly not intended to see the light of day, the low-cut chemise was sheer and clingy and radiated a presence all its own. It seemed to be no color at all until she moved. Then it became a muted, silvery explosion of every color in the damn rainbow, caressing her all over and driving him to distraction.

The blasted candles only made it worse, he decided. Dozens of them had been placed around the room, their light bathing her skin with a warm glow, making her look like a soft, ripe peach just begging to be devoured. This time when his mouth watered it had nothing to do with the aroma seeping from the silver domed lids on the serving table.

He had to hand it to her, this was a very effective countermove. But was it intended as a taunt or an invitation? It did not matter, Adrian told himself firmly. Whatever her motive, this languorous mood could not last. As soon as Leah heard what he had come to say, the fire in the hearth would not be the only thing shooting off sparks.

"What is all this?" he inquired, lifting one lid to reveal slices of rare beef, fresh asparagus with cream sauce and tiny white potatoes speckled with parsley. It was a shame he would not be there long enough to eat.

"Dinner," she replied, lifting another cover. "To tease your appetite beforehand, there is also Russian caviar, Spanish olives, and these delightful little Bolognese sausages." She picked one up with her fingers and eyed him enticingly. "Shall I feed you?"

He could almost feel the beads of sweat popping out on his forehead. His appetite was not the only thing being teased. He shook his head and slipped Christiana's note from his pocket, lest he forget his purpose for being there.

"I can wait," he said, his tone straining for credibility.

Leah smiled knowingly. "At least have some wine." She poured a glass and handed it to him. "I believe it is a particular favorite of yours."

He tasted the full-bodied red and nodded.

"I dismissed the servants so I could serve you myself this evening," she told him. "I hope you don't mind."

Mind being alone with her in that dress? Within an easy tumble of that bed? Sipping his favorite wine and nibbling spicy sausages from her long, elegant fingers?

"Not at all," he replied smoothly. "But tell me, is Thorne really responsible for all this?"

She nodded. "I discovered a week or so ago that he was a far better cook than poor Snake would ever be, but tonight he has amazed even me."

"And to think I've been forcing down mutton two times a week for years."

"That is entirely your own fault," she chided, making it sound more like a compliment. "All you had to do was open your eyes and see the potential all around you."

"Perhaps I liked things the way they were. Did you ever stop to consider that?"

"No," she answered. "But if that is the case, I shall ring and have a plate of mutton brought for you immediately."

He grasped her hand as she reached for the bellpull. "That won't be necessary."

It seemed foolhardy to stand on principle when you had no idea when the next decent meal would come along. And it occurred to him that Leah might take the news of the elopement better on a full stomach.

Without removing her hand from his, she laughed up at him. "Admit it, Adrian. You like the changes I have made."

"I will admit to liking what I see under those lids better than mutton, does that satisfy you?"

"No." Her smile softened seductively. "Is that the only thing you see that you like, Your Grace?"

He shook his head, taking the bait willingly, losing himself in the mysterious green pools of her eyes.

"I like this," he said, running his hand over the filmy wrapper she wore over the chemise. "And this . . ." He trailed one fingertip down the length of her throat and hooked the center of the neckline, drawing it lower, exposing the upper swells of her breasts. "And I like these very, very . . ."

As he spoke, he raised his other hand to share in the bounty and from the corner of his eye he saw he was still holding the note from her sister.

"Damn," he muttered, and froze.

"What is it? Is something the matter?"

"No. Yes." Dropping his hands to his sides, he took a step away from her. "There is something I must discuss with you and there is no sense in delaying any longer."

"What is it?" she asked, her tone wary.

He clutched the note more tightly, hating the damage he was about to do. Forcing himself to look her in the eye, he said, "A messenger arrived this morning . . . from Baumborough."

Her face lit up. "With news of Christiana? Do you know when she will be arriving?" Noting his expression, her own became shadowed. "Oh dear, nothing has happened to her, has it?"

"No, nothing has happened *to* her," he assured her and watched her relax, trusting him, believing him. "It's just that she . . ." He tightened both fists around the blasted note, crushing it the way he was about to crush her fondest dreams.

"She's been detained," he heard himself say. Damn. Talk about backing into something the long way around.

"Detained how? For how long?" Her brows furrowed in that familiar V, and to his disgust, he found himself making another adjustment in his approach.

"Not too long. I'm sure of that much. It's the weather that's holding them up. So bloody unpredictable at this time of year. Shall we eat?"

"How was your day?" she inquired, over a meal that rivaled any he had sampled from chefs renowned the world over.

"Tedious." He snapped the one word reply, to repay her for making him feel things he did not want to feel and for exposing his weakness. All he had done with his trumped-up excuse about the weather was postpone the inevitable.

He took another succulent mouthful of beef and chewed in silence.

"How are your plans progressing for the House of Birds?"

"Rapidly." Her silence was expectant, demanding that he elaborate. Fine, he thought, she wanted details, he would give her details. "Colin's property proved to be perfectly suited to my needs. The public areas have been completely refurbished, the various cages built and decorated. Lavishly." He met her gaze. "All that remains is to hire the ladies to fill them."

She shook her head. "I suppose I should have known better than to ask. More wine?"

He held his glass while she filled it, deciding there was a great deal to be said for dispensing with servants now and again.

"Now tell me about your day," he urged, because it was the polite thing to do. "Tea at your aunt's, I believe?"

"Yes. Tedious sums it up nicely. At least as far as

the tea itself. A bunch of dreadful bores, sitting around trying to keep each other awake."

He laughed with genuine amusement. "A very apt description, and one with many applications. I've sat through any number of sessions of Lords that could be described the same way."

"Really?" she said with feigned astonishment. "And here I pictured the House of Lords as a place where the noblest of men debate matters of great import."

He snorted. "Not quite. I'll bring you along one day and you can sit in the gallery and see for yourself . . ." He lowered his gaze to his plate. "That is, of course, if you're here long enough."

"Of course," she replied, with a little smile.

He did not like that smile at all. In fact, he deplored it. Almost as much as he deplored having to be the one who, very shortly, was going to wipe it from her face for good.

"I did have a very interesting conversation with Michael Holt this afternoon however."

"Him again? He seems to be underfoot nearly as much as Will and Colin lately." He took a bite of beef and chewed vigorously. "What did he have to say that you found so fascinating?"

"We talked about my mother," she replied. "I've told you they were great friends."

"Yes, and he seems to feel he can pick up with you where he left off with her."

"He's being kind," she insisted, then frowned. "What is that look for?"

"What look?"

"That look. You're . . . glowering."

"I am not glowering. I'm thrilled my wife has made so many new friends so quickly after arriving in town, and all of them men."

Her frown slowly gave way to that smile once more. "If it makes you feel better, I also spoke with Lady Williams, and my cousin Jenny, and Aunt Millicent. All females. Oh, which reminds me, I've a favor to ask of you, a rather sizable one, I'm afraid."

"Go ahead." The look of consternation he mustered was a pitiful sham, an attempt to hide from himself the truth of the matter. There was nothing within his power to grant that he would deny her tonight.

"I believe my uncle recently submitted a business proposal for your consideration," she said.

Adrian nodded. "It arrived on my desk last Thursday morning, the same day I returned it—unopened—with a letter of regret. As I distinctly recall promising you I would."

"I know." She flashed him a beguiling smile, which made him think that in a real business negotiation with her, he would be lucky to walk away with his skin. "But do you think you might possibly ask to see it again? And actually look at it this time? And, if at all possible, approve it?"

He eyed her suspiciously. "Why?"

"Because, according to Aunt Millicent, they are in the most dire financial straits. And I find, quite to my own amazement, I assure you, that I do not want to see them ruined when it may be within my power to help."

There was a little popping noise in his head. Blood vessels most likely, he thought, seeing red. What a fool he was, to think, for a moment, that this laborious scene represented anything as innocent as a desire to have dinner with him. He flung his napkin aside and stood.

"So, that's what this is all about. The candles, the wine, that ridiculous excuse for a . . . a . . ." His gaze locked on her breasts, rising and falling rapidly inside the diaphanous silk.

"Gown?" she suggested.

"Gown," he growled. "And that nonsense about dispensing with the servants and serving me yourself . . . sausages, of all things. Well, I'll have you know it was all a waste of time."

"Do you mean you won't reconsider the proposal?" she asked softly.

"No. I meant all you had to do was ask. I'll agree to his damn proposal, whatever it is. But I would have done so even if you had not gone to such ridiculous lengths, and, I might add, put yourself in more danger than you can possibly know of ending up in precisely the same spot you did last night. Do you understand?" He somehow managed to lift his gaze from her breasts to her face.

"Yes," she said, standing and stepping away from the table. "Except . . ."

What now? he thought.

"Except what?"

"Except none of this had anything at all to do with my aunt and uncle."

He gazed at her, bewildered. "What are you talking about?"

"I'm talking about the wine, the candles, getting rid of the servants, even this gown . . ." The mere mention of the gown jerked his gaze back in that direction, as if it were on a damn string and she was the puppet master. He was powerless to stop it from sliding lower, past her breasts, down her stomach to where the material formed a shallow, enticing pool at the V of her thighs.

"Especially this gown," she amended. "None of this was for their sake. It was for yours."

Reluctantly he dragged his gaze back to her face,

where, to his bewilderment, a small smile tugged at her beautiful mouth.

"Why?"

"Because it occurred to me this afternoon that two can play your game. Or, at least a version of it. You set out to seduce me into bed and it was wonderful, the very best thing that has ever happened to me. I've decided I am going to return the favor by seducing you into falling in love."

Adrian gaped at her in disbelief. "That will never happen. For God's sake, woman, after everything I told you this morning, why would you even contemplate such a thing?"

"Because I love you," she answered, and the open, guileless look on her face left him no doubt that as insane and impossible a notion as it was, she believed it.

He went cold inside, and wished he had sat down a moment ago when his legs had first started feeling shaky. Panic, great smothering waves of panic, was crashing over him.

"You don't have to say it," she went on. "I know what you are thinking, that this is madness. But it is true just the same. I love you."

Adrian braced himself, half expecting her to throw herself at him, but instead she merely folded her arms. "The devil alone knows why, since you do not make it at all easy and, truthfully, you show no promise of being worth all the effort. But apparently love is one of those things that defy common sense. Like gambling or taking snuff."

Hearing himself compared to other notable vices went a long way toward restoring his equilibrium.

"Aren't you going to say anything?" she asked quietly.

"Two things. You certainly have a unique way of expressing your affection. I should hate to hear what you would liken me to if you did not feel so tenderly."

"And the second?"

"You are wasting your time, madam."

"It's my time." She took a step closer to him. "And until Christiana arrives, I have a great deal of it to waste."

Tell her, ordered an unfamiliar voice inside. Tell her that her sister won't be coming, that there will not be any happy ending to this story, that nothing is going to turn out the way she hoped it would.

Tell her.

Then her hands were on him and it was too late.

She unbuttoned his waistcoat and he let her, relishing the feather-light brush of her fingers, even as he hungered for more. When she'd finished with his waistcoat, she went to work on his shirt, creating an opening between his still neatly tied neckcloth and his waist.

He looked on, intrigued as she leaned closer, then he felt her warm breath on his bare chest and was swept by a rush of something he was afraid to name. Her mouth touched him next, her soft lips slightly parted, her tongue hot, wet, inquisitive.

"Leah," he uttered, "what do you think you're doing?"

"Tasting you," she whispered against his skin. "The way you tasted me last night. Do you remember? My throat and my tummy and my—"

"Sweet Jesus." He gripped her shoulders and hauled her up, bending to capture her mouth and stop it with his own.

He was not a needy man. For him, that was not a matter of pride. It was sanity. It was survival. For years he had been honing to perfection the qualities of detachment and self-sufficiency, and a take-it-or-leave-it philosophy that ran right to the bone. But he needed something now, Adrian realized. He needed it badly, and it scared the hell out of him.

He needed what she had surrendered to him last night. He needed the sweet hot taste of her all over his tongue and the liquid fire of her fingers moving on his skin. He needed to devour, to overwhelm, to possess . . . again and again until he had conquered this need. Her sister be damned; there was no way on earth he could let Leah leave until he had quenched his lust for her.

He kissed her hard, then dragged his teeth along her throat and the curve of her shoulder. Hooking one finger inside her gown, he tugged, roughly, until the straps fell below her breasts, giving them up to his hungry gaze and eager mouth. He raked her with his teeth and pressed his mouth to the sweet valley between.

He licked her there, and groaned. She tasted of soap and salt and woman and he couldn't get enough. If the moment went on forever he would still never get enough. Desire, white-hot and sparking, hissed inside him.

He straightened and locked gazes with her, and she smiled.

"Lovely coat." She playfully slid her hands inside, caressing his chest with her palms. "The question is, shall I take it off or will you?"

"Neither," he growled, feeling distinctly unplayful. "There isn't time."

She had started this game, but they were going to finish it his way. He took her by the hips, feeling the tantalizing curve of bare flesh beneath the silk, and hurriedly backed her up against the wall, pressing her there with his body. Burying his face in her shoulder, he inhaled her scent, drinking her into his senses until it hurt to breathe, and all the while his fingers were shimmying over her gown, gathering it up on both sides in a frantic rush to get at her.

With the fabric bunched at her waist, he slid his hand between their bodies and pressed his splayed fingers to her belly, reaching for the softness and the gentle curve that sloped down to the silky cloud of curls where her thighs met.

His fingers curved into her, greedy, wanting. Needing her. Needing more. He tangled his fingers in her soft, fragrant curls, stroking deeper and lower, seeking the fragile petals of flesh beyond. When at last his fingers uncovered what he sought, he released a rough groan. She was hot. Wet. Heaven.

She quivered against his fingers and another, all-new need rose up inside him. He needed to feel that sweet quiver again, to hear her small cries of amazement, to give her the closest thing to love he had to offer—raw, physical pleasure.

He thrust his leg between hers and felt a shudder that began in her and traveled through him, as though they were already one, sharing flesh and sensation. The very idea thrilled him and scared him and made him tighten his grip on her. He bent his head and as he suckled her breast, she groaned and groaned, her head turning from side to side.

She tossed her arm across her face, concealing her eyes from him, and drew a knee up. The movement, at once so guileless and so utterly erotic, made his blood run thick. Adrian wasted no time in releasing the buttons of his trousers.

He plunged his shaft between her thighs, not daring penetration, not tonight, with his senses so ravaged he was fearful he would not have the presence of mind to withdraw in time. This would have to suffice, he told himself, as she closed around him like a satin glove, her firm flesh sheathing him.

He levered upward, pressing and stroking that small mysterious nub where her pleasure was centered. Leah cried out with surprise and delight, and clamped her legs closer together, creating a sweet, moist suction that made him desperate.

His breath came in short, harsh pants as he rocked against her with ever greater demand, moving faster and harder. He cupped her buttocks and pulled her to him, too deep into it now to slow down, to wait, to do more than feel and let the feeling take him.

"Yes," she whispered against the damp skin of his throat, kissing him, licking him. She was like a volcano, all pent-up heat and energy.

She braced her hands on his broad shoulders, holding on to him as the storm inside drove her higher with its primitive, lusty rhythm. They slammed together and pulled apart, their sweat-slick bodies straining together, arching higher and higher together, until there was nowhere higher left and as one they tumbled off the edge of the universe.

Adrian felt the wild clutching of her muscles. He heard her low, primitive rumble of satisfaction mingle with his rough gasp of pleasure as he found his own release, and he would have been supremely content if it all just ended with that.

But no. As soon as she had recovered sufficiently to smile, she ran her fingers through his hair, and finding him with that dazzling, direct gaze of hers, she said the very last words he wanted to hear.

"I love you, Adrian," she whispered.

He managed not to wince, or pull away, opting instead to drop a kiss on her enchantingly swollen lips. Then he offered the only reply a gentleman could under the circumstances.

"You'll be sorry."

16

—❦—

"I shall not be sorry," Leah told him, without a trace of doubt. "Ever. No matter how it ends up, I shall never be sorry for following my heart."

Adrian snorted, as she had known he would. There was something comfortable about that, though she refrained from telling him so. She thought it best not to subject him to too many sentimental concepts all at once.

"Following it straight into disaster is what you're doing," he insisted. "Did you ever wonder why it's called a heart and not a brain?"

"Don't be so cynical," she scolded, but with a laugh that reflected the way she felt inside, all loose and easy.

"Don't *you* be such a bloody romantic."

"I'm not. I'm being quite practical actually. I have proof, you see."

"What sort of proof could you possibly have?"

Breaking contact with her body, he shifted his weight and glared down at her.

"Step aside and I'll show you."

He did as she asked and Leah quickly shimmied her gown back into place. Adrian, watching her, absently righted his own clothing. She retrieved the black velvet pouch from her drawer and brought it to him.

"Do you recognize it?" she asked eagerly, once she had unwrapped the legendary necklace. In the candlelight, the ruby's fire burned with a softer, but no less spectacular glow, and the diamonds glittered brightly.

"Of course." He lifted his gaze to meet hers. "A more interesting question is, how do you happen to have it tucked away in your drawer?"

"Michael gave it to me this afternoon."

His dark brows rose. "My my, that *must* have been an interesting conversation. Should I bother asking how *he* got his hands on a priceless heirloom that had been in my family for generations prior to its mysterious disappearance?"

"There is nothing nefarious about it, if that's what you're thinking."

"Of course not. Just one more example of old Holt simply being a *friend.* Careful, Duchess, if the man gets too friendly, I may be the one in dire straits and it will be you going to your aunt, hat in hand."

"That's unfair. If Michael had wanted to profit from this in some way, he could have sought a private buyer years ago. Instead he has kept it safe all this time."

"Safe from its rightful owner, you mean."

"Here." She thrust it at him. "You have it back now. Take it."

He eyed her for a few seconds, as if gauging her

temper, then shoved his hands in his pockets. "Keep it," he drawled. "It's sure to look better on you anyway."

"Do you want to hear about it or not?" she demanded.

"Desperately," he replied, his tone bored.

Leah sighed, thinking it would serve him right if she didn't tell him and just let him go on running around in circles in the little world of bitterness and half-truths he'd been living in for years. And she would have, if she hadn't gone and fallen in love with the scoundrel, and if somewhere along the way, his suffering hadn't become enmeshed with her own. She wanted that suffering, all of it, to end.

He listened, silent and expressionless, as she related what Michael had confided about the relationship between her mother and his father and how the necklace had been a farewell present to her mother as she embarked on her new life.

"Don't you see?" she prodded, when he persisted in looking underwhelmed by the tale. "He *gave* this to her."

He shrugged. "It was his to give. As I recall, the piece is not entailed in any way."

"Just the same, it was an extraordinarily personal and extravagant gift for a man to give to his mistress," she concluded bluntly. "Can't you see what that means?"

"That your mother drove a hard bargain?"

"That's crude." Yesterday, the remark would have slashed straight to the heart of her vulnerability, but a great deal had changed since yesterday. Today, she recognized the pain behind his cynicism and anger. "To have given her something so precious means that, for all his faults, he truly loved her. He was capable of that much, at least."

"Rubbish." He sneered at the necklace in her hand. "The family vault is full of jewels. What's one more or less?"

"Not jewels like this," she argued. "This piece is priceless, if only for its personal significance to your family. You're just too pigheaded and set in your ways to admit it, and I know why."

"Why?"

Ignoring the warning glitter in his midnight eyes, she answered, "Because if I am right, it proves your father was not a completely coldhearted bastard and it is far easier for you to just go on telling yourself he was."

"I'm happy you have found reason to defend him," he countered harshly, "but I—"

"I am not defending him," Leah interrupted, her voice rising. "Make no mistake, I despise him for what he did to you and that will never change. But what I despise even more is what he is still doing to you, what he has cost you and what he goes on costing you, every single day that you choose to go on living in the shadow of *his* mistakes.

"Think about it, Adrian," she pleaded, taking his arm when he tried to turn away. "Your father did not steal just one woman from you, he stole *all* women, everywhere and forever. He did not take only one child, he took any number of them, all the babies you might have had . . . that you might still have. The damage he did that day was only the beginning. He takes from you every single day, he takes away possibilities, and you let him. You just go on letting him."

He kept his gaze averted. A muscle quivered at his jaw. "I cannot undo what he did."

"No, but you can stop allowing something that happened years ago to keep on hurting you. You can stop thinking of your father as some malevolent ogre, so horrid, so unrelentingly evil, that you must dedicate every day of the rest of your life to avenging yourself." She let go of his arm and held the necklace in both hands. "You can stop yourself from making the same stupid mistake he did, finding a woman he loved and letting her go, failing her just as he failed you, just as in the end, he failed himself."

"Failed?" he challenged, turning on her. "He got exactly what he wanted."

"Did he?" She let the question hang in the air, before adding, "I think not. I suspect he got what he *thought* he wanted, or perhaps, what he'd always been told he should want. I think he chose all the things that are *supposed* to matter over the things that really do, and ended up with nothing. Where were you when your father drew his last breath?"

His eyes narrowed, then gleamed with comprehension. "As far away as I could get."

"Don't you see? He gave up on love in favor of duty and some narrow sense of family tradition, and lost his only son in the bargain."

"Forgive me," he said, withdrawing behind that shuttered look, just when she thought she was reaching him. "I must have missed something crucial in all this. How, precisely, does this prove you are justified in following the foolish dictates of your heart? It occurs to me your mother chose that route, with disastrous results."

"And your father chose not to listen to his heart and, in my opinion, suffered an even worse fate." She held up the necklace once more. "This is symbolic."

"Of what?" he countered with biting cynicism. "Man's infinite capacity to delude himself?"

"No. Of . . . of . . . courage," she said, at last settling on the word that came closest to capturing something that was pure emotion. "Michael said the necklace first came to your family as a reward for some clandestine, and no doubt dangerous and courageous, act on the king's behalf. Your father gave it to my mother to wish her well in her new life. He understood what she was doing and why, and how much courage it took."

"Nice story, Duchess. But it strains credulity even more than Olivia and Nevar's does."

"Sometimes *life* strains credibility," she shot back. "Lord knows, we are nothing if not proof of that. Think of it, Adrian, what were the odds of us coming together at all? Much less in the curious manner we did. And now, because of us, the Sun and Stars is at last back where it belongs . . . as if this was always meant to be."

"A perfect ending. Why not use it for the princess and old Nevar?" He stretched mightily. "Personally, I'm much too tired tonight to undertake the complete abandonment of rationality it would take for me to believe any of what you've said."

He reached for her hand, the one holding the necklace, and brought it to his lips. His stubbornly opaque gaze locked with hers as he dropped a perfunctory kiss on the back of her hand, and murmured, "Night, Duchess. Dinner was . . . delectable."

Not until he was alone in his own chamber, the closed door a solid barricade at his back, did Adrian abandon the facade of nonchalance he had somehow maintained in her presence, and at no small cost. His palms were sweating and his head felt as if it had been kicked around.

Leah's statements suggested that his father, for all his miserable failings as both a father and a human being, had at least practiced what he preached. That is, *if* he had ever truly loved Dava. Personally, Adrian was still not convinced the man had had it in him to love or cherish anyone except as pawns to fulfill his vision of what life ought to be.

He dragged both hands through his hair as he paced the floor. The roomy chamber suddenly seemed reduced to the size of a cell. His gaze darted about like a caged bird. He briefly considered visiting his club, only to discover that neither drinking nor gaming held the appeal it usually did when he found himself in a restless mood.

His wandering gaze at last came to rest on the bed. The Raven Wedding Bed. He had a sudden impulse to summon Thorne and order the useless thing carted outside and burned. But though destroying the bed might provide momentary satisfaction, it would not eliminate the niggling suspicion that was already eating away at the edges of his resolve. Why would his father, a man who had scrupulously adhered to the family tradition surrounding a frigging bed, have given the equally revered Sun and Stars to a woman for any reason other than he loved her beyond reason?

The fact that he could not come up with a more likely explanation than Leah's did not make him like hers any better. It made him angry. And more resolved than ever to keep his guard up around her.

Again he berated himself for failing to tell her about her sister's elopement. If he had, all this would be behind him and his life could return to normal. The longer he waited, the more difficult telling her was going to be, and the angrier Leah was going to be that he had withheld the information from her in the first place. She would doubtless feel used and betrayed and rail at him for being the most conniving, unprincipled, cold-hearted bastard alive. In other words, he thought, exactly what he was.

His wife thought he was redeemable, that he could be seduced as easily as an overripe spinster. But she was wrong, and he was going to prove it to her.

News of the elopement could wait a few days, he decided. He would indulge her little scheme and, in the process, prove to her once and for all that she was sadly mistaken if she thought she could overhaul and rearrange his thoughts and beliefs as easily as she had everything else around Raven House.

At least, she could not alter them any more than she already had. Though he could not put a name to what he was feeling, for the first time in a decade, he felt *something* for the man who had sired him other than pure, unmitigated hatred. Some might consider that an improvement. He had no doubt Leah would. But they could not possibly understand.

In the darkest days of his life, following the double betrayal by his father and Charlotte, it was hatred alone that had sustained him and given him a purpose to go on living. He had nurtured and developed it, given it shape and direction and carried it with him always, as a knight always carried his shield into battle.

The more it grew, the more room it commanded inside him. Other feelings gave way, feelings he no longer had any use for, no longer *wanted* to have use for, feelings like trust and innocence and need.

Eventually there was nothing left inside him but bitterness. It was at the center of who he was. If he lost that, what would he have left?

17

"That's seven pins down for me," exclaimed Leah, "and five for Will. Add to what we had at the start of this round . . ." She paused, nibbling her bottom lip in a way that Adrian, observing from a shadowed corner of the house, found most tempting. He was sorry when she completed the computations in her head and looked up. "Drat, Will. It means Colin is still beating you by double digits and edging me out by three."

"Didn't I warn you that I was a master at Dutch Rubbers?" Colin teased.

"Some master," she scoffed. "It's simply that your legs are so much longer than mine and that your *two steps and throw* is double what I can manage. Besides which, I still say my skirts get in the way."

"And I still say, be that as it may, I am not donning a skirt. Of course, what the rector consents to wear is entirely his own business."

"Very funny," muttered Will.

The three of them joked and laughed easily together as they went about setting up the lawn game for another round of play. It had been years since Adrian had seen the long, narrow, wooden enclosure, with its frame at one end to hold nine small pins. He had a vague recollection of his mother playing Dutch Rubbers with her friends on summer afternoons. Never this early in the season however, and never had they appeared to be having so much fun. Despite her playful grumbling, there was the same mood of breezy lightheartedness Leah seemed to evoke wherever she went.

Except with him, of course. For better or worse, when they were alone together, both their passions ran too high and hot to ever be described as anything resembling light or breezy. That had been truer than ever for the past several days, ever since she had thrown herself into this campaign to seduce him into falling in love. And he, in turn, had launched a private counterattack guaranteed to put an end to any and all romantic fantasies involving him and happily-ever-after.

He spent his days accelerating plans for the House of Birds and his nights taking everything Leah offered him, knowing, as all good soldiers did, that a two-pronged attack was most effective when your aim was to bring the enemy to his knees. As he watched her laughing with such abandon, he resisted the faint tug of what could only be conscience, telling him that as cruel and calculating as his actions might seem, he was actually doing her a favor. Leah was too generous, too optimistic, and too damned romantic to be discouraged by anything less.

"Silence," ordered Colin, as he made a great show

of lining up his next throw. "No whistling while the master prepares."

"That's not us, Master," Leah retorted. "It's the birds. Shall I clear the skies for you?"

"If it's not too much bother," he shot back over his shoulder.

Leah giggled.

"A real man rises above the birds," decreed Will, prompting groans all around.

"No, a *real* man would wear a skirt and even things up."

Ignoring them, Colin took two long strides and hurled the ball along the wooden planks, knocking over all nine pins.

"Perfecto." He threw both arms in the air and grinned. "It appears a real man lets his performance speak for him."

Adrian could no longer resist.

Stepping forward into the sunshine, he strolled toward the corner of the narrow lawn where they had set up play.

"You're using the wrong strategy, Duchess," he said, taking all three of them by surprise. "Forget the skirt and have these gentlemen grant you three extra steps to compensate."

"That's brilliant." She smiled broadly at the sight of him. She smiled at him often these days, all part of her scheme to break him, he told himself, renewing his determination to prove to her that he could not be broken. "How about it, gentlemen?" she asked.

"One step," Colin responded grudgingly, then shot Adrian a disgusted look. "Traitor. She's frighteningly good as is and I don't fancy losing at Dutch Rubbers to a slip of a female."

"Two steps," Adrian put forth on her behalf. "It's either that or the skirt, barrister, take your pick. Unless you fancy having it get around that you forfeited a match to a slip of a female?"

"Two steps," Colin quickly conceded.

"I married a genius." Leah stretched onto her toes and looped one arm around his neck to reward him with an exuberant kiss on the cheek.

It was a totally spontaneous gesture, which apparently did not strike anyone but him as remarkable. He could not recall the last time any woman had planted so casual a kiss anywhere on his body . . . if indeed anyone ever had. It was, he decided, a subtle, different sort of pleasure than any he was accustomed to. And one he did not need.

"How long have you been watching?" she inquired, smiling up at him.

"Only a moment," he lied. Thinking quickly, he added, "I only came out to ask Will and Colin if they're up for Newmarket on Thursday. How about it?"

"My pockets are empty until the first," replied Will, "but I'll come along for the show. I hear Biswell is going to run the filly he got from Mother of Pearl. It'll be her first time out."

Colin whistled. "Gives me goose bumps just to think of the killing to be made on that. And, as luck would have it, my pockets are full. I ran into young Wickerson again last night. I'll stake you," he offered Will.

"What's at Newmarket?" she asked.

"Turf," replied Will.

"The sport of kings," said Colin.

"And suckers," added Adrian dryly. "Newmarket boasts the best horse racing anywhere. This Thursday will be the Fawley Mile for two-year-olds, a straight course over some of the most taxing terrain there is."

Leah's green eyes brimmed with excitement. "I'd love to go," she declared.

All three men chuckled.

"Sorry, Duchess, but Newmarket is no place for ladies." Adrian saw her jaw set. "It's usually endless mud, for one thing. If you think Dutch Rubbers is no place for skirts, you'd abhor Newmarket."

"I should like the opportunity to decide that for myself. I happen to love a good horse race."

More low-pitched chuckling.

"There are also no stands, or facilities," he went on. "You have to watch from your mount. All in all, it's a long day in the saddle and not at all, I'm certain, the genteel sort of horse race you've witnessed at country fairs. Now I shall leave you to your game."

"Why not join us?" she invited, the challenge still in her voice.

He smiled indulgently. "I don't play lawn games. Where on earth did you dig up that old relic anyway?"

"Brewster found it when he took over the stables, along with a number of other items that have probably been missing from the household for years." Her mouth curved merrily. "You'll be happy to know the fireplace in the library now has a matched set of andirons."

"Happy does not begin to express my sentiments," he drawled, resigning himself to the fact that there would not be a single corner left untouched when she was through.

"It's not a difficult game," she assured him.

"That's not the point." That she thought the reason he would not play was because he lacked confidence irritated him. "I have work to do."

"Surely your work can wait a half hour." She was cajoling now, gazing at him from beneath a lush fringe of dark lashes, her ploy so obvious it was laughable.

Did the woman really think *he* could be taken down with such an unskilled maneuver?

She stepped closer and placed her hand lightly on his arm. "Please, Adrian? It will be fun."

Fun. She was dredging up all sorts of buried memories that day. When, he wondered, was the last time he had done anything simply because it promised to be fun?

"I won't even ask you to wear a skirt," she teased. "And it will give us an opportunity to discuss my deep and abiding love of horse racing."

"Don't waste your breath," he advised. "There is not a chance on God's green earth of my showing up at Newmarket with a woman."

"Are women officially precluded?" she persisted.

"*My* woman is." His hard tone drew curious looks from Will and Colin. He ignored them, and the injured look that flashed in Leah's eyes. "Your place in my life is limited to this house and my bed. Don't forget it."

18

Olivia decided . . .

Olivia thought if only she . . .

Olivia was certain of one thing and one thing only . . .

Frustrated, Leah tossed aside her pen and propped her chin in a cupped palm. It was no use; she had written herself into a corner. If Olivia had any inkling of what she was up to, she was not sharing it with her creator.

Leaning back in her chair, Leah closed her eyes and imagined herself in Princess Olivia's place. She had just seen the man she loved at his worst, scarred and . . .

Her lips pursed in concentration, she straightened and began rummaging through the manuscript pages piled at the side of her desk, quickly finding the one she was looking for. Ordinarily when she was working on a story, she was so deeply involved she had practically every word committed to memory. Recently her life had been anything but ordinary, however. Preoccupied with the convoluted affairs of her own heart, she seemed to have lost the thread of Olivia and Nevar's story.

Still, she could not believe she would have forgotten so critical a detail, and her suspicion was right. Nowhere in the scene in which Olivia saw Nevar without his mask did she actually come right out and say he was scarred. It was Adrian, reading over her shoulder, who had jumped to that conclusion, and she had gone along with him.

Now she let her imagination wander in a different direction. What if Nevar was not scarred? What if there were some other reason he kept his face hidden behind that leather mask? Such as . . . such as . . .

Such as he believed himself to be scarred even though he was not, she thought with a surge of excitement. Because . . . because he was laboring under some sort of awful curse of his own . . . a curse that blinded him to his own beauty and kept him from seeing himself as he really was.

Like Adrian, she mused, her thoughts abruptly taking a more personal turn. In a way, Adrian was as good as cursed, cut off from his own feelings, completely blind to his capacity to love, and his need to be loved in return. She had vowed to change that, but she had not made much progress.

In some ways he had been more moody and difficult than ever since she'd revealed her love for him. Oh, on the surface things were fine. He continued to play the part of devoted husband in public, and in bed. And he no longer protested her preparations for Christiana's arrival. In fact, he occasionally made suggestions or proposed the name of a suitable young man to be added to one of her pile of guest lists.

The problem was that his cooperation made her uneasy, especially since it was frequently accompanied by a scowl. She couldn't help wondering what he was up to.

If only Christiana would arrive, she would have something else to occupy her. But just yesterday Adrian had received word that her sister's carriage had lost a wheel and would be held up for at least a day or so while repairs were made. As eager as she was to see Chrissie, she couldn't decide if that was a blessing or a curse. It would hardly do to have her arrive and find Leah's supposedly devoted and head-over-heels in love bridegroom walking around like a bear who'd stuck his paw in a hornet's nest.

Sighing, she reached for her pen and forced her attention back to her work.

Olivia knew she must somehow find a way to make Nevar see himself as she saw him . . . as the only man she could ever love.

But how?

Good question, Princess, she thought, replacing the pen in the stand. If you figure it out before I do, be sure to let me know.

Deciding she was finished for the day, she went downstairs to see if Adrian had returned from an afternoon meeting with his solicitor. It was absurd, she knew, but the house always seemed quieter and a little darker when he was not there. For that reason alone, she sensed he was still out.

Perhaps she would arrange for a bath to coincide with his arrival. He was bound to be weary after a long day of finalizing plans for the aviary, and she had some new bath salts that would pamper every aching muscle. And then, when he was naked and relaxed and at her mercy, she would go about taming him in ways not available to princesses in fairy tales. It was, she thought wistfully, the only time he really let her close to him lately.

Smiling wickedly in anticipation, she paused on her way to find Phelps and looked through the morning mail gathered in the Chinese bowl by the front door. It consisted of the usual letters for Adrian and an array of invitations addressed to them both. But it was the wrinkled note at the very bottom of the pile that instantly commanded her attention.

It was from Christiana, and had traveled the devil's own route to get to her, judging from the looks of it. She impatiently broke the seal and opened it.

The note was brief and to the point and so absolutely devastating, Leah forced herself to read it a second time.

Christiana wrote that she was married, or would be by the time her letter arrived. She had eloped . . . with the Grisholms' nephew, that sheep farmer from Wentworth. Leah shook her head as if dazed. This was just not possible. Why, she had vouchers for them to attend Almack's a week from that night. She had made plans . . . lined up invitations . . . arranged for every last detail . . .

This could not be true, she thought, twisting the note in her hands. She would not let it be true. She would return home and put a stop to this outrage at once.

How fast could she possibly get there? she wondered, her mind a jumble as she frantically smoothed out the crumpled note in order to check the date.

No date. Of course not. She hissed through clenched teeth. Oh, this was just like Christiana, acting in haste, without bothering to date a letter or give a thought to the fact that she was throwing her entire life away.

Eloped. The word alone made her ill. Oh, Brian St.

Leger was nice enough, but he was not the man for Chrissie. She deserved more. She deserved someone who would excite and challenge and cherish her. Someone like Adrian.

Poor Adrian, thought Leah, horrified anew. He had been taken in right along with her. All those phony excuses and delays. Though how Christiana had managed such an elaborate hoax about the carriage was beyond her. More of St. Leger's doing, most likely. He'd apparently thought of everything. But she was not about to give up hope yet. Not until she had found Adrian and told him everything. If anyone would know of a way to save Christiana, he would.

"Phelps," she cried, at the same time she was tugging on the bellpull.

Phelps came running.

"Yes, Your Grace?" He saw her expression and blanched. "Is something wrong?"

"Yes. Everything is wrong," she replied impatiently. "Do you know the address where the Duke was to meet with his solicitor?"

"Yes, Madam."

"Good. Write it down for me. And do you know if the Duke took the carriage?"

"He did, Madam."

"In that case, summon my driver and have my carriage brought around at once." She paused at the bottom of the stairs and glanced back over her shoulder. "I'm going to fetch my wrap. Please see that the carriage is waiting out front when I get there."

"Shall I send in the next applicant, Your Grace?" inquired Gates.

"Why not?" Adrian replied, rubbing his hands together in a show of anticipation, and wondering whom he was trying to convince, Gates or himself.

He ought to be enjoying this, savoring every moment. And he was, he reassured himself. He simply wasn't savoring it as much as he'd expected to and he couldn't figure out why. For over an hour he had been interviewing the "ladies" Gates had lined up to inhabit the cages at the House of Birds. Though they were, without exception, comely and overtly sensual, exactly the sort of women he had once sought out on a regular basis to satisfy his carnal desires, he was bored. And would say so if the very idea wasn't utterly ludicrous.

He glanced around as he waited for Gates to bring in the next overly eager applicant. Ringing the area where he was seated were the various cages, each designed to display a different "bird of paradise." There was the Canary Cage, with bright yellow sateen sofas, a soft saffron rug and brass accents; the Cardinal Cage, done entirely in shades of red; the Ebony Parlor, featuring black satin and lace; and Bluebird's Retreat, where the centerpiece was a vivid blue satin swing suspended from hooks in the ceiling.

He ought to be pleased. The workmen, who had been handpicked by Gates and well paid for their discretion, had executed every detail exactly as requested.

He turned as the door leading from the reception area opened. A smiling Gates stepped just inside and with a flourish, said, "Your Grace, I present to you Miss Gloria de Pardieu."

Miss de Pardieu entered with all the subtlety of a brass band. She was plump and blonde and smiling an invitation no male over the age of fourteen could misread, the perfect specimen to grace the Canary Cage. Adrian could not have been less interested.

Before he could say so, Gates had withdrawn, leaving them alone. It was a situation Miss de Pardieu was not at all uncomfortable with, he realized, as she began to saunter toward him, hips swaying and a determined gleam in her eyes.

Miss de Pardieu stopped directly in front of him and cranked her come-hither look up another notch. "Your Grace, this is indeed a pleasure to end all pleasures. I have heard such wonderful stories about you."

Adrian forced a smile, irritated that he had to force it. The fingertip she was suggestively trailing down his chest should have been all the invitation he needed. What the hell was wrong with him?

Leah, that's what. He was so busy plotting strategy to counter her every ploy that he couldn't even enjoy himself with a woman. He refused to think about the fact that he had no trouble enjoying himself with Leah. This had to end. He had been luring her deeper into the trap, waiting for the perfect moment to tell her the truth about her sister and about the true nature of the House of Birds, waiting for that moment when the damage he inflicted would be most complete and irrevocable.

But he was through waiting. With each passing day, Leah seemed more content, more at home where he did not want her. And he, who was supposed to be masterminding the counter-assault, felt more out of control.

"You flatter me," he told Miss de Pardieu, dislodging her hand gently. It was not her fault he had temporarily lost his taste for all this. "But now is not the time—"

"Now is always the time," she broke in. "Here is always the place. A clever woman is always, always amenable to the situation at hand."

"Look, Miss de Pardieu," he began as she sashayed around him and plopped herself in the swing a few feet away.

"Look all you like," she invited, leaning forward to display her considerable charms to full advantage. "And call me Gloria. How about giving Gloria a little push while you're at it?"

"Sorry, Gloria," he said drily, "no push. The interview is over. Mr. Gates will be in touch."

"Well, I like that." She was clearly miffed. "After getting myself all done up in yellow, like that Gates fellow said, you don't even give a girl a chance to show you what she has to offer." She curled her fingers around the satin ropes and smiled coquettishly. "Sure you don't want a little sample, Your Grace?"

With that she lifted one stocking-clad foot and planted it in his crotch. Then she wiggled her toes.

Adrian grunted and grabbed her leg, Miss de Pardieu giggled, and the door behind him opened.

He heard Gates's frantic voice.

"Please, Madam, I've told you that His Grace cannot be disturbed. If you will kindly wait—"

"And I told you that I cannot wait. I must see—"

He turned his head and met Leah's stunned gaze, then watched as it carved a horrified path from his face to the foot he must surely appear to be pressing against his genitals.

"Oh, my God," she said.

Perfect, he thought.

He had been waiting for just such a moment, a chance to demonstrate to Leah exactly what kind of man she had married.

This was what he had planned for, what he wanted. So why did he feel as if the bottom had just fallen out from under him?

He dropped Miss de Pardieu's foot.

"Leah, believe me, this is not what it appears to be."

Believe him? He couldn't believe he'd even said it.

Obviously, she didn't believe it either.

She dragged her gaze around the room, her brow furrowed, her posture so tense he was afraid if he touched her she would shatter. Suddenly he saw his surroundings not through the eyes of a jaded, self-centered libertine, but through Leah's eyes, and the garish scene made him cringe.

"If it is not what it appears to be," she said, "what in God's name is it?"

She could not seem to tear her gaze away from the sight of Miss de Pardieu in the damn satin swing. When at last she stared directly at him, Adrian flinched from the accusation that blazed in her eyes.

"Because what this appears to be, *sir*, is a brothel. Am I wrong? Tell me I am wrong." Her voice trembled at the end, her fierce demand giving way to a heartrending plea.

"You're not wrong," he said quietly.

She did shatter then. Not on the outside. Her shoulders remained square, her jaw high, her gloved hands firmly clasped at her waist. But she shattered on the inside, and it showed in her quick, brittle smile.

"You weren't teasing," she said. "All those times you told me you were planning a brothel and I laughed so knowingly, you weren't teasing. And I wasn't nearly as smart as I thought I was."

The self-recrimination in her tone tore at him. He was the one to blame for this, the only one.

"Please, Leah," he said, quickly covering the distance between them. "Let me explain."

"No." Her voice suddenly simmered with rage. "This place and that woman are explanation enough. I was wrong, wrong to come here thinking you could help me, wrong to ever think, for a moment, that you had changed. You are beyond redemption."

The words, precisely the words he had wanted to force her to say, filled him with sudden, fierce desperation.

She shrank back as he reached out to touch her, the contempt on her face enough to stop him even if she had not moved.

"Don't touch me," she ordered. "Don't speak to me. Don't come near me. I never want to see you again, is that clear?"

He shuddered, her rejection falling like a lash across old wounds. He hated himself for letting it happen, and for that one instant, he hated her as well.

"Very clear," he said with a quick bow. "I won't importune you further, Madam. You may count on it."

19

He was a jackass, he told himself, and anyone else within earshot, as he left White's alone later that evening.

A pompous, pigheaded jackass.

Leah had had every right to be enraged and to say the things she had said to him, and he no right to feel anything at all other than remorse, and a soul-searing desire to beg her forgiveness.

He was still a jackass.

But he was not a fool.

The irrefutable proof of that, as far as Adrian was concerned, was that it had taken him only a few hours to come to his senses this time, instead of ten years.

He hauled himself into the back of the carriage and called to the driver. Who said he was beyond redemption?

He was not. He was most redeemable. And with the absolute clarity of several too many brandies, he knew exactly what he had to do. He had to come clean with Leah. No easy task. Fortunately, those same brandies gave him the courage he needed.

He was going home and he was going to tell her the truth. About everything. First he was going to tell her that he had ordered Gates to see to the permanent dismantling of the blasted House of Birds. Or at least what remained of it after he'd spent his anger on the place.

Then he was going to tell her about her sister's elopement. He would tell her he had been wrong to keep the news from her, but that he had done so only because he had not been ready to give her up. And that he was still not ready and might never be. Somehow he would find the courage to tell her that, too.

Then if she still insisted she never wanted to see him again, he would . . .

He sighed and closed his eyes. He would jump off that bridge when he came to it.

"Has the Duchess already retired for the evening?" he asked Phelps, who had materialized before him with his usual quickness and was helping him off with his jacket.

"Why, no, sir." The servant looked perplexed by the query. "The Duchess is gone."

"Gone where?" Adrian demanded, a knot of alarm forming in his gut. He ran through all the possible places Leah might have gone for the evening—the theater, the opera, any number of balls. His gut knew that she had not been in a mood for any of that. "Gone where?" he repeated.

"Why, home, sir," Phelps answered, his uneasiness obvious.

"Home?" snapped Adrian. "This is her home." His

eyes narrowed accusingly. "You don't mean home to Baumborough?"

"Why, I, she . . . yes, I believe so. I assumed you knew, Your Grace. She left shortly after returning from her meeting with you earlier today. At least, I thought she met with Your Grace." He rattled on uncontrollably as Adrian's expression grew darker and more ferocious. "She asked the whereabouts of your meeting with your solicitor and I provided her with the address. I hope that was all right."

"Yes, yes, it was fine," Adrian told him, leashing his temper. None of this was Phelps's fault, any more than it was Leah's.

"It doesn't make sense," he said, thinking out loud as he struggled to clear his head. "Why would she leave London now? With her sister supposedly due here any day."

Phelps cleared his throat. "If I may be so bold as to suggest a possible explanation, Your Grace?"

"What is it?" he asked, willing to listen to anything.

"Perhaps the Duchess's decision to leave had something to do with this." He removed a wrinkled sheet of parchment from the pile of mail nearby and held it out.

"Perfect," said Adrian.

"It was directly after reading this that the Duchess first became upset."

Adrian stared at the note from Christiana Stretton without touching it. Oh, he'd wager Leah had been *upset,* all right. Which explained why she had come looking for him. Where she'd found him, and with whom, could only have fueled her ire.

"Where did that come from?" he asked, his tone flat.

"One of the upstairs maids found it tucked behind the leg of the dressing table in the Duchess's chamber. She gave it to the housekeeper, who brought it to me, and I in turn placed it with the incoming mail where—"

"Where the Duchess would be sure to find it," Adrian finished for him.

"Exactly," Phelps said proudly.

"Perfect," said Adrian again.

He wandered toward the stairs. Perhaps things would look brighter in the morning, but somehow he didn't think so. His one chance to redeem himself had been to tell Leah the truth *before* she discovered it on her own. The way she had walked in and discovered him with a harlot's foot in his crotch, he thought disgustedly.

He could see no reason now why she should ever believe anything he had to say, much less trust him enough to give him a second chance, a chance to go back and do things over the way he should have done them from the start.

There was too much to explain. And too much to forgive.

It seemed fitting, the perfect end to the most wretched day of his life, to find the Sun and Stars tucked under his pillow when he crawled into bed. The message was short and to the point. Leah had given up on him, the same way her mother had given up on her dreams years before.

Adrian closed his eyes for several moments before throwing off the covers and getting to his feet.

Perfect ending, be damned. Nothing was ending. Least of all his bloody marriage.

He started for the door, prepared to bellow, then remembered the bellpull and used it instead. If this new, wretchedly efficient household of his was going to work against him, turning up letters that inadvertently fell from his pocket while he was making love to his own wife, then it could damn well be of service as well.

Phelps and his valet appeared quickly and simultaneously. Adrian grinned, thinking he could get used to this.

"I want to dress. Clothes suited for riding," he barked, sending the valet scurrying to the closet. "Have my horse saddled and brought round," he directed Phelps, who disappeared with equal haste.

Leah was his wife. He had schemed and lied and risked deportation to get her. He had connived and wheedled and put up with cupids and buttercups in order to bed her. He had appeared at balls and sat through recitals and allowed himself to be paraded down Bond Street like a besotted bridegroom, and he was not, by God, going to give her up. Not for any reason, but certainly not because of some stupid . . .

Misunderstanding.

The House of Birds had been an unfortunate misunderstanding. Clean and simple. Married couples had misunderstandings all the time, and went on. He would apologize profusely for the harlot, and her foot, and he would inform her he had already abandoned the whole misbegotten scheme. Better yet, if it pleased Leah, he would open a damn aviary on that site in her honor.

The sister's elopement was another matter. It could not accurately be described as a *misunderstanding,* he decided, after twisting and turning the facts every which way in his mind. A mere apology would not do here. Groveling appeared to be the only way to go. Perhaps it was lucky Leah had a head start on him. The chase would give him plenty of time to rehearse.

He encountered the first scattered, heavy drops of rain just outside of town. As the road narrowed and curved into the countryside, it rained steadily harder and the wind picked up, until he was riding blind through blowing torrents.

Cold and drenched, he arrived in Westerham and gave up for the night. He would seek shelter at the rectory at St. Anne's, he decided, and start out fresh first thing in the morning. With luck, he still ought to overtake her carriage before noon.

Turning into the rectory, he circled the darkened house and rode directly to the stable. No sense dragging the poor groom out in this weather when he was already soaked to the bone.

It was only after he'd dealt with the rain-sodden saddle and blankets and settled his horse for the night, that Adrian realized the carriage closest to the stable door belonged to Leah.

His heart constricted, with relief, with joy, with trepidation, and he took off running through the rain.

Shoulders hunched against the water pouring off the overhang above his head, he pounded on the front door until an upstairs window opened and the curate, Cole Brindley, appeared.

"Quiet down, my good man," he called. "Have you any idea of the hour?"

"I couldn't care less about the hour," Adrian shouted up to him. "And I'm not a good man. I'm Raven, and I've come for my wife."

Brindley sputtered something. The window closed, and within minutes the front door opened.

Leah stood framed in the light from a single candle. Her hair was loose and she was wearing a simple ivory wool robe, the ruffles of her cotton nightgown visible at the neck. In a heartbeat, Adrian forgot how cold and wet and scared he was.

"You're beautiful," he said.

She pressed her lips together, extinguishing the flicker of soft welcome he had already seen.

"You came all this way in the rain to tell me that?" she asked frostily.

"No." He stepped closer, bringing the cold and the rain to the threshold that separated them. "I came all this way to tell you that I love you."

She was in his arms, a soft, clinging bundle of warmth and blessed dryness. Her open mouth was wet, but it was hot and sweet and Adrian wanted to go on kissing it forever, even if it meant spending the rest of his life on the rectory steps in the rain. It was only when he gripped her head and felt the moisture already in her hair that common sense returned.

Still, he couldn't wait until they were inside to ask.

"Does this mean you're not still angry with me?" he asked with a hopeful grin.

"Not at all. I am furious with you," she retorted, a fire in her green eyes which, he figured, could be from anger or could be from kissing. "But it is not every day a woman sees a mountain move," she added. "I thought that merited commemoration of some sort."

"I shall consider myself duly commemorated," he drawled, and followed her inside.

Mrs. O'Hara appeared to help him shuck his coat and everything else that was wet, down to his shirt and breeches. Brindley had already stoked the fire in the small sitting room to a welcoming roar, and placed a bottle of brandy and a glass by the chair closest to the fireplace.

Adrian glanced at it wistfully, then turned to the housekeeper with a rueful smile. "I know it's late, but would a cup of tea be too much trouble?"

"Hot tea coming up," she said and bustled from the room.

He wanted what was in his head to be as clear as what was in his heart.

At last he was alone with Leah, and all those convoluted excuses and explanations he had rehearsed on his way there. He looked into her eyes and abandoned them all.

He loved her. This was no longer a contest. She was no longer a prize. She was his life, and he wanted it back.

They sat in chairs flanking the fireplace, both of them up straight, poised, as if ready to take flight . . . or give chase, he thought wryly.

He leaned farther forward, resting his forearms on his thighs, and turned his hands palms up to her.

"May I hold your hands?" he asked when she ignored the gesture.

"No."

"To warm them," he persisted, "that's all."

He promised himself it was the last lie he would ever tell her. He just needed to touch her, to hold on to some part of her, if he was to get through this.

Reluctantly, she leaned forward and placed her hands on top of his. Adrian watched his fingers close over them. Her hands were smaller and paler than his, different in every way, her bones delicate, her skin smooth and unmarred. Yet they fit together perfectly.

It occurred to him that with almost no effort at all, he could crush her hands and break those narrow bones. With a single, rash move, he could mark her fragile flesh. It would be as swift and easy as breaking a heart or scarring a soul. The knowledge did not make him feel strong or powerful. It made him feel fiercely protective, and woefully inadequate. It also filled him with determination to never again hurt her.

"I'm sorry," he said. "So damn sorry for so many things that I hardly know where to start." He took a deep breath. "So I shall start at the beginning. I'm sorry for tricking you into marrying me, Duchess, and in doing so, stealing your dream of gallant princes and fairy-tale weddings and happily-ever-after endings."

"That was never my dream," she protested. "At least, not for myself. It was always for—"

"Quiet," he ordered, the gentlest command he had ever issued and still he felt compelled to soften it further by rubbing his thumbs across the back of her hands. "It was your dream. You were simply too blind to see it. Nearly as blind as I have been, I would say.

"I'm sorry too for ruining your plans to have our marriage annulled. It was deliberate and calculated, just as you accused. I suppose I should also be sorry for taking what you can only give once. If you had gotten your way, you might have saved that gift for a better man, a man who could love you the way you deserve to be loved. But I am not sorry for that," he declared, tightening his grip on her hands, "and I never will be."

She listened in silence, her expression still.

"I'm sure I'm skipping over hundreds of small infractions here, but that brings me more or less to this afternoon."

She remained motionless. The only indication that she recalled the incident to which he referred was the flush that appeared high on her cheekbones.

His voice was deep, ragged with regret. "God, Leah, I am so sorry that you walked into that . . . scene."

"But not at all sorry for creating it, I take it?"

"I didn't create it," he protested. "That is, not *all* of it."

She quirked her brow skeptically.

"The brothel was my idea, I admit that."

"And the cages?"

He shrugged. "A joint effort."

"You're very . . . creative," she drawled. "Were all those feathers real?"

"Yes, no . . . I really couldn't tell you." He exhaled heavily, his awkwardness seeming to please her, if the glint of satisfaction in her eye was any indication. "I didn't have anything to do with the actual details," he explained, hoping to skirt over as many of those details as possible. "And I definitely did not invite or in any way encourage that woman to . . ."

"Fondle you?" she suggested when he hesitated.

"Exactly. I intended only to interview her . . ."

Again her brow quirked.

Adrian ignored it and forged ahead. "And I had already informed her the interview was over when she . . . Then you walked in. Hell, Leah, I think at that point I had already decided to call off the whole damn thing, to close up the House of Birds before it opened."

"Why?"

His gaze narrowed. "Why?"

"Yes. Why did you decide to call it off? Because you suddenly realized that it was a childish, malicious prank? I'm assuming it was that, and not a serious business venture . . . and that your motive for lining up such a renowned group of benefactors was to make them the very public butt of your joke? Am I right?"

"Close enough," he admitted, with a self-deprecating air.

"And did you change your mind because you suddenly realized that what you were doing was tasteless and despicable?"

He hesitated, then gave her a small, rueful smile. "That's the right answer, isn't it?"

She simply stared, forcing him to figure it out on his own.

"I know it is. And I know it's what I ought to tell you, but . . ." He took a deep breath and tightened his grip on her hands. "I made up my mind I am never going to lie to you again and I'm not."

"You didn't exactly lie about the House of Birds," she allowed, her tone heartbreakingly bleak.

"Close enough," he said again. "You said this afternoon that you were wrong to believe that I had changed, and I came after you prepared to tell you that you weren't wrong, that I had changed. I was armed with a long list of arguments to prove it to you. But the fact is, I haven't changed."

He felt her fingers stiffen, but she didn't pull away. Her hands had become a sort of barometer for him. He held them loosely now, attuned to the slightest tremble, the smallest change in temperature.

"I'm the same man who carried you across the road to that church and married you without your consent, the same man who made love to you knowing it was not really what you wanted." He lifted one finger to silence her half-formed protest.

"Deep down, there's part of me that still thinks the House of Birds would be a brilliant comeuppance for that bunch of stodgy hypocrites. I decided not to go through with it not for their sake, or mine, but for you and you alone. Because I suddenly realized how it would look to *your* eyes, and how it would make *you* feel, and *that* is all I care about. I never, ever want to do anything that will hurt you in any way again.

"That's the truth of it, my love. I abandoned the plan, and I am prepared to give up a great many other things as well, whatever is necessary to make you happy."

Her hands were cool.

"That is very charitable of you," she said stiffly, "but I wouldn't dream of so severely hindering or restricting your own pursuit of happiness. So I—"

"You aren't," he broke in. "I've made a mess of explaining it, I'm sure. All I'm trying to say is that I can take no credit for any of this. I am not a better man than I was. It's only that you make me wish I were. You make me want to be a better man, better than I ever can be, perhaps, but for the first time in so long, you make me want to try."

"Oh, Adrian." She leaned closer, her hands sliding free to move to the inside of his wrists, her fingers breaching his ruffled cuffs. Her mouth looked soft and kissable, but Adrian forced himself to resist and finish.

"Riding in the cold and the dark, you do a lot of thinking to distract yourself. I thought that my life is like a kaleidoscope. The bits and pieces have always been there, but it took you to move them around and make something of it, to make me come alive again." He ran his hands up to her elbow and held her that way. "Dont' you see, Leah? That's why I came after you, that's why I cannot let you leave me. I haven't changed, but everything around me has, thanks to you, and I don't want to let go."

He kissed her lips, keeping the pressure light, even when he sensed she would accept more. He brushed his mouth across her cheek and ran his hand through her hair, letting the moment spin out as his feelings churned inside.

"I once thought there was no pain worse than being betrayed by someone you love," he said, his voice rough, his mouth buried close to her ear. "I learned tonight that there is a pain much worse. That's losing someone you love and knowing you have only yourself to blame."

That was the pain his father had to live with, he realized, feeling another small, grudging sliver of understanding. It was a pain he never wanted to feel again.

"When I came home and found you gone, and knew I had driven you away, I went a little crazy," he whispered.

She pulled back and looked at him in surprise. "You didn't drive me away." Her gaze widened. "But you still don't know . . . Of course not, how could you? That was my reason for going to see you in the first place, to tell you and ask what I ought to do next. Then I walked in and . . ."

"Tell me what?" he prodded, puzzled as to what else could have sent her fleeing.

"It's about Christiana," she said, her mouth tight.

"What about her?" he asked, eyeing her cautiously.

"The worst possible news." Her bottom lip trembled, jerking heartstrings he didn't know he had. "She's eloped."

She didn't know. The realization was a massive jolt to his nervous system. He quickly pieced it all together as she went on about the folly of impulsive girls and opportunistic sheep farmers.

Leah believed that the letter from her sister had arrived only that day. She had no idea of his role in it, how he had diverted it and then fabricated messages to explain Christiana's continued delay.

Perhaps she never had to know, his brain thought of its own volition, as his brow gathered itself in a properly sympathetic frown. How simple it would be to pretend he had never seen the note. The footman who'd brought it could be dispatched elsewhere. The gift of an extra herd or two ought to persuade his new brother-in-law to take full credit for those troublesome messages.

All he had to do was say nothing.

20

Poor Adrian, she thought, he looked nearly as devastated by the news about Christiana as she was. But then, she'd had longer to come to terms with it.

"Of course, I am still hoping to arrive home in time to stop them," she told him. "Failing that, I'm praying for a miracle, anything that might prevent them from doing the deed, and leave open the possibility of an annulment."

He nodded, but his grim expression did not hold out any more real hope for that than she felt.

"It's not that St. Leger is a bad man. He's perfectly nice, and respectable," she allowed. "He's pleasant looking and speaks French fluently and plays the mouth harp."

Her lips curved in a reluctant smile. "Chrissie once told me that he can play for over two minutes without pausing for breath. She had stars in her eyes when she said it," she added, recalling the moment. "I suppose I should have known then."

"A dead giveaway," he agreed, without a trace of humor.

She sighed. "When you come right down to it, I feel a bit the way you described a moment ago, as if I've lost someone I love and have only myself to blame."

"You are not to blame," he said, his tight, hard tone coming as something of a surprise.

"I mean for leaving her home alone and unsupervised. I thought that was the best way to handle it at the time. Now I'm not—"

"Stop." He got to his feet so suddenly the teacups rattled in their saucers on the small table beside him. "You are not to blame, do you hear me? This was your sister's decision to make all along and she made it. This may not be what you wanted *for* her, but it was apparently what she wanted for herself."

He was breathing harshly, pacing the small room like a caged lion. One would think it was *his* sister who had eloped and ruined all *his* plans.

"If anyone is to blame for anything," he said, turning sharply to face her, "it is I. The fact is, I received word of their elopement days ago and I said nothing. Worse, I hid the note your sister left for you. I assure you, it was only by chance it turned up where you found it today."

Leah got to her feet. "You knew?"

He nodded. "A footman brought the news last week . . . and even then it had been delayed due to your staff's reluctance to admit to mine that their young mistress had run off."

"Then it really is too late." Her feeble hope slipped away.

"I'm afraid so. Though it may hearten you to know

the villagers mounted a valiant search for the couple on your behalf."

"The footman relayed all this to you?" She felt suspicion growing where hope had once been. "And you said nothing at all to me?"

He nodded.

"But why?"

"What would you have done if I had told you?"

"I would have left for home at once, of course."

"Precisely. I was not ready to have you leave me." His jaw was rigid. "Not then. Not now."

"So you kept the truth from me?" she demanded, her voice rising. "You commandeered a letter addressed to me? What makes you think you have the right to meddle in someone else's life that way? I don't care if I am your wife," she said before he had a chance to answer. "I will not allow you to decide what I ought to know and when I ought to know it, do you understand?"

"Yes."

She took a deep breath. "And I will not be treated like . . . like chattel, as if my wishes do not count every bit as much as yours."

"Understood."

"That is why you did it, isn't it?" She found it difficult to keep her fury going full force when he was being so damn conciliatory. "You wanted to keep me there because you were not through playing games with me?"

"Yes, but only at first. Don't," he ordered, shoving a chair aside to stop her as she moved toward the door. He held her by the arm and turned her to face him. "I'm not going to let you run away until you hear what I have to say."

"I've heard enough," she said, wanting the privacy of her own room before she gave in to the grief building inside. How easily she had been taken in by him again. All he'd had to do was offer the words she wanted so desperately to hear. Words like love and forever. Clearly, the things he *said* were only half the story. She wished now he had never come after her. "How can you say you don't want to hurt me and then do this?"

"I said it because it's true, dammit." He shook his head. "I know it sounds crazy, but it's *because* I can't stand the thought of hurting you that I kept the truth from you long after I knew it was only going to lead to worse disaster."

He cupped her face. Leah didn't pull away, but she kept her jaw taut beneath his fingers.

"I couldn't stand to be the one to tell you, knowing it was going to break your heart," he said quietly. "I didn't tell you because I knew your eyes would go all teary the way they are right now, and that your chin would tremble, just this way," he said, touching her there with the rough pad of one thumb, "and because I knew I would be destroying the hopes and dreams you cherish more than anything.

"Not simply the dream of finding the perfect husband for your sister," he went on, as she anchored her watery gaze on the top button of his shirt and tried to keep her resentment from melting away. "I mean the secret, private dream all your own, the one you don't even acknowledge to yourself, your dream of a perfect world, where love makes everything right."

He gave a weary smile that she refused to acknowledge. "You'll never know how tempted I was not to tell you the truth tonight. Not to lie, exactly. To simply keep my mouth shut and let you go on believing that I'd had no knowledge of the elopement until you told me."

"Why didn't you? The odds are I never would have known the truth."

"Ah, but I would have," he said with a wry laugh, and at that moment Leah knew he was wrong. He *had* changed. The man he had once been—the man who would blithely wed a dying woman—would have had no compunction about turning her trust in him to his full advantage. He would not have confessed to anything unless his back was to the wall. And he would not have ridden half the night to tell a woman he loved her.

She was suddenly deliriously happy to be that woman, and very, very grateful she'd had the stamina to outlast that other man and be rewarded with this one.

He wound his arms around her and she let him.

"You must be rubbing off on me," he said. "I'm still no prince, but I want a shot at the happy ending. And I know that isn't possible if there are lies and secrets between us. This time I want everything right from the start." He grinned, that wicked, boyish grin that made her dizzy, and said, "Marry me, Duchess."

"We are married," Leah reminded him.

"You call that a wedding?" he scoffed. "I want flowers and music and a church, no, a cathedral full of people. I want you in the most beautiful dress you can imagine. I want to watch you walk down an aisle a mile long, smiling at me all the while, and I want to stand with you at the altar, before God and man, and vow to love . . ." He kissed her eyelids as they fluttered shut. "Honor . . ." His lips slid along her cheekbone and down her throat as his hands moved on her back. "And cherish you . . ." His warm, open mouth hovered over hers. "Every day, every night, every blessed moment for the rest of my life."

Leah felt as if she were shimmering inside as she

listened to him put into words the most secret longings of her heart.

With his hands in her hair, he kissed her mouth, sweetly, delicately, as if she were something fine and rare that had been entrusted to him for safekeeping.

"Say yes," he urged, barely lifting his mouth from hers, "and I'll tell you what comes next."

"Yes." She struggled to breathe and laugh and kiss him all at the same time. "Yes, yes, yes."

"After the cathedral, and a wedding breakfast fit for a duchess, I shall take you home and take you to bed," he told her, sending a thrill along her spine. "*My* bed. Where I shall make love to you properly, fully, and for as long as it takes to consummate every sweet inch of you and make you mine, well and truly and forever."

This time his kiss was harder and more demanding. Leah could feel his heart pounding against her breast. In spite of his light tone, she sensed his need for her to know exactly what he was offering, and what it meant to him for her to accept.

He was asking for more than her hand. He was asking for all of her, body and soul. He was asking for forever.

"How about it, Duchess?" he drawled softly. "Do you fancy giving me a son?"

Leah took his face in her hands and gently traced the curve of his smile. "I'd love to. But only one?"

He pulled her hard against him, his chuckle edged with relief. "I thought we'd switch to daughters after that, little girls with beautiful green eyes and their mother's laugh, who can play outside my open window and distract me from my work."

"Two little girls sounds perfect," she agreed.

"Actually I was thinking more along the lines of three."

"Three then. Just so they are judiciously spaced."

"Already worrying about your figure?" he teased, spanning her waist with his hands.

"No, about their seasons overlapping. I want to be able to devote myself to planning one wedding at a time."

He groaned. "On second thought, Madam, sons and only sons will do nicely. I've seen you at work and I do believe that living through one wedding—ours—will be my limit."

"In that case, we shall have to schedule it for when Christiana and Mr. St. Leger can come to London. That way we can all confirm our vows together."

His mouth softened with gentle indulgence. "Would you like that, sweetheart?"

"Very much." Her smile grew thoughtful. "Perhaps you're right, and all the dreams I had for Christiana were really mine all along, only I was too afraid to reach out for them for myself. This way it won't really matter whose they were. It will be a celebration for all of us."

"Then it's settled, a double wedding it shall be." He cherished her with mouth and hands, his touch slow, heavy, stirring to her senses and her heart. "That is what I want, Leah, to make all your dreams come true."

"You already have," she told him. "I love you, Adrian, and I promise that after this I shall content myself with *writing* happy endings for others. Starting with Olivia and Prince Nevar." Her eyes sparkled up at him. "I have at last figured out what she must do to bring him around."

"Dare I ask?"

"Wouldn't you rather be surprised?"

He laughed, resignedly, adoringly. "Do I have a choice?

EPILOGUE

Baumborough, England
One year later

"Are you alone?"

Leah looked up from her plate of dry toast and smiled as Christiana entered the room. Her sister was wearing a simple yellow dress, her golden curls caught in a black ribbon at the back of her head, her beauty all the more arresting because it was so effortless.

Though Chrissie had proven to be a confident and gracious hostess, she appeared thrilled to find the dining room otherwise deserted that morning. Leah understood why. She, too, had looked forward to having a quiet moment to themselves.

"It's just me and the coddled eggs," Leah replied, then winced and gripped the edge of the table as if to steady herself. "Ooh, why did I say that? The word alone makes me queasy."

"Which word? Eggs?" Chrissie chuckled sympathetically as she helped herself from the chafing dishes on the sideboard.

"That's the one," answered Leah through gritted teeth. "Please don't say it again."

"It won't pass my lips for the remainder of your visit, I promise." She sat and reached for her napkin, her expression rueful as she saw Leah shudder at the sight of her full plate.

"For me the word was gravy. The mere thought of the stuff made me green. As luck would have it, Thomas happens to be the world's foremost gravy aficionado."

"What did you do? Come to dinner blindfolded every night?"

"Don't be silly. I simply barred gravy from the table for the entire nine months I was pregnant." The gleam in her blue eyes was defiant, and very familiar to Leah, who suddenly felt even more of a bond with her new brother-in-law. "I decided since my pregnancy was a joint project and I was carrying most of the load, so to speak, it was the least he could do. Of course now he feels that Catherine Anne is more than ample compensation."

Leah wondered how she could ever have doubted that her headstrong sister knew exactly what she was doing when she ran off with Thomas St. Leger. Thomas might not be very handsome or very witty, but he was strong and solid and he adored his wife. Marriage to such a man provided a secure environment for a butterfly like Christiana, and she had bloomed in ways Leah had never envisioned. She now possessed the ease of a woman truly content with herself and her life, and Leah could not be happier for her.

"You might consider having Raven give up you-know-what for the duration," Chrissie suggested. "It will make him feel a part of things, as though he's doing something of great import to the success of the venture. You know how men love that sort of thing."

"I just might do that. It's odd, isn't it?" she asked, her tone bemused. "After all these years, *you* are suddenly the one giving *me* advice."

Chrissie wrinkled her nose. "I don't think I like the idea of dishing out advice any more than I liked being on the receiving end. No, I much prefer to think of this as sharing what I've learned about the care and management of expectant fathers. Don't you agree that sounds better?"

"Much. But does this mean I have to stop sending you those ten-page letters filled with unsolicited snippets of advice on marriage and housekeeping?"

"Of course not." Chrissie grinned. "If you did, what would I use to line the bird's cage?"

They were still laughing as their husbands entered the room, back from their early morning ride to a neighboring estate to check out some livestock Thomas was considering buying. They were followed by Colin and Will, who had accompanied Adrian and Leah to Baumborough.

Having met Chrissie and Thomas a year ago, Colin and Will had claimed they wanted to be present for the christening of their firstborn. But Leah suspected their desire to tag along had more to do with another baby than with Catherine Anne. Perhaps she was in greater need of Chrissie's advice than she first thought, since she sometimes felt as if she were dealing with not one, but *three* expectant fathers.

"So tell us what struck you ladies so funny this morning," said Colin as the men joined them at the table. A footman appeared to pour coffee.

Adrian claimed the seat beside Leah, smiling a lazy, private smile as he bent to give her a good-morning kiss and a pat on the tummy. The two gestures seemed to be inexplicably linked in his mind, and for months she had not received one without the other.

"We were discussing the trials and tribulations of impending motherhood," announced Christiana, her mischievous gaze meeting Leah's across the table.

The men responded with a general clearing of throats and exchange of apprehensive glances, as if the dining room carpet had suddenly turned into quicksand and they were searching for the safest route around it. Only Thomas looked completely at ease, leaning back in his seat and gazing indulgently at his wife.

"Fascinating," said Adrian at last. Leah couldn't be sure if his tone was dry or simply cautious. Either response was possible when Christiana was setting the pace. "It is a great comfort to me to know that Leah has someone experienced to give her an idea of what to expect."

"You might benefit from my knowledge, as well, Raven," Chrissie admonished. "Forewarned is forearmed and all that."

"Thank you." He smiled as he reached for Leah's hand and carried it to his lips. "But I believe my wife's condition gives testament to the fact that when it comes to being a father, I am already well-armed."

Leah might have been able to take one smug male smile in stride. Perhaps. But there was no way she could tolerate a quartet of them.

With a sugary smile at Adrian, she said, "She's talking about being a *father,* sweetheart, not supplying *stud* service."

His cheeks darkened. "I know exactly what your sister is talking about, and I have no need of lectures on the subject."

"Good," she said. "Then you won't mind naming

for us one thing you know about being a father and caring for an infant."

"Not at all. I know . . . I know . . ." His jaw clenched as he swung his gaze toward Thomas. "Let him name one first."

"Burping," said Thomas without hesitation. "That's my domain, burping. It's not too complicated or too messy." With a self-conscious shrug, he added, "That is, once you get the hang of not whacking, I mean patting, the back too hard."

"Burping," declared Adrian as if he'd invented it. "I have no doubt I will be at least as accomplished a burper as Thomas is."

Her voice brimming with barely suppressed laughter, Chrissie said, "I seriously question whether a man of your lofty position and rather, shall we say, self-indulgent past, can ever hope to achieve the same level of expertise as my husband."

"Now, Chrissie," chided Leah, "it's not fair to draw conclusions before Adrian has had a chance to demonstrate his technique."

"That's right," agreed Colin. "Show them your technique, Rave." He stood, snatched a porcelain urn from a table in the corner, and carried it to Adrian, who looked absolutely befuddled.

"Think of it as fencing," suggested Will.

Colin curled his lip. "Fencing?"

Will shrugged. "Just trying to help."

Adrian glared at Leah. "Is this really necessary?"

"Crucial," she replied, giving him the look that men married to pregnant women never understood, but quickly learned to heed.

He held out his arms. "Give me the damn thing."

Amid a barrage of instructions and observations, Adrian finally managed to position the urn on his shoulder and burped it to everyone's satisfaction.

"Can I give it a try?" asked Will.

"Certainly," said Leah. "In fact, if you and Colin are going to be underfoot all the time after the baby comes, you could probably use a few lessons yourselves."

"Lessons?" Colin looked wary. "Lessons in what?"

"Pacing, for starters," said Chrissie. "That will be critical at the time of delivery. We can't have you all stumbling about, bumping into things."

"And rocking," added Leah. "Rocking a baby is an even more highly refined talent than burping."

"And we haven't even touched on nappies," said Chrissie.

"Nappies?" Adrian's hand froze on the urn he had been absently patting. "You're not suggesting . . ."

Leah smiled. She couldn't help it. The sight of the Wicked Lord Raven burping an urn and contemplating the more rudimentary aspects of fatherhood warmed her heart. If she had needed proof that Adrian would take to his new role as father as thoroughly and enthusiastically as he had to being a husband, she had it.

All in all, it was an ending so absolutely perfect, she might have planned it herself. But she hadn't planned any of it, and she had learned that sometimes it was better that way. Besides, it wasn't really an ending. As she gazed around the circle of people she loved most in the world, Leah knew this was only the beginning.

ABOUT THE AUTHOR

Patricia Coughlin is a former English teacher who quickly discovered she would rather make up stories of her own, thus ensuring happy endings. The award-winning author of over twenty-five novels lives in Rhode Island with her husband and two teenage sons.